# CONTROLLING

## Robert Seckler

Brighton Publishing LLC
435 N. Harris Drive
Mesa, Arizona 85203
BrightonPublishing.com

# CONTROLLING

## ROBERT SECKLER

BRIGHTON PUBLISHING LLC
435 N. HARRIS DRIVE
MESA, ARIZONA 85203
BRIGHTONPUBLISHING.COM

COPYRIGHT © 2013

ISBN 13: 978-1-62183-206-5
ISBN 10: 1-621-83206-6

PRINTED IN THE UNITED STATES OF AMERICA

## First Edition

COVER DESIGN: TOM RODRIGUEZ

ALL RIGHTS RESERVED. THIS IS A WORK OF FICTION. ALL THE CHARACTERS IN THIS BOOK ARE FICTITIOUS AND THE CREATION OF THE AUTHOR'S IMAGINATION. ANY RESEMBLANCE TO PERSONS LIVING OR DEAD IS PURELY COINCIDENTAL. NO PART OF THIS PUBLICATION MAY BE REPRODUCED OR TRANSMITTED IN ANY FORM OR BY ANY MEANS, ELECTRONIC OR MECHANICAL, INCLUDING PHOTOCOPY, RECORDING, OR ANY INFORMATION STORAGE RETRIEVAL SYSTEM, WITHOUT PERMISSION IN WRITING FROM THE COPYRIGHT OWNER.

## Dedication

To three of my many friends from
Houston Air Route Traffic Control Center

Gary Beller
John Jordan
Ronnie Lancaster

May they rest in peace.

Also to the love of my life
My chief editor
My wife
Julie Seckler

Without her, this book would not have been possible.

# Chapter One

## Out of Control

Had I known that being fired by President Reagan would transform my best friend into the biggest pain in my ass, I would have voted Democrat.

Over the past five weeks, I'd watched him fall deeper and deeper into depression. He'd mentioned revenge more than once and, since he had more destructive skills than anyone I knew, he was scaring the hell out of me.

Walking into the living room, I purposely chose the chair furthest away from my roommate, Earl Baker. Neither he nor his sweats had been washed in four days, and I counted six empty beer cans on the table beside him. He had a full one in his hand.

Earl was unable to talk without thrashing his hands about, so I took particular notice of the beer he was holding. It was the one splashing out onto my recently cleaned tan sofa. Having lived with Earl's unnerving mannerisms for two years, my tolerance was diminishing with his ever-increasing quest to drink the breweries dry.

He held a cigarette with a precariously long ash teetering above my orange shag carpeting. As the ashes started to fall, I reached out for them, but my reach was short, and I could only watch as they joined the many others that had fallen before them.

It was 1981, and non-smokers were but a small minority. That minority included me—Rob Silvers.

Over the past two years, Earl and I had been roommates in my home. We had joined forces to keep the house clean and comfortable, and we had agreed to split the expenses. Everything worked well until the day we were both fired. That day marked Earl's last day of assisting me with household chores. He suddenly lost all pride, including the desire to have a well-kept home. Due to his depressive mental state, I assumed his share of the cleaning instead of making it an issue. I made it a point to always keep his bedroom and bathroom doors firmly closed, and I requested he do the same.

Earl and I had both loved our jobs as air-traffic controllers, but when we lost them, he was far more devastated than I. His depression was pushing us further apart, and his daily use of alcohol was serving more as a medication than a beverage.

Our final checks from the FAA were substantial, so money wasn't yet an issue, but Earl showed no signs of looking for a job. I tried to be rational when I talked to him about getting help for his growing problems, but that only served to piss him off. I was fed-up with Earl's pity me attitude, and I had reached my breaking point.

I should have known better, but I said loudly, "Earl, when are you going to get off your lard ass, start helping out around the house, and look for a job?" The words no sooner left my lips, than I wanted them back. Earl was notorious for his quick temper, and he could be a mean son of a bitch when he was pissed.

I could feel the snap of Earl's head as he shifted his focus in my direction. He threw his feet to the ground, and we stood up together. As we made eye contact, I could see the look of fire flickering across his beer-glazed eyes. I knew I was in trouble.

Earl took a step closer to me, and said, "Don't worry about me, asshole. I can get a job anytime I want. What I do is none of your damn business."

With his face only inches from mine, I took a step backward. "It sure as hell is my business as long as you're living under my roof. And I'm damned sure if you don't start helping out around here you need to start looking for a new place to live."

I dropped my voice a notch or two, and added, "Earl, you just need to find a job."

Earl stood his ground, and I could see it was taking everything he had to keep from throwing a punch. He was still within my personal space, so I stepped back another foot. I could feel the edge of the chair behind me, and I knew I had retreated as far as I could.

At 6' tall and 200 pounds, I could hold my own against most other men, but I didn't want to push my luck with Earl. Although we were close to the same height and weight, he had the advantage of a quick temper, and a well-deserved reputation as a proven bad ass.

It had been over ten years since Earl had finished number one in his physical training to become a Marine Corps Special Forces Officer. Before the controllers strike, he'd kept in shape by going to the gym four times a week for a demanding two-hour workout. Twice a week he'd followed his session with a five-K run—regardless of the weather. At thirty-seven, Earl was as buff as he could get, but now he was drinking his six packs instead of maintaining them.

We stared at each other for a long moment before I saw him relax his facial muscles slightly, and I knew the confrontation was over. It was only our long-term friendship that had saved my blood from becoming another major stain on our ugly orange carpet. To my great relief, Earl turned slowly, and went back to his sofa and beer.

I had an 8:00 dinner reservation with my girlfriend, Jewels, so I used that as my excuse to leave.

Walking toward the door, I turned back to Earl. "I know I pissed you off, but you need to take a good look in the mirror. Your life is on a downhill slide."

With a light rain, I walked away from the house quickly, crossed the courtyard, and went into the garage. I sat in the darkness of my car knowing I had to shake off the tension from my encounter with Earl before seeing Jewels.

When he'd first moved in, after being kicked out of his house by his second wife, I couldn't understand what her problem was. Earl had a constant smile on his face, and a happy-go-lucky personality. I had agreed to let him move in until he could find a place of his own. That had been two years ago.

Earl's initial presence seemed to have spurred somewhat of a mid-life crisis in both of us. We each bought new Corvettes and Kawasaki motorcycles. The following year, we had more than our share of wild parties. At sunrise, we would often wake to find friends still lying around the house. We consistently exceeded our reputations as wild-ass controllers.

Then I met Jewels. We fell in love, and most of the heavy partying came to an end. Earl still threw a bash now and then, but when that happened, Jewels and I would stay for a couple of hours, and then go to her apartment. Those were good memories, and they made me realize that the Earl in my living room needed help, not ultimatums.

Jewels and I were going out to dinner to celebrate our first year of dating. If all went as planned, this would be a significant evening. I was going to ask Jewels to move in with me. If she said yes, we would soon be helping Earl find a new place.

Backing out of the garage, I was hit with another batch of heavy rain. It was only a fifteen-minute drive to Jewels' apartment, but splashing through the puddles had me thinking about how a Corvette might be fun for a single guy, but not so much for my thirty-three-year-old girlfriend.

Jewels occasionally registered her complaints about how there was no lady-like way to get in and out of a Corvette, especially with a skirt on. A bigger car was on my short list of changes that I needed to make. But Earl held the number one position.

I grabbed my umbrella. As I walked to Jewels' door, I knew I could expect a comment or two about my car before the evening was over. We were going to a nice restaurant, and I knew she would be well-dressed for the occasion. She had instructed me to wear slacks and a sport coat to guard against my showing up in jeans and a T-shirt. I guessed that she would be wearing a skirt, and some sort of fancy top.

Jewels saw me coming, and held the door open as I reached her porch. She was slim, but not skinny, and her shoulder-length, dark brown hair suited her well. As I'd suspected, she had on heels, a tight skirt, and a low-cut blouse that showed just enough cleavage to make me want to skip dinner, but I knew better than to suggest that. She looked gorgeous. Just the sight of her completed the mood change I was looking for.

As we pulled away from her apartment, Jewels looked over to me with a "happy anniversary," and we met in the middle for a quick kiss. I knew we were both looking forward to dinner at Landry's, our favorite steak house. When I called in our reservations, I'd requested a booth and, as usual, we both sat next to each other on the same side of the table.

After being served our wine, and placing our dinner orders, Jewels said, "I was thinking how your Corvette is almost two years old. Are you thinking about getting something a little bigger one of these days soon?"

I'd nailed that one for sure.

Knowing where she was going with the car thing, I replied, "You know, if it wasn't for possibly losing Earl as a roommate, and the extra expense associated with that, I might think of getting something a little bigger."

"Earl's moving out? When?"

I smiled, and paused to set the mood before saying, "It all kind of depends on you. I don't suppose you'd consider moving in with me... would you?"

"Let me think about this... OK, I can move in this weekend if that works for you. I'm on a month-to-month lease, so the sooner the better."

I could see it was time to get a little more serious. "I haven't talked to Earl about this yet, and I don't know how long it will take him to find a place. I love you, and I want you to move in as quickly as possible, but the timing will depend on him. I think a month should be plenty of notice. He's paid me for September, and I'll tell him to forget about October."

Jewels thought about it for a moment, and then said, "It would be OK with me if it had to be the three of us for a while, but just until he found a place."

I knew I needed to derail that train of thought. I said as emphatically as I could, "No. That wouldn't work. It's because I love you that I say Earl has to move out before you move in. Sleeping over is one thing, and you can still do that on the weekends, but moving in fully with Earl still there, that just wouldn't be a good idea. Earl has a mean streak you haven't seen, and I'd feel better if you never did."

"OK, I get it. But he's always been nice and friendly to me."

"Let me tell you a story about Earl. Three years ago he got into a bar fight. He let his temper get the best of him and, before he realized what was happening, it was him against four guys. Five minutes later he was the only man standing. All four of them went to the hospital, and two had to stay overnight."

She wasn't looking convinced, so I continued, "Almost anyone would have been fired from the FAA immediately after being charged with felony assault, but Earl has friends in high places within the government. I don't know the whole story, but when Earl was in Vietnam he was part of a six-man team that performed top-secret missions across enemy lines into Cambodia. Their orders came directly from the White House, and they were all sworn to never disclose secret contracts. Anyway, the bar fight was totally covered up."

"What happened in Vietnam?" Jewels asked.

After a sip of my wine, I replied, "On one of their missions they got ambushed, and were forced into hand-to-hand combat. He saw his best friend die from having his throat cut open by a Cambodian solder's knife. Earl was only ten feet away when it happened. He told me he put at least ten rounds of ammunition into the Cambodian's face. Earl's favorite reply to questions about Vietnam is, 'We killed many, and destroyed much.' Those times had to be very trying for him."

Putting down her glass, she said, "Thanks for telling me. I understand why you want me to wait until he moves out. I feel badly for him, and I can't imagine his having to carry that heavy burden through life."

We both had to work the following day so I didn't stay over. But I did go in for a congratulatory drink, and more than a few kisses before heading home.

## Chapter Two

### Troubling Thoughts

On the way home I thought about how the past five weeks had gone for Earl and me. We had both gotten fired at the same time, and we had both received similar retirement refunds from the government. The only obvious difference was that I had a job, and Earl had yet to update his resume.

I was a pilot in the Navy before joining the FAA, so I considered being fired as my forced opportunity to go back to my first love—flying. My biggest regret was not taking that route directly after my Navy years. At the age of thirty-nine, I could only hope that it wasn't too late for me.

A week after being fired, I called Harold Weston, the owner of First Flight Aviation. I asked him if he had any openings for a flight instructor. His response was, "When can you start?" I'd often rented planes from his company for my recreational flying, and Harold and I'd become good friends. Occasionally, after a few hours of buzzing fields of spring bluebonnets, or the forever miles of Texas beaches, we would sit around drinking beer and telling lies about our flying adventures. Although it was a significant cut in pay, I was happy to be flying for my living.

Earl had a master's degree in business management, and lacked only finishing his dissertation for his doctorate. More than any former controller I knew, Earl had all the tools to easily find more than just a job, but a career position that would pay him more than he could ever make as a controller. Earl's problem, as I saw it, was his belief that controllers were victims of a slick double-cross by President Reagan. He was pissed at the world, and he wasn't ready to move on.

## Controlling – Robert Seckler

On occasion, usually after several beers, Earl would drop a casual threat of revenge. Had it been anyone else I would have just blown it off as the typical bullshit people say after being fired, but this was Earl Baker. If anyone had the motive and skills to do something bad, really bad, it would be Earl. I had heard him make threats before, but I never knew of him making an idle threat.

Recently, I'd started to find new items around the garage, and it added to my worries about Earl. There was a pair of long-handled bolt cutters, a spool of gray wire, and a motorcycle battery that wouldn't fit either of our bikes. I had no idea what he was planning, but I was fairly sure he wasn't building a flower box for his mother. Earl was up to something bad.

It was about 10:00 when I pulled into the garage. I was happy not to have to worry about Earl tonight. He'd finished off far too many beers to do anything drastic. I just hoped he'd made it to his bedroom before passing out.

Crossing the courtyard, I could see the lights were out in the living room. Inside I could hear the washing machine running in the laundry room, and that got me thinking, *This can't be right; Earl takes all his laundry to the dry cleaners, even his socks and underwear.*

Curiosity got the best of me. The first item I pulled out from the washer was a black, hooded sweatshirt. It looked new. As I dug deeper, I found jeans, socks, and tennis shoes. They were all black, and they all looked new. The last item was a wool stocking cap. I couldn't think of any reason why Earl would buy these clothes, especially since he seldom wore black.

Was this about his depression? Or was this something more sinister? These were the kind of clothes someone would wear to hide in the shadows of a dark rainy night. Tonight was a dark rainy night.

I put the clothes back in the washer, and closed the lid. Starting down the hall, I passed Earl's bedroom. The door was open, and his bed was empty. The next door was Earl's bathroom, and I could hear running water again. This time it was his shower.

Earl didn't normally shower at night but, in light of the fact he hadn't showered in four days, I thought this was a good thing. I hollered out to him, "Hey Earl, I'm going to bed."

"OK, see you tomorrow."

In bed I tossed and turned, thinking about what Earl might have done. I rationalized he bought a new outfit, and was just wanting to wash it before wearing it. A lot of people did that. I've done that myself, but not at 10:00 at night. I didn't know what was going on, but it just didn't seem right. It was after midnight before I finally fell asleep.

Wednesday morning I hit the snooze alarm a few too many times. When I finally focused on the clock, it read 6:45. I pushed myself out of bed, ran a comb through my hair, and skipped my shower. I had a 7:00 appointment with a student, and I was going to be late.

As I backed out of my drive, I pushed *Queen's Greatest Hits* into my cassette deck, and cranked up the tunes. Late or not, I had to have my morning jolt. I pulled into the drive-through lane at McDonald's, and stopped at the order speaker. With "We are the Champions" as my background music, I ordered an Egg McMuffin and a large coffee. At the pickup window, the young girl that handed me my order was singing along with my music. They all knew my morning routine.

It was 7:10 by the time I pulled into my usual parking space next to the hangar at Hooks airport. My nineteen-year-old student was leaning against the entry door with his arms crossed, and a pissed-off look on his face. *What the hell*, I thought, *I'm only ten minutes late*.

As I got out of my car, I said, "Sorry. Untie the plane, and start your preflight. I'll just be a moment." A couple of minutes later I came through the door with my paperwork in one hand, coffee in the other, and a mouthful of muffin. I walked quickly around the Cessna trainer to double-check my student's work. After washing down the last of my breakfast, I said, "Looks good, hop in."

We climbed into the plane and, as my student continued his preflight check-off, I picked up the microphone, and called the tower, "Hooks Tower, First Flight November twelve-ninety-six, ready to taxi to runway one-seven-right, over."

The tower controller must have seen me getting into the First Flight plane, and he knew who I was. "Rob," he said, "you aren't going anywhere today. Someone bombed Houston Center."

Shock traveled through my brain and body as I thought immediately of Earl. The controller continued, "Houston Center's completely shut down, and the FAA has closed about a million cubic miles of South Texas airspace. Didn't you hear about it on the news?"

My hand was shaking as I replied, "I was listening to music on the way over, and this is the first I've heard anything."

"It wasn't a huge explosion, but it did a lot of damage to the north end of the building," the controller's disembodied voice continued. "It knocked out the power, including backup power. It could be several days before we're back in business, maybe even longer."

His description of the damage made me feel a little better because I knew the control room was at the opposite end, but I'd heard enough. I told my student to make sure everything was shut down, and I stepped out and started tying the plane back into position. When he got out, he locked the door and threw me the keys. I said, "You heard what I heard, so I guess you'll need to call ahead to make sure things are operational before your next lesson. Of course, there'll be no charges for today." The kid left, and I went into the office.

Harold had slipped inside while we were in the plane. It was a small company, and our hangar was only large enough to hold two of our three aircraft. We had a twin Beach, a Cessna 310, and the trainer. The trainer got the tie-down spot.

Harold was a big guy, probably 300 pounds—maybe more. He was an old crop duster who had scared death more times than he could remember. That was pretty typical. It would be hard to find a crop duster over forty, but Harold had stopped dusting years ago. It was hard for him to fly at all anymore because of his weight, but he still went up now and then.

I filed my paperwork, and then headed into Harold's office. I could hardly see him behind the large stacks of paper on his desk. I knew there had to be a lot of jobs that needed to be billed, and bills that needed to be paid, but this wasn't the time to question Harold about his efficiency.

Harold looked up at me between the stacks, and said, "I guess you heard about the center?"

I nodded.

Harold paused for a moment, and then, without cracking a smile, asked, "Did you do it?" Harold and I often kidded around with each other, and I knew him well enough to know he was joking with that question, so I took my time with my response.

There was a small TV sitting on top of one of the shorter stacks showing live coverage of the bombing. I watched it for a moment before saying, "No, Harold, I didn't bomb the center. But with your many issues with the FAA over licenses and inspections, your name certainly crossed my mind. Was anybody hurt?"

Harold laughed a little before saying, "I guess a guard was injured, but I don't know how badly."

I wanted to get out of there to check on Earl's whereabouts. "According to the controller, it'll probably be a few days before we can fly again. OK if I take the rest of the week off?"

Harold replied, "That's fine, but check in every day, just in case."

On my way home, I thought of Earl. He'd been home last night when I'd left at 7:30, and he had been there when I had gotten home around 10:00. It didn't seem likely for him to be able to run out and bomb Houston Center in the two and a half hours I had been gone.

Then there was his drinking. When I'd left for dinner, Earl was on beer number seven, and there were plenty more in the fridge. There was no way someone could, or would, bomb the center after having that much to drink. The opportunity just wasn't there.

Pulling into the garage, I parked in my spot to the left of Earl's car. His car was still dry and, if anything, a little dusty. It was another element in his favor. With the rain lasting through the night, there was no way that car had gone anywhere. His bike was gone, but he must have left after the rain stopped about an hour or two ago. Earl never, ever, rode his bike in the rain, not even in a sprinkle.

Earl couldn't have done this.

Despite all that, I couldn't help but take a few minutes to look around the garage. Noticeably missing were the long-handled bolt cutters, the spool of gray wire, some bailing wire, and the motorcycle battery. I also remembered two small wooden boxes that had sat on a top shelf. They too were now gone. I had planned to ask Earl what he was working on, but I never got around to it. Whatever it was, it was apparently finished and gone now. I told myself it was no big deal.

I went inside and sat down in front of the TV. A local station was broadcasting live from Houston Center. I could see there was a hole in the north wall big enough to drive a small car through. They also showed an area of the chain-link fence that had been cut through, and then wired back together with bailing wire. That was where the bomber had gone through the fence.

I thought about Earl's bolt-cutters and bailing wire. My first impulse was to call the FBI, but I couldn't do that. What if there was a logical explanation? Our friendship was worthy of my giving him the benefit of doubt, at least for now.

When the news broke for a commercial, they said, "When we return we'll have our report on the status of the injured security guard." I knew most of the guards, so I was concerned.

The news returned after a few commercials. "Clyde Roberts, a long-time security guard at Houston Center, was killed this morning at five-thirty. Mr. Roberts is believed to have been within a few feet of the explosives when they were detonated. The blast is thought to be an act of terrorism. It knocked out all power to the facility, and crippled or stopped all air traffic into, out of, or through South Texas. Houston Center was the major air traffic control facility for flights south of Dallas between New Orleans and Lubbock."

I knew Clyde well, and so did Earl. Along with many others, we'd occasionally stopped and talked with the guards when we'd walked around the building during breaks. I knew he had a wife and two young children.

The news of the bombing was gaining worldwide attention and the coverage was changing from local to national. The next announcement was concerning the FBI's initial investigation. They indicated four separate sticks of dynamite had been strategically placed in a manner that would destroy not only their main commercial power, but also three sources of backup power. The FBI believed that whoever was responsible must have had inside information.

The FBI was in full force at the center. Special Agent in Charge Cartwright was the senior agent in charge of the Houston office. By order of the director, he would be the main spokesperson for this crime, and he set aside all other matters to direct his full attention to the bombing. It was now considered the FBI's number one priority.

Agent Cartwright stated that a persons-of-interest list had been put together, and the list included any possible terrorist suspects that could be in the Houston area. Also, and to the surprise of many, the list included all air traffic controllers who'd been fired from Houston Center by President Reagan five weeks ago. "Many of our agents are calling on those people as we speak," he said. "Both agent Woolsey and I will soon be participating in that portion of our investigation."

*If Earl did this*, I thought, *he'd better be hauling his ass to Mexico or someplace else remote. It won't take long for the FBI to put the pieces together.*

Then it hit me. *That meant the FBI would be swarming around all terminated controllers—including me. We all had motives, and there were over two hundred of us fired from Houston Center. If Earl was a suspect, I would be too.*

I thought it might not be a bad idea to warn Jewels about what was happening. She worked for an attorney whose office was located between her apartment and my house.

"I'm glad you called," she said. "What do you think about what's going on?" Before I could answer she laughed, and continued, "I hear you and Earl are suspects."

I didn't find it too funny. "No kidding. Earl's out, so I don't know what's going on with him. His car's here, but his bike isn't. I just needed to share this with somebody, so I called you." I paused, my eyes on the TV, and said, "News is back on. I'll call you back later."

# Chapter Three

## A Midair Collision

Although the national news was on all major channels, it was the local guys who were covering the on-site broadcast. The next breaking report got my immediate attention. "We've just received notification from the FAA, that there's been a mid-air collision between a corporate jet inbound to Houston Hobby airport, and an Eastern Airlines flight from Orlando, Florida, enroute to Las Vegas, Nevada."

I could feel my stomach cringe.

The reporter continued, "We're still gathering details, but all indications point to the collision being a direct result of the power outage at Houston Center, and the center's subsequent loss of their radio frequencies. We have no information about the fate of the business jet, but the Eastern flight is still airborne, and it has been rerouted to San Antonio. We're shifting our coverage to our sister station there. We join KSAT reporting live from San Antonio International Airport."

I found I'd been holding my breath, and I let it out as the reporter said, "Eastern Airlines flight seven-eleven was en route to Las Vegas when it was hit by another aircraft at twenty-eight thousand feet. If you look closely at the center of your screen you'll see the Eastern aircraft on its final approach to the airport. The plane is now less than a quarter-mile from the runway. Fire trucks and ambulances have lined both sides of the runway to enable an instant response."

The reporter paused as we all watched the aircraft grow closer. "We have just been informed that the Eastern aircraft's rudder is totally inoperable."

My first thought was that the people in the emergency equipment next to the runway should be getting their asses out of there. Without a rudder, there's no telling where this plane might touch down. The skies were clear, and the runways were dry, but the grass was still wet from overnight storms. A grass landing would require the gear to be up, but I could see it was fully extended.

The reporter continued, "The aircraft is well to the left of centerline, but moving to the right." He paused for a second, and then began shouting, "Did you see that? It looked as if the landing gear was going to catch the perimeter fence! They couldn't have cleared it by more than a foot or two!"

After getting his voice under control, he continued, "All we can do is watch and pray, but it looks like it will miss the runway and land on the grass. There are several vehicles parked on that grassy area."

The wheels were about to hit the ground, and I had to agree with the reporter that the plane was going to land on the grass. Suddenly, the nose of the aircraft was jerked sharply to the left, and the wing gears hit the runway hard. The nose was still high, but coming down quickly as the thrust reversers kicked in with a loud roar. The nose gear hit, and bounced back up a few feet before hitting again and sticking to the runway. Smoke immediately rolled from the wing gears, and I knew they must have blown a tire or two.

The aircraft was slowing fast, and all three gear extensions were smoking. The pilot must have been standing on the brakes as they slowed down enough to make the first high-speed taxiway. The emergency vehicles were pulling onto the runway, and following close behind.

The reporter said, "The Eastern flight has been directed to the gate closest to the main terminal building to allow access for injured passengers. The captain's latest report said there were no deaths, but up to sixty passengers and crew members have been injured. A doctor on board reported three of the injured were in serious to critical condition."

The Eastern flight stopped short of the passageway. Some of the tires appeared to be on fire, and the fire trucks immediately began spraying foam on the gear and the underbelly of the fuselage. It took a couple of minutes before they deemed it safe enough to extend the passageway to the forward door. Rolling stairs were placed at other exits for passengers capable of using them.

Being both an air traffic controller and a pilot, this was exciting stuff for me. I found it hard to believe they were able to get cameras in place in time for a live broadcast. As everything seemed to be under control, people started coming down the stairs to the tarmac. One of the last off was a flight attendant, and a reporter stopped her for an interview.

He asked, "The plane doesn't seem to have any major damage. What caused all the injuries?"

"It will probably be weeks, or months, before NTSB has their official report, but we experienced sudden, and very extreme, changes in altitude. The nose of the plane shot up about forty-five degrees, and it had no sooner reached its peak, when it dropped about ninety degrees. It threw a lot of us around the cabin like rag dolls. I was luckier than most, I only got a few bumps and bruises, but it scared the crap out of all of us, including me."

It was hard to believe that people were actually walking away from a mid-air collision, however slight, and to be watching it all on live TV was remarkable. The whole thing was surreal.

As I considered the size of the two aircraft, along with the reported loss of rudder, I decided the tip of the corporate jet's left wing must have come within a few feet of the Boing 727's cockpit when it passed on its way to clip the upper tail section and rudder. Had the captains of both aircraft been looking, they could have counted the stripes on each other's epaulets. They were that close to the death of all.

The instant rise and fall of the nose was likely caused by wake turbulence from the other aircraft's close proximity as it clipped the tail of the 727, and knocked out the rudder. It was unbelievable that no one had died on the Eastern aircraft.

I was sure the corporate jet could have never survived the effects of the overwhelming wake turbulence from the three larger engines grouped on the tail of the 727.

The reporter ended his coverage from San Antonio by saying, "Additional reports will continue from your local stations after our commercial break."

I went to the fridge for a snack and a drink before returning to the Houston coverage.

When the special report continued, the first thing on the screen was a young girl and an older man standing on a make-shift stage inside a hangar. Lights flooded their faces, and a few feet behind them sat a Lear Jet with a slight crease in its left fuel pod.

I couldn't believe what I was seeing. I stood up, and hollered at the TV, "Unbelievable! They made it!"

"We're south of Houston, in a hangar at Hobby Airport," the reporter said. "As you can see, there are numerous reporters and cameramen gathered to question the pilot of Lear Jet four-twelve—the aircraft that collided with the Eastern Airlines flight. The pilot is Megan Kaye, a twenty-five-year-old with eleven years flying experience."

She was blonde, very cute, and had a nice figure, but I thought there was no way she was twenty-five. Seventeen or eighteen was more like it. I couldn't believe they had actually made it.

The owner spoke first. "Our flight attendant and two passengers won't be available for questioning, and their names won't be made public at this time. To be clear, this accident was a direct result from the bombing of Houston Center. Those explosions knocked out the frequencies, and made it impossible for controllers to relay their instructions to aircraft. It was Megan's instant reflexes that saved the lives of people on both aircraft. She is the sole heroine of this collision."

He paused and then continued, "Please don't let Ms. Kaye's youthful appearance fool you; she is a highly qualified pilot with more experience than pilots twice her age. She started flying with her instructor father at the age of fourteen. She received her pilot's license before her driver's license, and she's certified in more aircraft that I can count. She holds the unique title of being the youngest person to receive an airline transport pilot rating."

He moved over so Megan could stand in front of the microphones.

Megan said merely, "I'll be glad to take your questions."

"Can you walk us through this collision, and the aftermath?" was the first question.

"We departed El Paso early this morning going to Houston Hobby. About a hundred miles west of Hobby we received a clearance from Houston Center to descend from forty-one thousand feet to twenty-four thousand feet. This was all totally normal." She paused.

"As we were descending, I glanced at my altimeter and noticed we were going through twenty-eight thousand five hundred feet. I remember this because I was thinking I needed to call Houston Center to request a lower altitude so we wouldn't have to level off during our decent for landing."

For once, reporters weren't trying to interrupt to get their questions in. They were mesmerized.

"I looked out the windscreen to check our weather, and that's when I saw the other aircraft. It was right in front of me. I remember pulling the yoke into my chest with all of my might, as my instinct also turned the plane hard to the right. I didn't feel fear until later when I realized I was still alive."

She cleared her throat before continuing.

"I don't remember seeing it happen, but my left fuel pod must have clipped the other aircraft. I lost control momentarily as we were being severely tossed around from the wake turbulence of the passing aircraft. I can't believe how very lucky we are to be alive."

Another pause. "My flight attendant, Elise, was a real trouper. I knew she had to have been as scared as the rest of us, but she was a rock.

"I tried to call Houston Center a few times, but I was unable to raise them, so I called Hobby Tower. They replied on my first call. They advised me of the Houston Center bombing, and they said they would clear all traffic and runways for our arrival. They took care of us the rest of the way."

I continued to watch as a few more trivial questions were asked, and answered. As I was getting ready to check other channels, a man dressed in a suit said, "I would think an extra set of eyes could have been valuable in this situation." He paused, but there was no response from Megan or the owner. He continued, "Isn't it true that FAA regulations require two pilots on this flight?"

Megan obviously knew he was right, but she said nothing. Instead she turned to the owner for his answer. The owner said, "Two pilots were assigned to this flight but, due to a last-minute emergency illness, and with the agreement of our passengers, we made a joint decision to proceed with one pilot. Thank you for your time."

The man who asked the last question was identified as a member of the National Transportation Safety Board. Like Megan and the owner, I also knew the answer, and I felt badly about the possible repercussions to Megan, and her company.

# Chapter Four

## Knock—Knock

About an hour after talking with Jewels, there was a knock on the front door just as I was heading toward the kitchen. The FBI hadn't wasted any time. Two suits with badges were standing on my porch. The bigger of the two must have been about 6'5" tall, and 250 pounds. The second guy was probably 6'3", and 210. Both were big compared to me, and I was more intimidated than impressed. "How may I help you?"

Showing his badge, the big guy said, "I'm special agent Karl Cartwright, and this is my partner, agent Don Woolsey. We're with the FBI, and we'd like to ask you a few questions. May we come in?"

I didn't think I had much choice in the matter so I pointed toward our beer-stained sofa and two chairs. As they sat down, I turned off the TV. Agent Cartwright said, "You must be either Earl Baker or Rob Silvers. Is that correct?"

"I'm Rob Silvers. My roommate is Earl Baker, but he isn't home right now. I saw you on TV not more than an hour ago." My palms were already sweaty. "I heard you say you would be going out to investigate people on the list, but I didn't expect to be one of the first you called on. How did I warrant that top spot?" I added, trying to be assertive.

"I guess you're just lucky. Is Mr. Baker expected home soon?"

"He was gone when I got home, and I'm not sure when he'll be back."

Agent Cartwright said, "That's fine. We can proceed without Mr. Baker."

Agent Woolsey set up a couple of pieces of recording equipment while Agent Cartwright read through my Miranda rights. I agreed to waive my right to an attorney and, after the general questions of name, address, and such, the questioning began.

"Can you give us your whereabouts between 5:00 p.m. yesterday, and 6:00 a.m. this morning?"

"Sure," I replied. "Yesterday, I got home from work at First Flight Aviation a little before 4:00. Earl was here, and he can verify that. I got ready for a dinner date, and left here between seven-fifteen and seven-thirty. Again, Earl was here. I picked up my date, Julie Rauen, at about seven-forty. We went to Landry's, our favorite steak house. We had reservations for eight, and we were on time. We left about nine. I stopped in at her house long enough for a drink, and I then came home. It was around ten, and Earl was here. I went to bed and woke up at 6:45. I was back at work at 7:10 this morning. I work at First Flight Aviation at Hooks airport."

"Thank you." He paused, and looked around. "That seems complete, but while we're here, I'd like to ask you a few questions about Earl Baker."

"OK." My palms continued to sweat, and I tried not to be noticed as I slowly wiped them on my pant legs.

Agent Cartwright said, "Just to be sure, you said Mr. Baker was here at the house when you left around seven-twenty, and he was also here when you returned at ten. Is that correct?"

"Yes, he was here when I left, and when I came back."

"Do you have any reason to think Mr. Baker may have gone out, and returned during your absence?"

I shook my head. "No. When I left he was lying on the sofa watching TV and drinking beer. I know he'd already had several, so I don't think he would have gone out. When I returned, I parked my car next to his. My car was wet from the rain but his was dry and dusty. If he went somewhere, he didn't take his car. He was in the shower when I went to bed, so I didn't actually see him, but I hollered to him, and told him I was going to bed. He answered, and I recognized his voice."

Agent Cartwright gave no indication of whether this was good or bad news. "I understand he has a motorcycle. Did you notice if the motorcycle was there, and if so, was it wet?"

"His car was between my car and where we park our bikes, but I saw enough to know his bike was there. I don't recall it being wet, but I probably wouldn't know what his bike looked like when it was wet. I've never seen it that way. He won't ride it if there's any chance of rain, not even a sprinkle."

Agent Cartwright's beeper went off, and he frowned at it. "Can I use your phone?"

I gestured toward the kitchen. "Help yourself."

Agent Woolsey was gathering the equipment while his partner was on the phone, and they left as soon as he was finished.

I wasn't feeling good about this. We had to be at the top of his list of two-hundred-plus fired Houston Center controllers for some reason. Why would they pick us first? I'd been honest about everything, but I suppose I could have mentioned the new clothes, or the missing garage items. But it wasn't my job to make theirs easier, especially when it came to giving up a friend.

Repair crews were already making progress, as they were everywhere around the north end of the center. With all South Texas airspace shut down, the public was demanding when they could fly again.

At noon the president held a special news conference to announce his appointment of Graydon Finn, a renowned engineer in Houston, to oversee the reconstruction of the center's power and cooling needs.

The president said that Mr. Finn had assured him that, with the help of local utility companies, the center would be operational within twenty-four hours. He also said Mr. Finn had been given the highest priority, with the full backing of the government. He received a rare authorization that allowed him to appropriate equipment from other non-essential government facilities as needed.

The FBI director, Doug Murphy, looked suitably grim. "We will continue to keep the full force of this agency focused on the apprehension and conviction of the person, or persons, responsible for this act. Our persons-of-interest list is being vigorously investigated and we have already interviewed over thirty people. Rest assured, we will capture and convict the people responsible for this bombing."

With the agents gone, my worries about Earl led me to the laundry room to see if the clothes were still in the washer or dryer. Both machines were empty, so I gave his bedroom a good search. I looked in the closet, dresser drawers, and under the bed. There were no signs of the mysterious black outfit.

I was sitting in front of the TV when Earl came through the door. He started talking the minute he came in. "What do you think about the bombing? Somebody must have been really pissed. I heard one person was hurt, a security guard, have you heard anything new."

"Earl, are you on speed or something?" I gave it a few seconds, and then said, "It was Clyde Roberts, and he's dead. He was my friend, and"... I paused... "I thought he was your friend too."

There was no expression on his face at all. "That's terrible. I always liked Clyde. I heard the blast occurred at 5:30 in the morning, and it was in the dock area. What was Clyde doing around the dock area at that time anyway? Do they think he's the bomber?"

That comment caught me off guard. I didn't think Clyde was a suspect. "What are you talking about? Clyde was the victim, not the bomber. As far as I know, he was making his rounds, found a cut in the fence, and called it in to the duty officer. The duty officer told Clyde to check out the dock area, and he was walking to meet him when the bomb went off. If he was a minute or two earlier the duty officer would have died, too."

Earl wasn't exactly reassuring me. "It's terrible about the bombing, but in a way, it's justifiable."

"What the hell are you talking about? How can you say Clyde's death was justifiable?"

"Not Clyde's death, but Houston Center getting bombed. Yeah. Whoever did this was just getting revenge for all of us. Take Clyde's death out of the picture, and I for one would thank the bomber."

It was quiet for a few minutes. Earl went into the kitchen, and brought back two bottles of beer. I was ready. I took a couple of sips, and said, "They're sure that whoever did it must have had inside information. They knew exactly where to place the dynamite to take out all four power sources." I paused again to look at Earl. "At least that's what the FBI agents told me about an hour ago."

That one got him all right. I watched the shock register on his face. "The FBI was here?"

"Agents Cartwright and Woolsey were in our house asking questions. They wanted to question both of us, but I told them I didn't know where you were, or when you'd be back."

Earl leaned forward in his chair. "Tell me everything about their visit. Did they have a search warrant or anything?"

I gave him a recap, but I didn't go over everything in detail. As I talked, I watched his emotions. He seemed to be especially interested in the times I told the agents about when I left and returned to the house. He was anxious to hear each question, and nervous about each answer. By the time I was finished, I decided there was a fifty-fifty chance that Earl was the bomber.

He seemed overly concerned about the bike questions, and he was definitely relieved when I said, "I told the FBI agent I didn't think your bike was wet."

"Do you think they believed you?"

"Of course they believed me. I told the truth."

Earl went to his room, and soon came back through the living room with a sack of clothes in his hands. "I forgot to pick up my laundry, and I have some to take in. You need anything while I'm out?" I shook my head.

I gave him plenty of time to get away from the house before heading out to the garage to look around. The back door was half open, and I could see Earl's car was still there. I turned and went to my bedroom where I had a better view of the drive. I waited twenty minutes before seeing him back out.

With Earl finally gone, I went back to the garage, and immediately smelled bleach. In the two years we'd lived together, I'd never seen him do anything that even vaguely resembled cleaning the garage. Not sweeping the floor, emptying the trash, nothing. The tools that normally showed a little dirt from use were now shiny bright and smelled of bleach. It was obvious why he took so much time in the garage. It appeared as though he had wiped down everything with bleach that he thought could be used as evidence.

Next, was his bike. What a beautiful thing it was. It smelled of wax, and hadn't looked any better on the day he'd bought it. Remarkably, there wasn't even dirt in the tire treads. He must have taken it to the detail shop while he was out this morning. I guessed there hadn't been a long line because not too many people would get a bike detailed on a rainy day. He must have dodged puddles all the way home, and then wiped it down again.

I walked back into the house knowing I should probably call Agent Cartwright with my suspicions, but I just couldn't do it. I kept thinking back to the good times we'd had, and the sacrifices he'd made in Vietnam. I could easily be persuaded for or against Earl, but I made up my mind not to beat myself up over this. I'd leave it to the authorities.

It was over an hour later when Earl returned, and I was waiting for him. I was determined to get back to the agenda I had before the events of the day interrupted me. "Sit down, we need to talk."

This wasn't the time to pussyfoot around, so I got right to the point. "Jewels is moving in with me, so I need you to find another place."

Much to my surprise, Earl smiled. "Well, congratulations. Don't think I couldn't see this coming. She's been sleeping over almost every weekend for the past six months. I just didn't know when. Don't worry. I've already made plans to move in with my dad in Huntsville."

Earl, sensitive? I hadn't seen anything like that since before the strike, and he kept on talking. "That's why I've been going up there every Sunday. I've already moved a few carloads of my stuff. I'm surprised you haven't noticed."

He paused for a change of thought. "My dad's been having a hard time taking care of the farm since my mom died. And being out of work and all, I thought this would be a good opportunity to move up there. All I have left are my clothes, and I can probably be finished with two more trips."

This was a welcome, and unanticipated, bonus. "If you're sure…"

"I'm sure, but I'll need you to follow me up to my dad's so I can have both my vehicles there."

"Of course. Just let me know when you're ready to go."

That Thursday I followed him to his dad's farm on the outskirts of Huntsville. We didn't go inside or anything; we just left the bike, and headed back. At the house, he loaded his car with the remainder of his clothes, and he gave me his forwarding address and phone number. We said our good-byes, but promised to get back together again soon.

I had mixed emotions about Earl. I was sad to see the end of a relationship that included a lot of good times, and I had no hard feelings. But I was still concerned about his connection, if any, to the bombing.

It was nice to have the place to myself, and I pushed aside all thoughts about Earl's involvement. If he did it, they would find out, and I would be saddened. But part of me would be a little understanding as well. If he didn't do it, I hoped he could finally move on with the satisfaction that someone had taken his revenge for him.

With Houston Center back open, I was able to go back to work on Friday, but I didn't have any students scheduled, so I didn't stay long. I hurried back home to continue my cleaning to get the house ready for Jewels' arrival.

We moved her in over the weekend, and it didn't take long before she started putting her artsy-fartsy things on the walls, and around the house. The orange shag carpeting was replaced the first week she was there. The sofa and chairs in the living room were professionally cleaned.

Like most of the world, I was still following the news about the bombing, but there were no announcements about the FBI's progress in finding the guilty parties. Mr. Finn had the center back online under his estimate of twenty-four hours, and he received a healthy bonus for his efforts. Although the center was operational, there were a lot of permanent changes that still needed to be put in place. Those would take several weeks. Motion alarms were to be placed along the perimeter fencing, and commercial power would be rerouted underground until inside the building. Both backup generators, and the cooling towers, were to be relocated to the rooftop.

Agents Cartwright and Woolsey must have scratched Earl and me from their persons-of-interest list based on my testimony. Earl was never interviewed or investigated. They had video of the bomber coming through the fence at 8:45, and leaving at 9:15, but it was so blurred they couldn't even tell if it was a man or a woman.

As the months went by, Special Agent in Charge Cartwright couldn't find enough evidence to either make an arrest, or call a grand jury. It turned out to be a huge black eye for Cartwright, and the FBI as a whole. The title of special agent in charge was a title reserved for the senior agent in an area or city. That title, along with the associated pay grade, was taken away from Cartwright. He was returned to his previous position as an agent, with no supervisory duties. But he pledged to continue his search.

Months later he thought he'd put enough circumstantial evidence together to present his case to a grand jury, but he still had no solid evidence.

Apparently—and we learned this later—when Cartwright had tried to get more background information on Earl, he had run into a solid wall. He'd traced Earl's military background to Vietnam, but that's where it ended. The White House had sealed his records. Cartwright was told that Earl was a Vietnam War hero who was instrumental in performing numerous missions that had helped bring the war to an end.

They also told him that, without approval from a sitting president, the records wouldn't be released. The only hope they had given him was in saying, "Should you find hard, undisputable evidence, we will reconsider."

Agent Cartwright remained determined to keep the case open.

# Chapter Five

## Twenty Years Later

Jewels and I were married in 1982, shortly after I received an offer to fly mail between Minneapolis and New York City. It gave Jewels the opportunity to return to the city she called home – Minneapolis. It gave me the opportunity to build hours in multi-engine turbo-jet aircraft. My next step would be multi-engine Pure-Jet aircraft. We sold our house in Houston, and moved into a townhouse in White Bear Lake, Minnesota. Jewels was happy to be near her three sisters in the area.

As the years went by, I had jumped from job to job to move into larger and more sophisticated aircraft, and better wages. On several occasions, I had borrowed money from our retirement funds to pay for training that would get me certified in the next-higher level of aircraft. I was competing for airline positions against men and women twenty years my junior. In hindsight, I'd often wished that I'd continued my flying career directly after my Navy days instead of becoming a controller.

Playing catch-up for lost years depleted most of our funds, but in 1999 Northwest Airlines hired me as a copilot on an Airbus A330. I was promoted to the captain's chair in 2000.

I'd achieved my career goal, but we'd spent our retirement funds along the way, and I was looking at federal laws that mandated retirement at age 60. I could still fly after 60 as long as I could pass my annual flight physical, but I couldn't fly aircraft carrying passengers for hire. I couldn't fly for the airlines. Our retirement picture was, at best, dismal.

One evening as Jewels and I were sitting around watching TV, I received a call from an old friend, and ex-controller, in Houston, Gary

Beller. He was also terminated for striking in 1981. We'd occasionally touched base with each other over the years. Last I'd heard, he was still in Houston, and was working as a sub-contractor for insurance companies. As far as I knew, he was doing well.

After a few minutes of updates about wives and kids, he told me he'd been recently re-hired as a controller at Houston Center. I was shocked when he said President Clinton had opened controller positions to those fired by President Reagan. He said about twenty were already working at Houston Center, but the program was dying down.

"I would have called you earlier," Gary said, "but I knew you were making a lot more than controllers anyway, and you always loved to fly. Last week Glenda and I were talking about how you had once mentioned that your retirement picture wasn't too great, so I thought I should make sure you knew about this program."

I replied, "I must be blind to the world outside of Northwest, because this is the first I've heard about this."

Gary continued, "Wait until you hear this: After President Clinton appointed Jane Garvey as Administrator of the FAA in 1997, NATCA, the new controllers' union, started working for a pay increase for controllers. It took a couple of years, but she approved a huge pay raise. Seasoned controllers are now making up to a hundred and fifty thousand a year, and supervisors are making a lot more than that."

Gary must have been able to tell that I was paying very close attention to what he was saying. "They're starting rehires back at around eighty thousand, and none of us will have time to work our way up to the hundred and fifty thousand some of our replacements are making, but it's a good retirement opportunity for us. Our military years and previous FAA time go toward the twenty years we need for retirement. They've waived the mandatory retirement age, which is now set at fifty-six."

"I think you're in about the same boat as me, and I only have four years to go before I can retire with full benefits. I guess President Clinton agreed that we got shafted when we were fired instead of receiving suspensions." Gary told me how to apply, and I was excited about the possible opportunity.

After I hung up, I sat down for a long heart-to-heart talk with Jewels. We ran the numbers every which way before deciding this was definitely worth checking into. I had four days off before my next Seattle run, so I went down to St. Paul tower, and talked to the human resources manager. She confirmed everything Gary had told me, and gave me the forms to fill out. "You should have received a package a few years back," she commented, "but we're still doing some hiring." I filled out the paperwork, and sent it overnight to the FAA's Southwest Region.

I knew how slow the government hiring process was, so I started making phone calls to old friends. I concentrated on supervisors I knew that hadn't gone out on strike. I found a couple that had worked their way into high places. I made a lot of calls, so I had no idea of where my help came from, but ten days later, I got a job offer for a controllers' position at Houston Center.

The offer called for me to be in Oklahoma City at the FAA Academy in a little over two weeks. Knowing Jewels liked being back in Minneapolis, I was pretty sure this would take some major sucking-up. I made a nice meal, bought a bottle of wine, and waited for her to come home.

While waiting, I went through the numbers again. The offer had a base pay of $86,000. I would get a daily allowance for expenses and temporary housing during my three weeks at the academy. That would easily cover my expenses, and I'd be paid mileage for my travel.

Jewels pulled into our basement garage about 5:30. She was working for Mohawk United Van Lines in north Minneapolis. That connection could be useful over the next few weeks. When she came up the stairs, I was waiting at the top with a rose and a glass of wine.

A few steps below me, she looked up and asked, "Did you wreck your car, have an affair, or are you just looking for love?"

I smiled. "No for the first two, and open for the third, but the wine is because I got an offer from the FAA for a controller's job at Houston Center."

Reaching the top of the stairs she took the glass of wine. "Really? That was fast!"

"That's the good news. The bad news is I have to be in Oklahoma City by April 23, and I need to call the Southwest Region tomorrow to confirm my acceptance of their offer."

Obviously, I was feeding her too much information to absorb instantly. "We need to sit down, and figure this out."

After dinner, Jewels picked up a calculator and a pad of paper, and we went to work. From across the table, I said, "OK, here's the way I see it. Our reason for cutting my income by almost fifty percent is for the retirement benefit, and no forced retirement at age sixty. We have nothing but Social Security now, and if I take the FAA's offer it will add about fifty thousand dollars a year to that. We'll also get health insurance at the government employee's rate for the rest of our lives." I waited a few seconds before saying, "Now for the down side."

"There's a downside?"

I nodded. "The downside is that I could wash out of the program. I've kept up with industry changes with my flying, but there are a lot more planes in the skies now. I was at the top of my class back in the day, but I'm not sure what to expect now. If I were to wash out, we could be left out in the cold. With real-estate fees and moving costs, we won't have much of a cushion.

She was frowning. "Well, you know I don't have a clue about your job requirements, either here or there, so you'll have to be the judge of that. Do you think it will be a problem?"

"I don't think so, but one of the biggest factors will be short-term memory. I haven't noticed anything with respect to a memory loss, short-term or long, but how do you tell. I've walked into a room a few times, and wondered why I was there. But it comes back to me quickly, and it doesn't happen often."

"I'll be fifty-nine in a few months," I said, "And everyone ages differently. My health is good and I feel about the same as I did when I was thirty. I do all the same things, and, you tell me—don't you think I'm fairly smart and quick-witted?"

She laughed. "I can't tell any memory differences in you over the twenty years I've known you, but maybe that's because I've changed along with you. Are you thinking you might not be able to do this?"

"I believe the question is: Am I as smart and quick-witted as I was twenty years ago, or am I smart and quick-witted for a fifty-eight-year-old? I'm sure there's a difference, but I don't know how it might affect me in that job."

Silence settled across the room for a minute or two before Jewels asked, "What difference does it make? We need to face the fact that you're scheduled to retire from Northwest at age sixty, regardless. We both know you'll be able to find something else, but whatever it is, it won't pay nearly as much, and it won't take care of our retirement problems. This looks to me like it'll probably be the only chance we're going to get to have a decent retirement. If you're reasonably sure you can do this, than I say, take the offer."

"OK, here we go!"

We spent the rest of the evening making to-do lists for each of us. The following morning, I called the FAA's Southwest Regional offices, and accepted the position. That evening we met with a real estate agent. She told us what she thought would be a fair asking price, and one that would likely sell our unit fairly quickly. We took her price, dropped it by ten thousand dollars, and told the agent, "We need it sold yesterday."

Jewels used her United Van Lines connection to take care of all our relocation needs. Before leaving on my last trip to Seattle, I turned in my resignation to Northwest Airlines. After I explained why I was doing it, they understood, and wished me luck.

Our house sold before I left for Oklahoma City, but to close the deal we had to knock another two thousand from our already-low asking price. I think they knew we were desperate. Jewels set up our moving needs before she left her job with Mohawk United. Except for the hit we took on our townhouse, everything seemed to be falling in place.

On my weekends in Oklahoma City, I drove to Houston to look for a house. I took lots of pictures, and sent them off to Jewels. We exchanged powers of attorney so we wouldn't have to be present at each other's closing. Jewels even agreed to buy a house close to my work without actually seeing it. I thought that was a sign of true love—buying a house based only on pictures.

Jewels found a job fairly soon after getting settled in our new home. In addition to my good friend Gary and his wife Glenda, we reunited with several other rehires that had shared our situation.

As the weeks went by I was required to complete written and on-the-job tests before I could move on to the next level. I took notice of the rehires that were further along in their training. Some weren't doing well at all. Occasionally, I would hear of someone washing out, and looking for other employment within the agency. I was beginning to get worried.

My fears grew when I saw that a friend, who I knew to be a great controller back in the day, was suddenly out of a job. My confidence took a big hit, and I was well-aware that confidence was a huge factor in being a good controller.

I reassured myself by recalling how this wasn't much different than it had been during the first time I had gone through the program. About half the applicants washed out and lost their jobs back then. The big difference this time was that all of these people had already made it through the program once, albeit twenty to thirty years earlier.

On the positive side, I also had two friends, Gary and Carl, who had made it completely through the program with certifications on all required positions. I used that fact to start building back my confidence. They became my role models.

## Chapter Six

### Earl's Highs and Lows

Twenty years had brought a lot of changes to the life of Earl Baker. He was one of a handful of ex-Houston Center controllers who had never been questioned or investigated for the Houston Center bombing.

Once he was settled in at his dad's farm, he had found a job as a manager of a small U.P.-Ex store there. He had passed over advancement opportunities with the company until he'd finished his doctorate in management of organizational leadership from the University of Texas in Huntsville. With that behind him, along with his ten years of aviation experience with the FAA, Earl's career took off like a rocket.

In 1995 Earl became chief operating officer for U.P.-Ex in Memphis. His position included a seat on the board of directors, and a Mercedes Benz for his company car. His total package was valued at over a quarter of a million dollars annually, and it was topped off with an office to die for. However, Earl wasn't nearly as well-to-do as many would expect.

As COO of one of the world's largest box and overnight delivery carriers, Earl's life became busy, and he lost all contact with Rob. It was just as well, since they no longer had much in common.

Earl had been divorced four times and each was financially demanding. Three of the four were receiving large spousal maintenance checks each month. The obligations were only valid until they remarried, but none of them were husband-hunting. The fourth was living in a five-hundred-thousand-dollar home that they'd once shared. Now she had the ownership, and Earl had the payments.

Few realized the extent of Earl's financial situation, but those who did thought he was probably the smartest idiot they knew. He fell in love at the drop of a skirt, and his longest marriage lasted eighteen months. He cheated, and got caught, with all of his wives. With Earl, it was all about the chase, not the capture. Problem was, Earl didn't consider the chase over until vows were exchanged. As soon as Earl was caught cheating, he started looking for his next chase. It never occurred to him to wait until the divorce was final.

Earl was a good-looking guy, with an enviable position, so he naturally had a following of women, young and old, vying for his attention.

By the time Earl saw his paychecks, the state had already taken about half of his net pay for spousal support. But that wasn't the extent of Earl's financial problems. He lived an extravagant lifestyle. His two-bedroom condo was on the twentieth floor of a high-rise in downtown Memphis. It overlooked most of downtown, and he had a great view of the Mississippi River. His clothes were tailored, and he wouldn't wear a shirt that wasn't monogrammed.

One of Earl's most frequently used benefits was his free access to the jump seat on any U.P.-Ex flight. Since these flights were considered management inspection flights, the company covered all expenses as long as he stayed in the same hotel as the crew.

On occasion, he would pick up the tab for a different hotel room when he expected to get lucky with someone other than his wife. He was smart enough to protect himself from the crew's inquiring eyes.

Shortly after being named chief operating officer, Earl was advised by the board that the new kid on the block had the additional duty of organizing the annual U.P.-Ex awards ceremony and Christmas extravaganza. He did it so well the first year that the job was made permanent. He was also host of the aviation division.

Earl knew how to delegate, so he made a standing reservation at the main ballroom of the Memphis Hyatt for the third Saturday of December each year. The hotel was to provide the evening meals, and bar requirements to Earl's demanding specifications.

The bars were open, and the booze flowed freely throughout the evening. He set up a taxi program that provided free cab fares for those who needed it at the end of the night. Of course, unbeknownst to those who took advantage of this free service, the hotel provided Earl with a list of user names. If you made the list more than three times, you would receive information about a company-sponsored, but mandatory, two-day alcohol rehab program.

No one ever used the taxi service four times, and it was a huge success.

The event for the year 2000 was to be U.P.-Ex's biggest event ever because of its record-shattering profits. Some stockholders openly complained about the enormous expense, but they couldn't complain about the revenue growth the company had enjoyed. Along with the revenue, their stock price continued to climb, and there was an increasingly high margin between them and their closest competitors.

The event was by invitation only. It included selected employees and their spouses or significant others. The board spent considerable time ensuring that their best-producers made the list. The top one hundred branches, based on their percentage to their bottom line, were invited. The invitation included round-trip airfare if jump-seats weren't available. The jump-seats went fast because it gave the managers a good look from the cockpit of the business, and they didn't have airfare deducted from their following year's bottom line.

The success of the extravaganza was proven when over twenty percent of the managers who missed the cut one year, fought hard to make the list the following year. Since Earl had put the program into effect, the branches had increased productivity by over ten percent. It was directly related to the competitive atmosphere enhanced by Earl's programs.

Top clients were also invited, and Earl recognized them in his opening remarks. Few would decline the invitation, as this was a company event geared for fun. Earl usually booked a comic, and always booked a dance band with a wide variety of music.

It was a black-tie affair, and the women, more than the men, loved an opportunity to dress to the nines. Earl was one of the men who enjoyed the dress code, and he wasn't to be outdone. All wore tuxedoes of some nature, but none stood out more than Earl's. Each year brought a new outfit for him, but this year he outdid himself. His tux consisted of a white silk jacket, finely tailored to his excellent physique, with well-fitting, black, silk pants. His shirt, also silk, was light blue with a white bow tie. His shoes were highly polished black alligator. He would have easily won the best-dressed award, had there been one.

Earl had gained a little weight over the years, but not enough to be noticeable. The company had a gym in the hangar below his office. It was open to all employees 24/7 and Earl used it often. At the age of fifty-seven, he was still a solid man.

Earl's ego was one of his most unflattering attributes. He thought every woman in the room took notice when he walked by. Fact was, most women, and men alike, thought he was far too much of an arrogant asshole. Earl had no close friends.

Having penned the evening's agenda, Earl got his keynote speaker and host duties out of the way quickly. He gave out his aviation awards, and was the first to be totally finished for the night. His speech was well-rehearsed, and his words flowed smoothly. He was comfortable in turning the ceremony over to the CEO and other board members.

Earl walked to one of the bars at the rear of the ballroom where people weren't as likely to count his drinks. His first drink of the evening was a stiff martini in a highball glass. He carried on small talk with the bartender while he was throwing it down. His second martini served as his traveler. He took it with him as he made the rounds greeting guests, and clients, while looking for a prospective lover for the evening.

About fifteen minutes later, as Earl was going back for his third martini, Katy Masters came up from behind him and said, "Can you buy an old friend a drink?"

He didn't see her coming, and was a little startled when he saw who it was. "Katy, I didn't see you. How the hell are you? Sure, I'll buy you a drink. What'll you have?

"Assuming you're drinking a martini straight up, I'll have what you're having."

"You're my kind of girl."

Katy and Earl sat down at an empty table. Their last meeting had been under the somber circumstances of her husband's death. Earl was glad to have this much-more-pleasant opportunity. Time and martinis flew by.

Katy wore a lime-green, strapless evening gown that was very low-cut, leaving little to the imagination. Earl tried to focus on other things, but that wasn't Earl. He caught himself telling her how gorgeous her necklace was for the third time. Realizing he was busted, he quickly looked away.

Katy was slightly overweight, but only slightly, and she carried herself well. They talked for over an hour, and by the end of the evening Katy had agreed to a dinner date the following Saturday night. Earl had consumed a martini or two over his limit, but he wasn't about to make his own free taxi list.

Once outside, the fresh air made him feel better as he gave the attendant his parking stub. His mind stayed on Katy. She wasn't only easy on the eyes, but she was also very smart, and well-educated. Like him, she had her doctorate. Hers was in economics. She had graduated college from Wellesley, but had done her post-graduate studies at Memphis State after marrying a pilot for U.P.-Ex.

The attendant pulled up with Earl's Mercedes, and he drove the four blocks to his condo.

In bed, his mind was still focused on Katy. He thought how easy she was to talk with. He had commented on that fact during their conversation. "I think you could talk with equal style and grace to a homeless person or the president."

She'd laughed. "That's because I've done so with both, on several occasions. One gets better with practice." Katy would be a good catch even if she hadn't been rich.

However, Earl was well aware that Katy received in excess of three million dollars from insurance and lawsuits resulting from her husband's death. He was flying for U.P.-Ex when he crashed in a thunderstorm while on approach to the Juneau, Alaska airport.

After his death, Earl had made himself point man for Katy's benefits. He had met with her on numerous occasions, and had gotten to know her fairly well. He was married at the time, but that only delayed his plans to follow up with her after an appropriate waiting period. He simply forgot, but he was happy to see her now.

Earl knew he would have to hide a lot of his history if he was to win Katy over, but he was confident his charm, position, and education would do the job. Those things had always worked well for him in the past, but Katy was considerably smarter than most. He looked forward to the challenge.

## CHAPTER SEVEN

### Romancing Katy

Earl called Katy at noon on Saturday, and he suggested a restaurant for their dinner date. "It's a nice place on the Mississippi with great steaks, and it's not overly dressy." She seemed pleased with his choice, and gave him directions to her house.

She answered the door wearing well-fitting, black slacks, and a tan cashmere sweater that accentuated her attributes. "Do we have time for a drink, or do we need to get going?"

"We have a reservation," Earl said. "But I take clients there several times a month, and I know the owner. They'll hold our booth until we get there, regardless of the time."

"Really? Aren't you the man about town."

Earl followed Katy through the double-door entry into the expansive great room of her home. Looking toward the back of the house, he could see a pool through the wall of glass. The great room opened to a kitchen on one end, and a large bar at the other. He followed her to the bar and, in doing so, noticed how well Katy looked this evening. Her few extra pounds were certainly in the right places.

Looking around the house he could see that there were two separate wings extending down each side of the pool. It was a beautiful home that was equally well-furnished. Katy had made a small pitcher of martinis, and poured them each a drink. As she handed him his drink, he said, "You have a beautiful home, and your pool looks like it'd be perfect for skinny-dipping."

"The water's a little cold right now. It's usually warm enough for swimming by late March or early April with the heater, but it takes a couple of days to get it warm enough for me." She paused and smiled, "But you're right; it's perfect for skinny-dipping."

When they entered the restaurant, it became immediately obvious that Earl did, in fact, have connections there. Although there were several people waiting in the lobby, the maître d' greeted Earl with, "Mr. Baker, how nice to see you again. I have your table ready." As they walked toward the rear of the restaurant Katy saw there were no tables at all, only booths with high backs.

The restaurant's calling card was its privacy and great food. Two of the largest booths held up to ten people. The booth Earl reserved was one of only a half-dozen that butted up to a window that looked out over the Mississippi. Earl had requested the table to be pre-set with both place settings on the same side.

While Katy sat down and slid across the heavily padded seat, Earl said, "I hope this seating arrangement is OK with you. I can sit across if you'd rather."

"It's perfect," she said with a smile. "I prefer it this way."

"This is my favorite table because of both the view and the intimacy. We can talk freely here without being overheard. " The waiter brought Earl's favorite wine, and left the bottle. He waited a visible distance until Earl's signal to return. Earl was known for leaving very large tips, and his waiter knew he would be well-compensated. They ordered dinner.

Earl had given a lot of thought to his first date with Katy. He went so far as to plan out questions that would lead to more conversation about her, rather than him. He also anticipated what he believed Katy might ask, and planned his responses. Some were true, some not-so-much, and some total fabrications.

"So," he said, turning to her, "tell me about the life and times of Katy Masters."

She smiled. "I'll give you the abridged version." After a drink of wine, she began. "I was fortunate, but sometimes not so much, to come from a well-to-do family. Both my parents were physicians. We lived well financially, but my parents were often absent from my life—especially, it seemed, when I thought they should be there for me."

She took a sip of wine before continuing. "I think I knew my nanny better than I did my mother. I was boarded at a Catholic school and, if I was lucky, I got to see my parents on the weekends. After that, I was off to Wellesley for college. I met my husband in Memphis the summer after I graduated. We were married a year later. With U.P.-Ex's hub being in Memphis, we made this our home, and I did my post-graduate studies at Memphis State."

She reflected for a moment. "I'm doing my best to see a whole lot more of my girls than my parents saw of me, but my oldest, Andrea, wouldn't hear of going anywhere but Wellesley. That's where she is now." The waiter arrived with their dinner.

After the waiter returned to his spot, they began eating their dinner. At the next break, Earl knew it was time for his contribution to their conversation. "I grew up on a large farm in Tahlequah, Oklahoma. After high school I went a few more blocks down the street to Northeastern State College. I got my degree in business management there.

"Since I had the financial benefits of being in ROTC throughout college, after graduation I paid the piper by becoming an officer in the Marine Corps. I was a Special Forces officer, and I spent time in Vietnam. When I got out I joined the FAA, and became an air traffic controller in Houston. There was a program with Prairie View A & M University whereas they provided the exact same classes during the evening as they did during the day. It gave us the opportunity to work our varying shifts, and still attend the necessary classes. I received my master's through that program."

He grimaced, "I was one of eleven thousand controllers who were fired by President Reagan in 1981. You may have heard about that."

Earl completed his mini life story around small bites of steak. "My dad sold the farm in Tahlequah, and bought a much smaller farm in Huntsville, Texas. After being fired, I moved in with him. That's where I found my first job after the strike. I became the manager of a small U.P.-

Ex store. I stayed there until I finished my doctorate through the University of Texas at Huntsville."

Although it was technically their first date, they had met several times when Earl was going over her husband's death benefits with her. He wondered if Katy realized that human resources personnel normally handled those discussions, not the COO. He'd jumped through a few hoops to shift those duties over to himself so he could get to know her.

When they got back to Katy's house she broke out the martinis. After a couple, on top of the wine at dinner, Katy said, "Pour us another; I'll be back in a few minutes." It was about five minutes before she returned wearing a floor-length nightgown. There was that cleavage again. She said, "You've had too much to drink to drive."

*So much for taking my time with Katy.*

After making love, they showered together in the biggest shower Earl had ever seen.

Over the next two months they saw each other several times a week. Andrea, Katy's oldest daughter, usually stayed in her sorority house at Wellesley, but she would occasionally fly home over long weekends. Her other daughter, Skylar, lived at home with Katy, but she occupied one wing of the house. That wing contained three bedrooms, each with a private bath, and a family room. The family room was equipped with a big-screen television, mini fridge, two sofas, and computer station. The only time she came out of her expansive cave was when she was hungry, and was looking for food.

Both girls were well-aware of Earl's growing presence, and Katy talked with them often about her relationship with Earl. Both supported their mother, and were comfortable with Earl.

On weekends, Skylar would either have a friend over, or she would go to a friend's house. Both girls had their own cars and, most importantly, they were both very responsible. Katy had raised them well. On occasion, Katy would go to Earl's condo, but she would always be back well before Skylar's weekend curfew of midnight.

Although only close friends and family knew, Katy and her husband had been separated for about a year before he was killed. They all approved of Katy's relationship with Earl. By March, Katy and Earl had decided to get married. They started preparing for a small and private ceremony. Katy had explained to Earl that, because of her girls, she would need him to sign a pre-nuptial agreement. Earl expected that, and told Katy it wouldn't be a problem.

One evening after work Earl walked in and found Katy sitting at the kitchen table with a woman whom he hadn't seen before. Katy made the introductions, and said her guest was a paralegal with her attorney's law firm. "She stopped by to deliver the pre-nuptial agreement. It's a little awkward, but I asked her to stay to see if you had any questions. I hope that's all right."

Earl, trying to be cool about everything, said, "Sure, I understand perfectly. Is it in this folder?"

Katy handed it to him. "Take your time to read it though, and ask any questions about what you see, or would like to change."

Earl quickly flipped through the pages until he reached the signature page. "Is this where I sign?"

The paralegal said, "Yes, that's the line, but you really need to read through it first. You may even want to take it to your attorney."

Earl was already signing. "I trust your needs for this agreement, and it's not a problem."

The paralegal stamped and notarized the document that Katy had already signed. It was official, and she left a copy for each of them.

Katy said, "Well, I hope that wasn't too bad, and I'm glad we have it behind us." She gave Earl a kiss, and said, "Let's get married."

Earl felt a little blind-sided but, regardless, he should have read the agreement, and given it to an attorney for legal examination. Katy had forewarned him about it, and he had agreed. She just hadn't given him notice that it would be that night. In hindsight, Earl knew he had just blown his only opportunity to make changes.

Without Earl's knowledge, Katy had had him investigated. It was that investigation, and her need to provide a safety net for the girls, that had led her to getting the pre-nuptial agreement. She knew more about Earl than he knew about himself. Although disappointed with the way Earl had hidden much of his past from her, she realized that in his place she might have done the same. She loved him, and felt him worthy enough to take the guarded chance... while hedging her bets.

Katy didn't share anything about the pre-nuptial agreement with friends or family, but she made sure Earl had no ownership of her assets, and that he couldn't hurt her family financially. She also included a provision that mandated terms for her receipt of spousal maintenance should Earl prove to be unfaithful. She called it her infidelity clause.

Signed and notarized, Earl knew there was nothing he could do, short of calling off the wedding, and he wasn't about to do that. He filed the document away with his other important papers. Fearful of what it might say, he didn't read a word.

Katy and Earl were married fifteen weeks from their first date. It was a small and somewhat secret ceremony, with fewer than twenty people in attendance.

Earl felt like he was king of the world. Although he had to take money to closing when he sold his condo, Katy's house was paid for, so he was mortgage-free. The little furniture that Earl had was nothing more than what his last wife hadn't wanted. He told the new owner he could keep what he wanted, and throw the rest away.

When he made his permanent move into Katy's place, he had little more than his clothes, but those clothes amounted to more than what ten normal men would have. He also had a lot of storage boxes full of his history and legal matters, so he rented a mini-storage unit to assure they were out of sight from unwelcomed eyes. With all that behind him, he had a very positive attitude as he looked forward to his new life with Katy.

Katy knew the truth about Earl's financial situation, and she felt a little sorry for him. She insisted, without objections from Earl, on paying all household expenses, including food. That left Earl with plenty of money to continue his extravagant lifestyle.

Earl arranged for a two-week European honeymoon. Katy's sister drove over from Knoxville with her two teenage kids. She would housesit, and watch over the four young adults while the newlyweds were gone.

     Earl and Katy visited several countries, and had a great time. Earl, being Earl, threw money around like a drunken sailor. By the time they got back Earl had liquidated a few more assets, but he was happy with the future before him.

# Chapter Eight

## The Setup

The first week of May, Earl was walking through the hangar at work, as he often did to touch bases with his employees. He liked to think it showed them how he was a hands-on boss that cared about all of his employees. He would glad-hand and talk with everybody about their jobs, and listen to any problems.

Seemingly out of the blue, a cute, young girl pulled up on a forklift. Earl thought she must be a fairly new employee because he didn't recognize her. She was wearing shorts and a tight T-shirt, so he was sure he would have remembered her if he had met her before. She leaned over toward him, and said, "I'm sure you know about the safety award we received."

"Yes, of course. Congratulations on a great job." Earl had no idea what she was taking about.

"Well, we're having a little celebration this evening, and we thought it would be a great gesture on your behalf if you could just stop by for a beer with us."

Earl felt trapped. He searched for a quick excuse, and said, "I'm going to be tied up until about eight, but let me give you some money to buy a round or two." He noticed her name tag while pulling a couple of twenties from his wallet. "Here, Shelby, take this, and use it for some drinks for the crew."

She didn't take his money, but instead handed him a card. "It would be better if you did it in person. The address is on the card. We'll see you at eight or so, but if you come later I'll have a seat saved for you. See you there."

She gunned her forklift and was back at the other end of the hangar before Earl could think of another excuse. He knew he should have known about the award anyway and, since others had heard their conversation, he felt obligated to go.

Earl called Katy to tell her he was going to be late. "I've got an awards thing that I forgot about. Some of the hangar employees got a safety award, and I told them I'd stop by at their celebration when I got through with my work." That wasn't anything new to Katy, since he stayed late two or three times a week. She knew it just went with the job.

Earl finished up in his office, and arrived at the address on the card at 8:30. It was a bar called Maxwell's. The parking lot was fairly large, and nearly full. As he scanned the lot, he could see there were few cars. The vast majority were pickup trucks and SUVs with either gun racks in their back windows, or National Rifle Association stickers on their bumpers. Most had both.

Thought to be obvious to Earl, Maxwell's was a redneck bar, and he was way overdressed. Appropriately enough, there was a bail bondsman's business in a building next door. Earl parked his Mercedes on the street in front of that business. He rationalized that the rednecks would think his car was the bondsman's car and, with the reputation of bondsmen being what it was, they'd leave his car alone. He tossed his coat and tie into the back seat, and rolled up his shirtsleeves.

Opening the door to Maxwell's brought the noise of a large crowd, and a thick cloud of smoke. After coughing his way inside a few steps, he'd seen enough, and decided it was time to go. As he turned toward the door he heard a loud voice over the crowd. "Mr. Baker, Mr. Baker, I'm over here, and I've saved you a seat!" He looked back to see Shelby standing on a chair above the crowd.

*Shit* was the only appropriate word that crossed his mind. He moved his wallet from his back pocket to his front, and kept a hand on it. He bumped and apologized his way through the tightly packed bar. He was pretty sure the building had to be at least double its legal capacity. Yelling fire would be suicidal. When he finally made it to Shelby's table, he sat down on the seat she had saved for him.

He immediately noticed the two other young girls at the table. He had never seen either of them, and was sure they weren't his employees. The three of them were wearing T-shirts—wet T-shirts with nothing under them. Shelby noticed the focus of Earl's eyes, and said, "What'd you think? I won the wet T-shirt contest."

Earl, still fixed on her breasts, said, "Well, had I been here, you would have got my vote." He looked up, and added, "How do you get a beer in this place?"

Shelby yelled across the room at the top of her voice, "Marcia! Four beers!"

Marcia was at their table with the beers within two minutes. Earl thought about how it took him about five minutes to fight his way from the front door. He wondered how she did it so fast. He was still having problems with the smoke. His eyes were watering, and he knew he wouldn't be able take it much longer.

Earl decided to shorten his stay. His revised plan would be to say a few congratulatory words about the safety award, give a token, "keep up the good work," and be on his way. He scanned the area for someone, other than Shelby, from work. Not recognizing anyone, he said, "Where's the rest of the group?"

"I was wrong about the time. It was six thirty, not eight." Shelby said, with a giggle. "They've all left. I met these girls at the wet T-shirt contest, and I'm the only one still here from work."

"You've got to be kidding me." Earl took a big swallow of his beer, and put the bottle down. "I've got to go. See you at work, Shelby." He placed a twenty on the table to cover the beers, and started for the door.

Outside, he stopped for a few deep breaths of fresh air before walking toward his car. Once again, he heard Shelby's voice. "Wait!" He turned to see her about three feet behind him. "I'm sorry. I'm always screwing something up."

"Don't worry about it. It's no big deal." He started for his car and Shelby stayed by his side. Earl stopped again. "Shelby, I've got to go home. What do you want?"

Looking as if she was about to cry, Shelby said, "I need a ride. The girl I came with left without me after I told her I had to stay and wait for you. I'm really sorry, but I don't live very far."

Shelby was a very cute girl with a great body, but he knew it was a bad idea when he heard himself say, "Come on." They got into his car, and she gave him directions to her apartment.

Earl parked his car outside her apartment building, and was looking around the area while waiting for Shelby to get out. He could see these were low-rent apartments, probably section-eight units. While he was looking off to his left, Shelby grabbed the keys from the ignition, and bolted out the door. Leaving her car door open, she hollered back at him, "You've got to come in for a beer for my ride home!"

Earl could see she was acting in a playful manner, but he was getting pissed. By the time he got out of the car and closed the passenger door, she was inside her apartment.

She left her front door wide open and, without keys, he had no option but to go in after her. He stood outside her front door, and said, "Shelby, this isn't funny anymore. Bring me my damn keys." Looking inside, he couldn't see anyone in the living room.

Getting madder by the minute, he hollered out again, "Bring me my damn keys, Shelby!"

This time, he heard her reply, "I have them right here. Come in and get them."

At Earl's best guess, Shelby was about twenty-five. He didn't know what to expect as he stepped slowly inside. He could see an open door to his left, and he was fairly sure Shelby's voice was coming from that room. As he slowly peeked around the corner he heard her say, "I'm in here."

There she was, lying on a mattress, with nothing on. The mattress had pink sheets, and the top sheet was covering only a minute portion of her lower body. She looked like a foldout from Playboy. "Your keys are touching my body. If you want them, you'll have to find them."

"Shelby, you're a beautiful, young girl, and this is all very tempting, but I need to go home to my wife, and you need to give me my keys."

She pouted. "You'll have a lot more fun in here, and you can't go home until you find your keys." Earl walked over, and sat down on the corner of the mattress. She immediately put her arms around his waist and pulled him back into the bed. That was all Earl could take. Only three weeks into his marriage and he surrendered to Shelby's advances.

A half hour later, Shelby told him his keys were on the passenger side floor of his car. With his fears about the neighborhood, he quickly looked out of the still-open front door. It was dark out, but he could see his car under a street light. He was relieved to see it was still there, and it still had all its tires. He left without further conversation.

Driving home, he thought, *here we go again*. He knew how stupid he was, but the more he thought about it, the more he wondered. *Why? Why would Shelby be so aggressive? She's half my age, with great looks, and a great body—so why would she come on so strong to me? It has to be about work. She must think she can screw her way to the top, and why not start with a COO with a philandering reputation? That has to be it.*

By the time Earl got home, it was after ten, and Katy was asleep. Earl walked lightly around to the bathroom, and washed up. He tossed his smoke-absorbed clothes to the back of his closet, and slid carefully between the sheets. He was under the impression that he had found his way to bed without waking Katy.

The following morning, Katy fixed breakfast while Earl was in the shower. It was ready for him when he came into the kitchen. The girls were both home, so there were four of them for a change. "I didn't hear you come in last night. Did your meeting run late?"

Earl, glad to hear her say she didn't know what time it had been, decided not to take any chances, and he stuck to the truth. "It was about ten or ten thirty, I guess." Earl did the right thing, because Katy had looked at the clock while he was in the bathroom.

"You're working too hard. You should hire another assistant."

Several days went by with life pretty much as usual, except that Earl went out of his way to avoid Shelby's hangar.

Having a large closet of his own made it possible for him to get his clothes to the cleaners and back into his closet without the smell of smoke ruining other clothes.

All was well until Thursday afternoon when Shelby called Earl's cell. "I'm off on Friday, and I thought we could go to lunch or something."

Knowing he needed to nip this in the bud, he said, "I'm glad you called; we need to talk. I'll pick you up at your apartment at eleven, and we'll go to lunch."

At Shelby's door, Earl refused her offer to come inside. On the way to lunch he asked, "How did you happen to have the address for Maxwell's in your hand when you stopped me in the hangar?"

"I had several of those cards in my pocket. I was giving them out to people I wanted to join us. Why do you ask? It turned out to be good for both of us, didn't it?"

"It was fine, but it has to end. I'm married, and I can't do this again."

She tossed her head. "I know you're married, but that's not a problem for me."

Earl was pulling into the restaurant parking lot, so he waited for a better opportunity before continuing. The restaurant was crowded, so he waited to finish their talk.

On the way to her apartment, Earl talked about the differences in their ages, and how she should find someone closer to hers. He also reiterated how he was married, and that he loved his wife.

"You don't need to worry about me with your wife. I'll be a good mistress, and it will stay just between the two of us."

"That's all good Shelby, and you're right; it has to stay between just the two of us. But you need to find someone else. I'm sure a trip or two back to Maxwell's should do the trick. "

It was quiet for a while, until Shelby broke the silence. "OK, I'll look for someone my age, but until then we can still enjoy each other's company every now and then. I get lonely, and I'm new in town. I need someone like you."

As Earl pulled up to Shelby's apartment, he made sure to keep his keys under his control. "Since we're here," Shelby continued, "Why don't we take advantage of our time together, and then we'll be done? I'll forget it ever happened. Right now, I can remember every single detail. I know you don't want me to remember all those details, do you?"

Earl had the picture now. "How do I know you'll forget?"

"I give you my word. One more time, and I'll leave you alone. We're right here, and we both have the time."

Earl said, "Let me get this straight. This is it, and you'll forget everything. It will end here today?"

"I promise that, unless you call me, this is it."

They went inside.

Late May came, and Earl hadn't heard anything more from Shelby. He was thinking about how lucky he was to have escaped her without a problem, but he did miss the sex. He decided she must have been honest with him after all, and he really didn't have anything to worry about.

# Chapter Nine

## The Knoxville Trip

Katy's sister, Anita Kenyon, was having a lumpectomy, so she decided to take the girls across the state to Knoxville to help with her sister, and her sister's kids. She was divorced, and their mother had died from breast cancer. She knew her sister could use a little hand holding. Her two kids were about the same ages as Katy's girls, and they had all enjoyed their time together when they had come to Memphis during Katy and Earl's honeymoon.

It was a six-hour drive from Memphis to Knoxville, but it was beautiful countryside, especially in late spring. They planned to drive over on Friday morning, and be back on Monday.

Earl had union contract meetings on Saturday that he couldn't cancel. Two previous extensions had led nowhere, and they had to work out their differences, or face a strike on Monday. It was ironic how Earl was now on the management side of a union bargaining table. He knew the pilots had been working without a contract for over a year, and the aviation division was highly profitable. Earl met with the CEO on Friday, and they agreed he could give the union up to five percent, even though they were asking for eight. Earl planned to push it as far as he dared, without having them walk out. If absolutely necessary, to avoid a strike, he was authorized to go up to the eight percent they were asking.

These talks were making front-page news in Memphis, so Katy and the girls knew the importance of Earl's meetings, and they understood why he had to say behind. They all kissed him good-bye, and wished him luck.

Saturday morning went much better than anyone would have thought. They reached a tentative agreement for an across-the-board six-percent increase.

Earl gave a short statement to reporters who were waiting for the results. "We have reached a tentative agreement that will go to the membership for ratification over the next few days. We are very happy with the results of our negotiations, and we look forward to moving on with no breaks in service. Thank you for your time."

After wrapping things up at work, he called Katy to tell her he could join her in Knoxville.

"Hey, we just saw you on the news." Katy said, "It looks like you're the hero once again."

"I'm just glad to have it behind us. Do you want me to catch a flight and come over?"

"No, honey, don't bother. You wouldn't have any fun anyway. We're just sitting around the hospital waiting. We'll probably leave here early Monday morning, and be back around noon."

"OK. I hope everything goes well. I'll check back with you Sunday afternoon to see how you guys are doing. Love you."

Suddenly, Earl was faced with being alone the rest of the weekend with no plans. The thought of Shelby immediately came to mind. After their second meeting at the apartment, she hadn't shown any signs of being a problem, and they both seemed to understand that it was a just-for-sex arrangement. Why not ask her over to the house? Katy and the girls wouldn't be back until Monday, and it would sure be better than sitting around the house alone. He gave her a call, and she was all for it. He picked her up at one.

Cheating on his wives was at first a game with Earl but, over the years, it had become more of an obsession. He had cheated so many times, on so many wives, that he no longer felt guilty–at least not until divorce court.

Earl decided this weekend would be one without worry. He knew Katy and the girls wouldn't be back, and he would take Shelby back by Sunday afternoon. That would leave him plenty of time to clean any tracks they might have left behind. This weekend was going to be a no-fear orgy for two.

When they walked into the great room, Earl noticed Shelby's nervousness. "Hey, are you OK?"

"Not really," she said. "Can we go outside?" Earl opened a slider for her, and they walked out by the pool. Shelby was wearing her usual T-shirt top and extremely tight jean shorts. She was still nervous as she sat down on a recliner, put her legs up, and kicked off her shoes.

After a few minutes in the sun it was beginning to get uncomfortably hot. Earl walked over to the outside fridge to get a couple of beers. When he turned back, Shelby had already taken off her T-shirt, and her shorts were on the way down. "Suits optional?" she called out, seconds before hitting the water.

Earl started scrambling to get his shirt and shorts off while walking toward the pool. He tripped and fell on the sandstone, scraping his right knee and left hand. When Shelby surfaced, and could see Earl's problems, she couldn't help but laugh just a little. He was slow to stand, but continued kicking his way out of his jeans and underwear before diving in to join her.

They swam for a bit, and made out for a bit, before getting out of the water. Not wanting to sunburn in all the wrong places, they put their suits on, and spent the next couple of hours outside.

Shelby was over her fears of being in another woman's home, and she seemed to be fine. Earl turned on the stereo, and switched it to the outside speakers. They baked in the sun, and listened to music. About every half hour they would jump in to cool off, but their time in the water was equally hot.

Katy's house had wetlands behind it, and the closest neighbor was a good hundred yards away. There was complete privacy, and no fear of disturbance to, or from, anyone. The twelve-pack of beer Earl had put in the fridge was going fast, and so was their afternoon.

After dinner they decided to watch a movie. Earl asked Shelby to pick one out of the hundreds on the shelves in the den. He was surprised to see her pick one of his favorites, *The Thomas Crown Affair*. She picked it based on Steve McQueen's looks; she had no idea what it was about. They watched the movie, and cuddled on the sofa.

When the movie was over, she said, "I can't believe someone with all that money would resort to stealing things just for the challenge."

"I can," Earl responded. "Everything in life is about the challenge. Wars are fought just for the challenge, and companies rise and fall for the challenge." He could see that Shelby's face looked like a question mark, so he dropped it and said, "Let's go to bed."

They slept until noon and, as Earl was getting out of bed, he noticed the flashing light on the phone indicating there was a message. From the caller ID he could see it was Katy calling, so he decided to wait until he was alone before listening to her message.

They went to Katy's amazing shower. Earl turned on the stereo, and put on a Rolling Stones CD. The music was vibrating from the four speakers above the shower as they stepped in. When he hit the switch, nine separate sprays of warm water came at them from every angle. "I Can't Get No Satisfaction" was rocking throughout the bathroom. As they were soaping each other's bodies, and singing along with the music, the bathroom lights suddenly flashed on and off several times.

There stood Katy, with Skylar on one side and Andrea on the other. Katy quickly ordered her daughters to wait in their rooms until she came to get them. Earl killed the water supply, and Katy threw them each a large towel. She stepped over to the stereo, and hit the power button. Shelby was trying to cover her body, as she suddenly started crying uncontrollably.

Katy raised her voice considerably to be heard over Shelby. "Somehow, I'm not too surprised, Earl. A lot of people warned me not to marry you because of your rotten reputation for sleeping around. I should have listened, but I actually believed we were in love with each other."

Katy paused, and Shelby covered her mouth to muffle her cries. Katy continued, "I'm going to be as civil as I can, considering your outrageous behavior. The girls and I will be gone for one hour—not a minute more. When we get back, you and your tramp friend will be gone from this house forever. I want everything of yours out of this house. If you can't get it in your car, put it at the end of the drive, but don't leave anything inside. If you do, it'll be burned."

Earl could only nod in acknowledgment, as Shelby continued to cry. He started to speak, but was stopped when Katy raised her hand within an inch of his face. "Not a damn word. If you want to talk to me, it will be through my attorney. I will never speak to you again."

By the time Earl and Shelby had gotten dressed and out of the bathroom, Katy and the girls were gone. Most of Shelby's clothes were already packed, so she had little left to do. Earl packed three large suitcases with suits and clothes he would need for work. By the time they were through, they'd filled the back seat and trunk completely. Earl then made several trips carrying more clothes and personal items to the end of the drive. He covered the outside items with a tarp from the garage, and put four large rocks on the corners.

At Shelby's apartment, she turned to Earl, and said, "Our good times are over. Good-bye, and don't call me again."

Earl said nothing as he turned and walked to his car.

Earl had nowhere to go, so he found a room at a Holiday Inn near his work. He didn't sleep much that night.

Monday morning he was walking through the hangar at 6:30. He kept an eye out for Shelby, but he didn't see her. Most everyone on the midnight shift did a double take, since Earl was seldom at work before 8:30 or 9:00.

He spent a couple of hours working in his office before going back to the hangar to see if Shelby had come in yet. She normally worked a 7:00 shift, so when Earl saw Shelby's supervisor, Kay Underwood, he asked her what time Shelby was due in today.

Kay replied, "You missed her, she's been here and gone. She came in about 5:30, and quit."

"You're kidding. Did she say where she was going?"

"Yes, but she made me promise not to tell anyone." Kay reached into a desk drawer, and handed Earl a letter-sized envelope. It was sealed, addressed to him, and marked "Personal." He took the envelope, and returned to his office.

Earl closed his office door behind him, threw the letter on his desk, and sat down. He propped his feet up, and leaned back in his chair. He had a great view of the tarmac where the U.P.-Ex planes parked to unload, and reload. He just sat there looking out the window for a good ten minutes.

He knew he had reached a new low in his life, but he was afraid it could get even worse if he were to read the letter. He was sure it was some kind of Dear John, but the more he thought about it, the more he thought how that would be a good thing. He might be alone again, but he knew she wouldn't have lasted anyway. His only real loss was Katy and her girls.

Short of the control tower, Earl's office had the best view of the airport. He had a large black walnut desk, and a low credenza that left him a full view above it. The windows on the back wall were all floor-to-ceiling, and looked out across the taxiways to the runways. Earl had planned the location of his furniture to be intimidating, and he often used it as a position of power when meeting with subordinates. In front of his desk sat two armchairs covered in deep, red leather. He also had a private bath with a shower.

Earl finally stopped his daydreaming, and pulled his legs down from his desk. He looked over to Shelby's envelope, and picked it up. He broke the seal, and slowly removed a typewritten letter with no signature. He started to read:

*Earl,*

*Sorry it has to end like this, but it's time to face reality. I can't believe how easy it was to lure you into my bedroom. Since I'm single, I didn't really do anything wrong. You, on the other hand, had everything to lose, but you did it anyway. After seeing your wife's house, car, and lifestyle, I was really surprised you would risk all that just for me.*

*Your reading this means you are aware that I quit work without notice. I also moved out of my apartment with five months left on my lease. I'm going to need your financial help. But, before you get mad, I'm going to give you something in return. My proposed agreement should serve both of us well as we move on with our lives. Kay, my* supervisor, is expecting you to bring her a large envelope, or small box, by noon on Wednesday of this week. She will forward it to me. She only has a post office box so there's no need to threaten her or anything. She knows nothing of our relationship.

Your package should contain fifty thousand dollars in cash. Please don't include any bills larger than a hundred. I told Kay the package would be some personal paperwork about a project I was doing for you. I think this is a fair settlement for the pleasure you had. I suppose that makes me a hooker, but at least I'll be a well-paid hooker, and I can live with that.

In exchange, you have my promise to keep our good times from the board of directors. I'm sure they would look harshly on your activities with a subordinate employee. They might even pay me more just to keep it from the media. I will also keep my new address secret from your wife and her attorney. She can't have me testify against you if she can't find me.

One more thing, I have video of us in my bedroom during our second encounter there. At that time, I was just going for ten thousand, but your plan for the weekend at Katy's sweetened the pot. I appreciate your help. If you'd like a copy, throw in an extra five thousand. The original will be ten.

The money must get to Kay before she leaves from work Wednesday or the board will get a letter from me. You may consider that both a threat and a promise.

Earl dropped the letter on his desk, stood up, and kicked his trashcan across his office and well into the adjoining conference room. When he turned back around he saw his secretary, Hazel. She was over seventy, and was standing outside his office looking at him with both hands over her mouth.

He knew he had to immediately say something to make this right. He walked to the door, and asked her to please come in. She ran her hand through her silver-gray hair and faked a slight smile as she slowly walked into his office. He motioned for her to sit in one of the two chairs in front of his desk. He took the other chair, and moved closer to her.

Calmly, he said, "I'm sorry you had to see that, Hazel. I had a really bad weekend. Yesterday, I found out a good friend of mine died, and now I read a letter that he wrote to me before he passed. As you can imagine, it was hard to read."

Hazel seemed to understand, as she put a compassionate smile over her previously confused face. Earl knew he'd said the right thing. He went on to ask her how her family was, and if her dog was still doing OK from a recent surgery on his hip. They talked a bit more about some work projects, and she then returned to her desk seemingly satisfied with his response. She closed his office door on her way out. Once again, Earl's charm had gotten him out of a tight spot.

Earl called his boss and CEO, Gordon Severson, and explained that he had some personal matters to take care of, and he needed to take most of the week off. He told him he would come in on Wednesday to finalize the weekend's union agreement, but it should only require a signature. Mr. Severson told him it wasn't a problem, but to keep his cell phone close in case they needed him. "To reconfirm, we'll expect to see you back at work on Wednesday to finalize the agreement, and be back on schedule next Monday."

Earl agreed.

Next he called his secretary back in to go over his schedule for the week. There wasn't anything she couldn't reschedule other than the Wednesday meeting.

Before leaving his office he tried to call Katy, but he got only her voicemail. The message had been changed to say, "If you're calling for Katy, Skylar, or Andrea, please leave a message, and we will return your call. If you're calling for Earl, he no longer lives here. Please try his cell." He was surprised she didn't say, "If you're looking for the asshole…"

Not having any luck reaching Katy, and needing to pick up the rest of his stuff, Earl decided to go there in person. When he arrived at her house he found a security guard blocking the drive. The guard got out of his car, and asked him if he was Earl Baker. When he answered positively, the guard handed him an envelope, and said, "You've been served." It was a restraining order forbidding him to get within a hundred yards of Katy, either of her two daughters, or their home. It was already effective.

Earl was pissed, but he knew better that to argue with a large man with a gun at his waist. He asked if he could get the rest of his things from the end of the drive. The guard told him that he could, and he helped him cram it all into his Mercedes. There were a few items that wouldn't fit so Earl told the guard, "Katy said she would burn anything that was left; tell her to strike a match."

As he drove out of the neighborhood, he realized it would be impossible for him to ever get back with Katy. His only hope was for her to take pity on him, and just let him walk away without hitting him up for money.

He made their bank his next stop. They had separate accounts, but they both had signature privileges to each. The banker pulled up his account, and Earl was glad to see his money was intact. When he checked Katy's account, he found it to be closed. He followed Katy's lead, and opened a new account without Katy's access privileges. He opened their safety deposit box to see Katy had also beaten him there. There was only his certificate of marriage, passport, and birth certificate. The certificate of marriage was on top, and it had a large, blood red, X marked across the page. He emptied the box, and closed the account.

Earl had money from investments, money in savings, and money borrowed from his 401(k) account. He liquidated everything, and came up with a little over one hundred thousand dollars. He asked the banker for sixty thousand in cash, and the balance to be placed in his new checking account. The only good news was the fact that he was debt-free outside of his divorce obligations.

The banker told Earl he was required to report a withdrawal of this size to the IRS and that the IRS might contact him requesting an explanation."

Earl replied, "I'll cross that bridge when it happens, but I need the money today."

The banker counted out sixty thousand dollars in one hundred-dollar bills and gave him a cheap, but lockable, briefcase to put the money in.

As he drove back to his hotel room, he entertained thoughts of killing Shelby, but they passed as he realized how stupid he had been to fall into her trap. He knew he would be immediately fired from his job if this became public; so he had no option but to pay her—at least for now. Not only could she get him fired, but she could also cause additional problems with his upcoming divorce proceeding. If he got fired for screwing a subordinate employee half his age, he'd be lucky to find a job anywhere.

He unloaded what he had in his car into his room, and picked up a paper in the hotel lobby. He started his hunt for a new place to live. It would need to be immediately available, and furnished. He hooked up with a real estate broker who had an agent who specialized in properties for lease. He expressed his urgency, and they spent the rest of his day looking at condos and townhouses.

This was an 'any-port-in-a-storm' type situation for Earl, so when they looked at a furnished townhouse, with a one-car garage, that was available today, he jumped on it. After paying cash for the first month's rent, and an equal deposit, he was given a key, and told he could move in whenever he liked. He had to sign a one-year lease on his half of the duplex unit that shared a common wall between them. The other unit was for sale, and not occupied.

He spent Tuesday morning moving his belongings from the hotel to the townhouse. His afternoon was spent buying the things he needed to set up his new place, and stocking the shelves and fridge with food. By the end of the day, he thought he had everything he needed.

He sat down in the well-worn recliner, turned on the twenty-six inch television, and popped the top on a beer that hadn't had time to chill. He took a big swallow, and said, "This has got to be the bottom."

Wednesday morning Earl realized he'd forgotten to buy coffee, and he had to settle on orange juice for his morning beverage. He had purchased a cardboard box to hold the blackmail money he would be paying to Shelby. He placed the money into the box, and used more than enough duct tape to secure the valuable package. As he got ready for work, he started a new list of the many items he'd forgotten to get on his shopping spree.

Earl was at his office at 9:00 to get ready for his 10:00 meeting with the union leaders. He knew it would be a short meeting, since the agreement was already in place. He called down to Kay to see what time she was leaving. It was a good call, because she was leaving an hour early at noon. The union meeting was complete at 11:00.

At 11:45, Earl was at Kay's desk with his box full of currency. Kay reached into a desk drawer, and pulled out a pre-addressed label. She pulled off the backing, and stuck it on top of the box. Knowing where her bread was buttered, Kay turned her head away with the label in full view of Earl. The address wasn't a post office box, as Shelby had indicated—it was a street address in Jonesboro, Arkansas.

Kay took her time to make sure Earl could read the address, and then looked back, and said, "Aren't you the sneaky one. You weren't supposed to see that." They both smiled, and Kay walked away with the box.

Earl was satisfied with what Kay had done to help, and with the knowledge that Jonesboro was only a couple of hours away. He could easily make the round-trip in a day.

On Thursday, Earl left early for Jonesboro, and arrived at 10:00 a.m. It was a small town so it didn't take long to find the address. The two-story, four-unit, apartment house had two sets of double glass doors at the entry. Access through the first set of doors was available to all, but the second set was available only through a coded entry pad. Earl entered the first set of doors, and looked at the names on the mailboxes. The name on unit number three was "Shelby & John Crosby." Obviously, Shelby had a male roommate or husband. All the mailboxes were keyed. Below the small mailboxes were two larger boxes. They were big enough to hold the box he had given to Kay.

Earl was finally seeing an even bigger picture of what was going on. Shelby had been working at U.P.-Ex only a couple of months, and Earl could see how she could have planned this whole thing with her roommate. It was all a big scam and he had walked right into it.

The parking lot for the residences was behind the apartments, so Earl circled to the back. Sure as hell, there sat Shelby's car. Not wanting to risk being seen, he took pictures of Shelby's car behind the apartments, and a picture of the units from the front. He'd accomplished what he'd come for, and he headed back to Memphis.

Following a friend's recommendation, Earl made an appointment with Scott Alan, an attorney who specialized in divorces. Earl had sent him a copy of the pre-nuptial agreement that he had signed. Mr. Alan had read it through twice before Earl had arrived, and had taken the seat in front of him. Mr. Alan asked, "Were you in any way forced or threatened into signing this agreement, or did you sign it on your own free will?"

"I signed it freely based on knowing she was the one with the money," Earl said, paused, and then continued, "To be honest, I haven't read any of it. I thought it better if I heard the bad news from an attorney so that I would get it legally straight the first time. I was afraid it might have kept me from marrying her and I planned on this marriage to be forever lasting."

"Nothing lasts forever, Mr. Baker. If you weren't forced to sign this, there's not much I can do for you. At this stage of the game, and with your admission of infidelity, I'm afraid you're going to be held responsible for the full terms of the agreement. I'm sorry, and I feel badly for you, but there's really nothing I can do. Feel free to get a second opinion, but you can expect to hear the same results. Next time, see me first—I'll save you a lot of agony, and a boatload of money."

Earl returned to his townhouse, sat in his recliner, and read the document for the first time. After he finished reading, he decided he was wrong earlier when he thought his life had reached bottom. He now knew that his life had no bottom.

Totally in the dumps, Earl turned on the television, and started flipping through the few channels he received. He stopped on a show about unsolved crimes. Its focus was on a hijacking that they referred to as the crime of the century. It was the B. D. Cooper hijacking.

Earl's head started spinning as he thought of how doable it would be to hijack one of his own company's flights. No one knew better than him about the lack of security at freight terminals, and he was the one who approved the authorizations for employee jump seat usage.

This wasn't the first time he'd thought about doing something like this, but previous thoughts were just casual, and never serious. But then, his life hadn't been in such a rut before.

He knew the Honolulu to Memphis run with U.P.-Ex would be the best option, since that flight was outside of radar and radio coverage for a few hours. It wouldn't be a walk in the park, and it would take a highly skilled pilot to pull it off, but he had an old friend in mind that might be perfect for the job. He was thinking about Rob Silvers.

Earl hadn't spoken with Rob for several years, but he had heard about his being rehired as a controller at Houston Center. He doubted that Rob would agree to any part of the plan he was considering, but he needed some time away from Memphis anyway.

He started making calls to track down Rob. It didn't take long to find his number in Houston.

# Chapter Ten

## Earl's Houston Visit

It was the last week of July, 2001, and Jewels and I were having dinner when Earl called. I had talked with him sparingly over the years, but I hadn't seen him since Jewels replaced him as my roommate. We had sent him an invitation to our wedding, but he had neither responded, nor attended. That was almost twenty years ago.

He started telling me his problems with his ex-wives and his ex-mistress. Obviously upset, it took him a minute or two before he got around to the purpose of his call. "I need a vacation, and I thought it would be fun to catch up on old times with you guys. I was wondering if I could come down for a long weekend in the next few weeks."

I had a full schedule with training on weekdays, and studying in the evenings, but I put my hand over the phone and asked Jewels. She said if it was only for a weekend—why not? We agreed on the dates of August 11$^{th}$ through the 13$^{th}$.

I still considered Earl a friend, but I hadn't forgotten that I'd once been very concerned about his possible involvement in the '81 bombing of Houston Center. I knew it would be best if I could think of that only as water under the bridge. Had he truly been guilty, they surely would have caught up with him by now.

There was still some talk around the center about Earl holding a spot on the FBI's person-of-interest list, but it was only rumors. However, I decided I wouldn't tell anyone at the center about his coming for a visit. I couldn't see what could be gained by throwing wood on a fire that was dead many years ago. We would reserve that weekend for rehashing old times, and having fun.

Earl came down in the jump seat of a U.P.-Ex flight. He arrived late Saturday morning and I picked him up at the U.P.-Ex airport terminal. It was only a couple of blocks north of the center, and we drove past the center on our way to the house. I was a little surprised when Earl asked, "Did they ever catch the guy that did the bombing?" He sounded like he was down-and-out, but I answered his question, "No, not to my knowledge." Then, after a short hesitation, I continued, "OK Earl, I know something's bothering you. What's the problem?"

Earl forced a slight smile and said, "It's a long story. Why don't we wait until we have more time?"

"Sure, no problem, but we need to concentrate on the good times we're going to have over the next couple of days, not the bad. If you want to get it off your chest, that's fine. If not, that's fine too."

When Earl and I came through the front door, Jewels was coming in from the back deck. She saw Earl and, as she walked toward him, she said, "Give me a hug."

Earl welcomed her hug and stepped back to look at her. "The years have sure been good to you, Jewels. You look fantastic."

"Thank you, but look at you. You look great. Unlike Rob, you've still kept your hair. It's good to see you."

I was feeling like burnt toast until Jewels finally leaned over and gave me a kiss.

It was a nice afternoon with temperatures forecasted to stay in the mid-eighties. We found a shady spot on the deck to sit, and Jewels brought out sandwiches and snacks. She had also put a case of beer on ice, and the cooler was within easy reach of all. The next few hours were set aside for talking about anything or anybody— yesterday, today, or tomorrow.

I started a conversation about where some of the fired strikers were today. Everyone we knew seemed to have gone in a different direction. Since I was back at the center, I'd heard more about the terminated controllers than Earl, so I said, "I heard a couple of guys became cops. Another guy, Dennis, went into banking, and did quite well. One of the guys bought a bar, but I heard that didn't work out too well. You probably remember Harold and Peggy, they both went out on strike, and both got fired. Last I heard, they were both back at the center working in the training department."

"One gal, I can't remember her name, opened a video store, and she and her husband were said to be making money hand-over-fist up until a few years back when they sold their business. They must have seen the writing on the wall because they got out before that business went south. I heard they made a big profit and are now very comfortably retired on the shores of Lake Conroe." I paused, and then said, "On the down side, I heard one of the younger controllers committed suicide."

Earl said, "I heard about that, and couldn't believe someone could be that depressed."

"You say that Earl, but I thought you were getting close in the weeks after the strike."

"I wasn't that close and I recovered." Earl paused to change the subject, and said, "I heard the training department is under a private contractor now. Is that right?"

"Yeah, that's right. I see Buster up there fairly often. They give manual and radar training problems to rehires like me."

Our memories ran dry of names so I tried to lift Earl's spirits by saying, "I felt like I did fairly well by making captain with Northwest, but you blew by everyone. No one can hold a candle to your being the chief operating officer for a multi-billion-dollar company."

"Trust me. It's not as fantastic as you might think. It's a very demanding job, and I have no problem spending more than I make. Of course, I get a lot of help from my ex-wives. The state automatically deducts their spousal support before sending me what little is left."

Jewels decided the conversation was going in the wrong direction, "Rob, tell Earl about your plans for tomorrow."

"We can cancel if you're not into it, but I've made us a tee time for ten o'clock tomorrow morning. I've got an extra set of clubs for you, and the weather is supposed to be good. What'd you think?"

"That's perfect, but I haven't played for a year or so. You'll have to put up with my poor performance, and promise not to laugh."

Jewels said, "While you guys are playing golf, I'll be spending Rob's money shopping. That way we'll all have fun. For now, I'm going to get our dinner ready."

Earl and I continued to gossip about anything and anyone while watching the planes go by. The wind was out of the east, and our house was along the approach to the east/west runway at Houston Intercontinental. On days like today there was a steady stream of aircraft passing behind our house at about two hundred feet with their gear down.

With our backgrounds in aviation, we enjoyed a game of identifying the aircraft types as they flew by. The noise caused occasional breaks in our conversation, but they lasted for only a minute or two.

Our house was well-insulated, so the noise was muted inside. We could still hear them when they were landing east, but they didn't bother us. How could we complain when we wouldn't have jobs without them?

We had a typical two-thousand-square-foot, brick rambler that was like thousands of others throughout the Houston area.

Before we knew it, Jewels was calling us to dinner. As with any out-of-town guest, she made her failsafe dinner of roast beef, mashed potatoes, gravy, and green beans. I could make a meal just out of her homemade rolls and butter. As we walked inside, the aroma from the kitchen hit our senses, and I said, "You're going to love Jewels' cooking."

While we filled our plates and poured our wine, I made the mistake of starting our dinner conversation. "Well, Earl, it's been a long time since we've seen you. Tell us what's good in your life nowadays."

It became immediately obvious that Earl either didn't hear the word "good," or he just decided to go his own way. He started with the meat of his problems. "Nothing good, I'm afraid. My latest wife, Katy, divorced me after catching me in her shower with a girl half my age. There's no possible way I can deny the fact that I'm a huge idiot when it comes to the women in my life. You'd think that after four divorces that turned out to be both financial and personal disasters, I'd learn something. But no, my fifth will go down as the most costly of them all."

Jewels made some sort of sympathetic noise, and Earl gave her a weak smile.

"She had millions," Earl said. "So I wasn't surprised when she had her attorney draw up a pre-nuptial agreement for my signature. It was several pages long so I just signed it like it was another signature page of a home mortgage. I filed it away for later reading, but I didn't get around to that until after I was caught with another woman. My attorney told me I was in deep shit and there was nothing he could do to bail me out.

"I thought I got hosed, but the few sane people I know thought, all things considered, that I was lucky to be alive." He shrugged. "They were right, and I know that now, but I have four large spousal-maintenance assessments being deducted from my check. There is painfully little left for me."

I couldn't miss such a great opening, "Sometimes you amaze me, Earl. You're the smartest guy I know when it comes to business, but when it comes to women you obviously let your dick do your thinking." I paused. "Anyway, we don't want to worry about anything this weekend. The golf course I'm taking you to is a great course, and I know you'll like it."

"That sounds great. Thanks. But let me tell you the rest of my story. The young girl sharing the shower with me was also one of my employees. She blackmailed me for fifty thousand dollars, and I had no choice but to pay her. She threatened to call my boss, and send letters to the board members. Of course, she also made a video of our bedroom adventures. I can get you a copy for five thousand dollars."

I knew Earl was joking, so I laughed. But Jewels was staring at him in astonishment.

"If I hadn't paid her," Earl said, "I would have been fired for sure. If I'd lost my job in that way, my degrees wouldn't mean shit. I'd be hard-pressed to find anything; and I need to hold on to this job for at least a couple more years." Jewels and I both smiled as he continued, "Overall, my life sucks. That's why I needed this getaway."

He was right. His life sucked more than I would have thought possible of anyone in his position. He had only himself to blame. "I'm really sorry to hear that, Earl, and I won't rag on you anymore while you're here. We need to concentrate on just doing fun things to keep your mind off all those problems."

Earl shrugged, "Like I said, I took a big hit financially, but I'm not broke yet. My problem is more long-term than short. I'm looking at nothing but Social Security for my retirement. Pretty sad, don't you think?"

I decided not to tell him we could be in the same boat, so I just shook my head. "Well, your money's no good here, and I haven't heard anything that can't be worked out. You've still got a few years before retirement, and I'm pretty damn sure that even half of your net pay would be envied by most people."

"Gross pay maybe, but probably not net. Anyway, that's the end of my troubles. I won't bring you down anymore."

We stayed up until about 11:00 talking. It was hard, but we worked to avoid all negative conversations. That led to a lot of dead space.

Jewels and I talked a little about Earl's problems after we were in bed, and we reached an agreement that we weren't going to feel bad for him anymore. We decided to assume 'you-made-your-bed' type of attitude, and went to sleep.

When Earl came out of the bathroom the next morning I reminded him of our 10:00 tee time, and told him the temperature would be in the nineties. "Shorts would be good."

"Sounds great; I'll be ready in ten."

Earl and I both loved to play golf, but neither of us was very good. When I called in for our tee time I was told we would be paired with another twosome. That was normal on weekends, but we were pleasantly surprised when we checked in, and were told the other players had canceled out. That made it easier for us to have some personal time without making fools of ourselves in front of better golfers.

After we hit off the first tee, Earl started talking about jobs he sometimes heard about that he thought might be of interest to me. "I occasionally have opportunities for short flying jobs. People call me every so often needing a pilot to fly from point A to point B because their pilot, for whatever the reason, can't make the flight. Do you think you might be interested in something like that?"

"I don't know. I can always use some extra money, but it would depend on how long I would be gone. As you know, I've got a forty-hour-a-week job, and I usually study at home for several hours more."

As we played on, my curiosity rose. "If it was just for a long weekend or something, I might be able to use a few days of annual leave if the pay was right. Of course it would need to be in an aircraft I was certified to fly. I'm still considered current in multi-engine jet aircraft, but I've only been type-rated in a half dozen or so. There would be a lot of variables I'd have to work out. Would they be U.P.-Ex flights? What kind of flying jobs are you talking about?"

It was my turn to hit so we broke our conversation long enough for us to finish the hole we were on. The next hole was a par three, and the group ahead of us was backed up.

"I usually find out about these flights from my pilots who have agreed to take a flight, but later needing to get out of it for some reason or another. Some U.P.-Ex pilots moonlight with other companies to ferry planes around, or take a leg of a flight when someone calls in sick. Most of them are along that line. You couldn't sub for one of our pilots without going through a lot of specialized training that includes weight and balance issues specific to our loads."

We were interrupted several times to hit our shots, but Earl continued our conversation when he could work it in.

"As an extreme example," Earl said, "One of our pilots was on his normal run from Memphis to Dubai and back, with a four-day layover in Dubai. It wouldn't take much of a detective to find out which hotel the U.P.-Ex pilots stay in. Shortly after he arrived, he received a call from a guy inquiring if he would be interested in making some extra money on his layover. When he learned what the job paid, and what he'd have to do for the money, he was persuaded to take the job."

I interrupted his story, and said, "Why do I get the feeling there might be some legality problems with these flights?"

"This specific flight had a lot of legality issues, but the pilots who tell me about these flights are in my circle of trust, so I turn a deaf ear to some of the rules they break. I'd deny it if it was ever brought up, but I sometimes get a percentage for brokering some of these deals… but let me continue.

"The flight the pilot in Dubai agreed to take was out of South Africa to the Maldives. That's an island off southern India. He told me the plane was an older 727 that looked a little worse for wear, but it flew OK. The plane was fully loaded, and fueled, when he picked it up. The manifest wasn't in English so he hadn't a clue what was listed to be on the plane, but it probably wouldn't be truthful anyway. After landing in Maldives, he taxied the plane into a hangar, and walked away.

"He was flown by corporate jet from Dubai to his origin, and was picked up by that same jet at the destination. He had plenty of time to do it all on his layover in Dubai. Of course, he couldn't log his trip or he wouldn't have the hours of rest to legally fly our flight back to Memphis. I have no idea how many laws he broke, but it had to be a lot. Of course, his compensation was considerable."

As we were driving up to the eighteenth green, I said, "Don't leave me hanging. What did this guy get paid for that little jaunt?"

Earl said, "Guess."

"I don't know… Fifty thousand?"

With a big smile on his face, Earl replied, "Four hundred thousand dollars."

"You've got to be shitting me—four hundred thousand for four days? He had to be hauling guns, or drugs, or both. If he got caught doing something like that he'd never see the light of day. And I'm sure he wouldn't like his new roommates."

"You're probably right, but I'm sure he weighed the risks. Besides, for that kind of money, wouldn't you?"

I shook my head. "No, Absolutely not. For one, I wouldn't have the balls to do something like that. Especially in countries I know nothing about. The risk-reward percentage is far too high. That guy may have lucked out on that trip, but sooner or later, he'll end up in some foreign jail. I wouldn't do that for any amount of money."

"Four hundred grand would pay a lot of bills, and he was paid in American dollars."

"I would never be interested in something like that, so you need not call if that's the kind of flight you have to offer."

Earl replied, "I was shocked to hear about that flight. I didn't have anything to do with it, and I was surprised the pilot even told me about it. We were at a bar, and he'd had too much to drink."

"I told you about that flight only as a worse-case example of some of the flying jobs that I hear about. I would never expect you to take something like that, and I was shocked that one of my pilots actually did. He quit U.P.-Ex shortly after that."

That evening we had another nice dinner, courtesy of Jewels. Afterward, we all sat around the living room, just shooting the bull, and getting to know each other again.

On Monday Earl had a noon flight back to Memphis, and I had to go to work about the same time. I dropped him off at the U.P.-Ex hangar and went to work.

# Chapter Eleven

## Thirty-nine vs. Fifty-nine

I was thirty-nine, and probably nearing my peak, when President Reagan terminated me from my job as a controller. At age fifty-nine, I found myself trying to keep up with all the young men and women hired to take my place. Most were twenty to thirty years my junior. I was constantly going over the flight progress strips to re-enforce my memory. But that didn't always work as well as it should, because it took time away from my need to scan the radar. The short-term memory problems I had feared were occasionally raising their ugly head. These weren't the kind of memory problems that would affect me in any other job. They were specifically unique to air traffic control.

Controllers must recognize a situation well in advance and compartmentalize those bits of information. Later, as the situation becomes closer to reality, that pre-stored information has to automatically resurface as necessary. With me, it was working at least ninety-five percent of the time, but not the one hundred percent I needed to do my job right. It was difficult to admit, even if only to myself.

By constantly refocusing my concentration back and forth between the flight progress strips and the radar, I was able convince my supervisors that I had enough ability to be certified on a couple positions, and that gave me more training time, but I knew the writing was on the wall because I couldn't convince myself. I had lost the confidence I had to have to be comfortable in my job. As feared from the beginning, my mind was simply not as quick as it once was.

In the first week of September, I failed a check ride on my third non-radar position. I was given forty hours of retraining on the position before being required to take another check ride.

## Controlling – Robert Seckler

On September 11$^{th}$, 2001, I was assigned training with live traffic between 7:00 am and 3:00 pm. My instructor was plugged in with me and monitoring my progress.

A little after nine we started hearing rumors about an aircraft hitting the north tower of the twin towers in New York City. At that time it didn't appear to be a terrorist attack. When a second aircraft hit the south tower, it started getting real serious real quick. Traffic going into or through New York Center's airspace was being diverted.

Even though our air traffic was over a thousand miles away from New York, you could feel the tension throughout the building. Everyone was on edge. Rumors were flying more frequently than facts as everyone seemed to have a different story to tell.

As more diversions were being mandated I was pulled off my training position and assigned to help with data entry to keep up with the changes that were happening by the minute. Everyone continued to get nervous as supervisors were updating controllers as new information was being received.

It was around ten when we received orders to land all aircraft at the nearest airport suitable for the size of the aircraft. This wasn't something any of us had trained for but, all things considered, it went fairly well.

I was entering new flight plans to new destinations as fast as I could get them in the computer. Over the next half hour aircraft were being funneled into any airport with a runway long enough and strong enough, to accommodate their landing, and later departure. The control room soon went from being chaotic, to orderly lines of traffic disappearing from the radar as they touched down at their new destinations.

The following day there was little for us to do, and then I was off for three days. When I returned everything was getting back to normal and I returned to my training. We knew we had been an active part of history that had never happened before, and we hoped would never be done again.

On September 29$^{th}$ I was scheduled for my next check ride. I was extremely nervous, and my confidence was low. That led to a simple mistake that turned out to be cause for my failure of my second, and last, certification test. They set up a training meeting to determine my fate. Although I might have been able to apply for an extension of my training, I knew it was time to throw in the towel.

On one hand, I was saddened to see my hard work end in failure, but I knew I had given it my best, and the stress release was welcomed. Unfortunately, that release was short-lived. I was now faced with the problems of telling Jewels, and finding a new job.

To assist me in finding a new job I was allowed to work as an assistant controller until November 19$^{th}$. If I hadn't found another position by that time I would be facing involuntary separation from the FAA for the second time.

I was optimistic and believed I would find something before the end of my grace period that would take me through to retirement. I made a decision not to share my problems with Jewels until I had good news to go along with the bad. There was no reason for both of us to worry. My pay would stay intact until I either transferred to a new position, or was out of a job.

I immediately started my search by going on the government jobs website on a daily basis. Most of the jobs I qualified for paid about half of what I was currently making - which was about half of what I was making at Northwest. Since my end goal was to retire from the government, and that retirement would be based on my high three years' average wage, that goal was fading fast.

I knew I could make more money if I could find a flying job that didn't include carrying passengers. Pilots working for those companies didn't fall under the age sixty forced retirement laws so I could work as long as I could pass the flight physical. I found several of those companies, and I submitted my applications.

After submitting numerous applications, I came face-to-face with the realization of age discrimination. Companies looking to hire pilots to haul freight would likely have up to a hundred applicants; maybe more. About twenty-five percent of the applicants had an experience level close to mine. Of that group, I was likely to be the oldest applicant. Of course, no company would actually tell me that, but I knew it to be true. I received no positive feed-back.

Time was passing, and I still didn't have a solid prospect for a suitable job. I called Earl, and asked about any availability for a flying job with U.P.-Ex, or even one of the flights he had told me about. I was embarrassed to tell him I'd washed out of training, so I left that part out.

Earl said, "I have so many well qualified pilots waiting for an opening with us, that it would be too obvious if I hired you over others twenty years younger and with more jet time than you have. It just wouldn't work. However, I will keep my eyes and ears open for one of the other possibilities. I don't know of anything right now, but sometimes those jobs just pop-up and they need someone right away. I'll call you if I hear of anything.

Hindsight was making it increasingly obvious that I should have known better than to, at the age of fifty-nine, accept a position that had a maximum retirement age of fifty-six – waived or not. We were all glad they waived the maximum age requirement since we couldn't have been rehired without it, but for those of us who had washed out, it also served as our enabler to fail.

Earl called a week later. "I've got a possible job coming up around Christmas, but I don't have any details about it yet. Do you want me to put you on my list of applicants?"

Suddenly the dim light at the end of my tunnel flashed brightly. I confessed my training problems to Earl, and said, "Yes I do. I might even be agreeable to a job that didn't cover every legal base, but nothing close to the one you told me about during our golf outing."

"I know better than to send you out on something like that. I'll put you on the top of the list for the December job if it comes through, and I'll call you either way when I know something."

I felt terrible about having walked Jewels down the proverbial garden path to disaster, and I had blown our opportunity for a decent retirement. I had to find a way to make it right.

It wasn't long before Earl called me back. "It looks like the flying job in December will be happening and, at least for now, the plane scheduled is an Airbus. I still don't know all the details, but I'll tell you what I do know."

Before I could say anything, he went on. "To start with, I want you to know that this flight will definitely be illegal. There's no question about that, but you will stay on U.S. soil and, most importantly, there will be no victims to this crime. I know that may sound unbelievable, but I'm serious about that—no victims. Your compensation for three or four days' work will be five hundred thousand dollars. Think about how a half-million dollars in cash would change your retirement picture."

That was a lot to take in, and I was a little bit dumbfounded, so I couldn't think of anything to say.

Earl continued, "That's it for now, but we will need to finalize details fairly soon. Does this sound like something you'd be interested in, or should I find someone else?"

I found my voice, and said, "I'm interested in anything that will pay me that much money, and the thought of a victimless crime is intriguing. I'll need more details before I can commit, but yes, I'm interested."

"You'll need to get a prepaid phone for our talks. We don't want our conversations to show up on our phone bills. Once that's done, we can talk longer and more freely. I'll gather my thoughts, and I'll be prepared to give you more details when you call from your new phone."

I really didn't know what to think, but I knew a half-million dollars would solve our piss-poor retirement dilemma. I was skeptical about the victimless part but, if it were true, it would go a long way toward my commitment to his plan.

I started thinking of what I would, or wouldn't, do for that kind of money.

There were several things that could keep me from doing this, but first and foremost would be Jewels' protection. She could have no knowledge of, or be party to, this crime. If I were to be caught, there must be nothing she could be arrested for, or found guilty of. If Earl couldn't assure me of that, it would end there.

Assuming we pass that obstacle, and it's true about the no-victims clause, I was fairly sure I would be good. I would take some chances, and cross the line of legality here and there as long as those things were met.

When it came down to stealing from someone or some company, I decided I could do that as long as I thought they were wealthy enough to absorb the loss with little disruption to their life. My logic being that these people were probably silver-spoon babies, and they should share the wealth. However, once again, the question of victims comes back up. I also added the fact that the odds of success would have to be significantly in my favor.

Earl had made it perfectly clear that I would be committing a crime and, for that kind of money, I would expect nothing less. I knew that, statistically, most crimes were never solved. However, I also knew how that statistic included a shitload of very trivial crimes, like speeding or jaywalking.

On a larger scale, the Houston Center bombing was declared the nation's number-one priority twenty years ago, but there was never an arrest, much less a conviction. The next large unsolved aviation related crime that came to mind was the B. D. Cooper hijacking in 1971. As hard as they looked, and some are probably still looking, they've never found him or the majority of the money he took from his hijacking. The Mafia boss, Jimmy Hoffa, is rumored to be buried in concrete somewhere, but he's never been found, and his killer never prosecuted.

Knowing our retirement years could easily exceed, the years Jewels and I have been together, I would go a long way to make sure those years were comfortable and enjoyable.

I had talked myself into a firm YES to Earl's plan.

The weekend came, and when I was sure Jewels would be gone for an hour or so, I called Earl with my newly purchased, prepaid cell phone. When he answered, I said, "Here's the deal. You can't say or do anything that will lead Jewels to finding out about my part in this plan."

Earl agreed.

With that, I said, "Tell me how you can guarantee there'll be no victims. If you can do that, then you can count me in."

"You and your actions," Earl said, "will be responsible for making sure there are no victims. If you do everything according to the plan, I guarantee you, there will be none."

I replied, "Let's hear what you've got."

Earl continued, "The most important thing about this plan is trust. Total trust between us is mandatory. I will tell you only what's required of you, and nothing else. You have to focus on your job, and let me focus on mine."

"It will be necessary for you to use your own money for some portions of the plan. You will need to have instant availability to about fifteen thousand dollars. You probably won't need that much, but it could be close to that, and you don't want to be short. Do you have access to that kind of money?"

"I have a 401(k) plan from an employer before Northwest that I've never rolled over. Last time I looked, it had a value of about twenty thousand dollars. I think I can cash it in without Jewels finding out about it, but the timing will need to be right."

"Before I go into too much detail," Earl said, "I'll quickly review the whole plan and give you your last chance to bail out."

Earl paused, but when I didn't respond, he said, "A U.P.-Ex flight will leave Honolulu for Memphis on December 21. I will give you a letter of authorization to board that flight as a new employee coming to work in Memphis. When you are outside of Honolulu's radar coverage, and the crew has made its last report to Honolulu Center, you will place a gas mask over your mouth and nose. You will then immediately release chloroform gas from a briefcase provided by me. It will cause no permanent harm to the crew, but it will knock them unconscious with two breaths."

I was just taking all this in, so I still had no response.

"You will then shut down all electronics, and turn the plane around. You will fly about a thousand miles west, and land on Johnston Island. It's a very small island with a big runway, and it will be uninhabited when you land. You will collect a shitload of worn currency from a container, and then go to the runway to wait for your ride. The pilot of a twin engine plane will land, pick you up, and fly you to a nearby island.

"You will then be pampered by all the amenities of a corporate jet flight. They will take you wherever you may want to go within the range of their aircraft. You will find a safe haven for the currency, and sit on it for at least six months. We'll then meet again to divide the money. That's all I have for now. My recap is over."

I was taking some notes, so it was a couple of moments before I said, "I can't believe you want me to hijack one of your company's planes. That's very interesting. Only yesterday, in anticipation of this possibility, I read about every hijacking that occurred over the past twenty years. Some were successful, but most were not. I was surprised to see how many of these hijackings weren't for money. They were for some political agenda—like those recent ones of September eleventh.

"I could find only one hijacking that involved a freight flight. It was the 1994 Fed-Ex flight that was hijacked by a disgruntled employee. He was going to use the plane as a missile to plow into their corporate offices, but he was subdued by the crew before he could do so."

I paused a moment while I thought more about it, and then said, "Maybe that's where the terrorists got their ideas for the twin towers. Anyway, don't you think this would be following way too close on the heels of that disaster to be successful? I would think the government would jump all over anything that even smelled like a hijacking."

"That's good. You've done your homework," Earl replied. "It is because of those attacks that this plan needs to be done soon. The feds are busy trying to get their new Transportation Security Administration up and running, and they're increasing all their security measures at every passenger terminal in the country. They are far too short-handed to mess with freight companies right now."

Knowing a little about what Earl was saying, I just agreed.

Earl continued, "If anything, they're relaxing, not building, their feeble security of freight carriers. They don't have the time, money, or manpower to do anything now, but as soon as TSA gets its shit together, freight carriers will be next. Now is our window of opportunity, and it won't be open that long."

He paused, and then said, "By the way, with the gas you'll be dispersing into the cockpit, you'll have no worries about the crew subduing you. They'll be fast asleep for the entire time you're around."

I took a breath and started to speak, but Earl continued.

"By the time the FAA will be expecting your check-in call to Los Angeles Center, you'll be on the ground at Johnston Island—the very last place in the world they'd look." Earl paused again before saying, "With all that, are you good to continue, or do you want to throw in the towel?"

I replied, "Jury's still out, but you go ahead."

"Not good enough," Earl said. "I need a commitment before I say any more. Are you in or out?"

"Under the assumption of no added surprises, and no victims, I'm in."

"Thank you. I'm counting on you. All expenditures must be paid in cash, or a pre-paid credit card under a bogus name. I will give you a schedule of where you have to be, and when you have to be there. You can be early, but you can't be late. You'll have plenty of time to make your scheduled rounds. If something should come up that prevents you from being where you're supposed to be, and you miss your pickup flight, you'll have limited escape options, and you'll likely need cash to cover such a possibility."

I agreed.

"There are only two times when you'll be dependent on someone to provide the next leg of your transportation. One is your pick-up flight from Johnston Island. If he fails to show you'll find an old, but capable, Beach Queen Air next to the terminal building. You may have to break in and hotwire it, but it'll get you off the island before the Fish & Wildlife people come back on Monday.

"I'm totally confident your ride will show on time," Earl continued, "But you might want to bring charts of the area to determine your safest destination with the Queen Air you will be stealing."

I cleared my throat. "Earl, you've got to know you're not saying anything to calm my nerves about this whole ordeal. You do know that, don't you?"

"Shouldn't I tell you of the options for any unplanned possibilities? You should realize that I'm going to do everything I possibly can to make this all go well. Think about it. You'll have all the money. If anyone should be worried, it would be me."

"Point made. Go ahead."

"The other time you'll be dependent on someone else is the business jet waiting to take you back to the mainland. You'll have a phone number to contact him if he's not where he's supposed to be. If you can't work it out on the phone, it'll be time to use some of that extra cash we talked about. You'll need to buy a ticket, and fly commercial. The only problem you might have will be the eight or nine pieces of luggage you'll have with you. But, you're a smart guy, you'll figure something out."

Earl paused, as though waiting for some sort of response from me, so I said, "I haven't heard something I can't live with, so let's keep going."

"OK. Well, we've got to end, except for a couple advisories. It's your choice, but if I were in your role, I'd want at least two or three good disguises, maybe even four. There are security cameras everywhere, and you can depend on being videotaped all along your trip. It's simply part of our everyday life. A good disguise can prevent anyone from recognizing you. A very good disguise can prevent facial recognition software from picking you out of a crowd."

That was all a new idea to me and I thought this was getting complicated.

Earl continued, "Also, unlike me, I don't know of any weird mannerisms you have, but if you have any that can be associated specifically to you, cover them up somehow because they can blow your cover even when you're in a great disguise. It's that type of little thing that could be picked up by someone, and be the death of us all."

Earl paused for a drink before continuing. "You'll need IDs and credit cards to go with every person you are disguised to be. I can take care of that for you, and they'll be perfect. Send me a picture and the information needed for each ID. I can provide a driver's license from any state, passports, and even a pilot's license with a matching logbook. In each case, I need all of the required information, and a minimum of two to three weeks' notice."

"I can do that," I said.

"You'll be responsible for getting the credit cards, but you'll need to have your new IDs to get them. Any bank will sell you a pre-paid card for cash. What sort of limit you will want to put on them is up to you, but hotels will run a card for more than the cost of the room, and rental cars will want proof of insurance. I can get that as well but, again, I'll need three weeks' notice."

"I get it."

"Moving on," Earl continued, "plan your trip to arrive in Honolulu in time to go shopping for luggage. You will need to buy two sets of luggage, and each set should have a large suitcase that holds at least two smaller suitcases nested inside. That will give you a total of six pieces of luggage, plus whatever you brought with you. For added room for the money, you'll also want to throw in a couple of dark-colored, nylon duffel bags that you can't see the currency through. That will give you a total of eight travel bags to hold the shit-load of currency you'll be taking home. The container holding this currency will be five cubic feet in volume."

That all sounded like a hell of a lot of baggage. But I held my comments.

"Don't think of taking any more suitcases than that, or you'll raise even more suspicion. I believe you can get away with eight by saying you've been working on the island for a few months, but don't try to push it. Any money you can't get in those suitcases will just have to be left behind."

"For that reason, you'll want to start with the bigger bills first and work your way down. You can do the math to figure out how many bills will be in the five-cubic-foot container, and how many will fit into those eight pieces of luggage. But not knowing the varying denominations of the currency, I can't tell you the total value."

Earl took a breath, and kept going. "I'm probably missing a few things, but we'll do another one of these sessions next weekend. If you need to talk about something before then, call me after eight p.m. But don't call me at work."

It was left at that.

# Chapter Twelve

## Confession Time

During dinner, Jewels asked, "How's your training going? You haven't said a word about it in a couple of weeks."

I knew it was time to come clean. "Not well at all, I'm afraid. I didn't want to tell you about it, but I failed a check ride for a second time. My program has come to an end. They are giving me until November 19 to pursue other government jobs. After that, I'm out."

She reached over, took my hand, and said, "I knew something was up with you. The last few weeks you've lacked your normal cheery attitude. I'm so sorry, honey, but we knew this was a possibility. We'll just have to settle on less money with the government, or maybe you should start looking for flying jobs outside of the airlines. You could work those as long as you could pass the physical, right?"

I smiled, and said, "Yes, but I have to wonder how long that will be."

She sighed. "Well, you know better than I, we can't pay our bills on my salary alone."

I told her, "We're OK for now, and I'm confident I'll find something before my time runs out. I've already started looking around the government jobs website. I haven't seen anything that jumps out at me yet, but something will pop."

Jewels leaned over, gave me a kiss, and said, "Don't worry about anything—it'll show in your interviews. Besides, you know we'll figure it out. We always do."

"I agree, but I think we should put our house on the market so we'll be flexible to go wherever a new job might take us."

She nodded. "As much as I hate to do it after such a short stay, I agree with you. We need to sell it, and we can live in one of those extended-stay hotels until we decide where our next step will take us."

I was surprised she was so willing to sell the house and move on, but I took advantage of the situation and said, "I'll talk with a real estate agent, and see what our options are."

On Saturday afternoon, Jewels was going shopping with Glenda. As she was walking out the door, she said, "Don't worry, I'm just going shopping, not buying." She knew the real estate agent was coming out and she didn't want to be present when we started this new step. "You can make our housing decisions, and I won't question whatever you do."

Knowing she would be gone most of the afternoon, I got busy with my research. I went to our files and dug out my last statement from the 401(k) program I still had money in. I called our representative and told him I wanted to close the account and cash out. He ran some quick numbers, and said, "After a ten-percent early-withdrawal penalty, and thirty percent in taxes, you will get around twelve thousand six hundred dollars. You realize you could avoid the early withdrawal penalty if you wait until January when you'll be fifty-nine and a half?" I told him I knew that, but I needed the money now. He told me he would get a check in the mail within two days.

I pulled up flights to Hawaii, and got depressed when I saw the prices. Houston to Honolulu would run about eleven hundred dollars one way. I knew that leg of my trip would be my responsibility and the money would have to come from the 401(k) money.

Our doorbell rang, and I greeted the real estate agent. She believed she could sell our home for the same price we paid for it, but we'd be out the cost of our improvements, and our closing cost. It was better than I thought, so I told her to sell it as quickly as she could. I also told her we would be flexible with our closing dates.

After she left, I was back on my laptop. I entered "actor disguises make-up" and I came up with numerous companies that sold the products I would need to change my looks. I decided I would need to make a cross-town trip to a couple of stores in south Houston, but just to look around.

Next I pulled up Johnston Atoll Island. I didn't mention it to Earl, but I had landed on Johnston Island five or ten times when I was in the Navy back in the sixties. I was stationed at Pearl Harbor, and I had often flown military and civilian personnel to and from the island over a period of about six months.

My mind wandered back to when they'd used Johnston Island as a launching pad for above-ground nuclear tests. I'd even had the opportunity to witness one of the rockets from Johnston climb out into the stratosphere well above us before it exploded. It was a forty-eight megaton blast and the country's largest above ground test. It was detonated about eleven pm on a moonless night. We had to wear dark glasses to protect our eyes, and I was glad I had them on. The skies instantly went from being pitch black to a brightness equaled to a welder's arc. The skies were suddenly brightened to make the darkness of night seem more like noon on a sunny day.

For the next half hour we watched the skies break into what looked to be millions of stars. These pieces of the blast slowly rose from the horizon to form an arch above us. We were told the magnetic poles of the earth were drawing the particles toward them. It was at about forty-five minutes before it was dark again. We wore dosimeters to track the radiation that was being absorbed into our skin – but we were never given the results.

From the Hawaiian Islands, the blast looked like a sunset, and pictures from Honolulu became the cover story of all the major news magazines.

I had many memories of Johnston Island, and I knew very well that Earl was right about the runway. It was plenty long enough, wide enough, and strong enough to accommodate most any aircraft.

I found out the island was currently being used for coral life and fish research by the Department of Fish & Wildlife. They had a team of six people on the island Mondays through Thursdays. They were working on various projects in the crystal-clear waters that surround the coral reef. Also, as Earl had said, they kept a Queen Air there for their aerial observations. I had to give Earl the credit he was due. This was the perfect island for his plan.

I finally got to the fun part. I loaded up my flight simulator, and flew the route Earl had suggested from about three hundred miles east of Honolulu to Johnston Island. Included in the program's various aircraft options was an Airbus similar to the ones used by U.P.-Ex. I took the plane off Honolulu on a direct route to Memphis. At three hundred miles east of Honolulu I reversed course and headed toward Johnston Island.

It wasn't long before I identified a problem. Although I was outside radar coverage from Honolulu, the radars on the big island of Hawaii would be able to pick me up. To avoid that coverage I would need to take a wide sweep to the east and south around the island. I also thought it would probably be a good idea to descend to a much lower altitude. These changes could add another half hour to an hour to my flying time, but I should be able make my scheduled connection with the pick-up pilot.

I made myself a note to purchase some aeronautical charts of the North Pacific to plot out the route changes I thought would be necessary. They would also be handy if I were forced into using the Fish & Wildlife's Queen Air for my departure.

Another possible problem I found was the landing itself. I doubted there would be any instrument approach equipment on the island, so I would need to make a visual approach. I could also make up my own GPS approach and use that to get me down below a thousand feet, but I wouldn't want to go much lower without seeing the runway. I would have plenty of room, since the highest building on the island was the control tower, and it was only thirty or forty feet above sea level.

The more I flew the simulator, the more comfortable I got, but it also pointed out some potential problems. Killing the electronics would most certainly include killing the GPS. Johnston Island was about eight miles long and under a half mile wide. The Pacific Ocean was huge. Finding that little island would be impossible without some sort of navigation equipment. I knew that dead-reckoning was named that for a reason.

I doubted the island would have an active radio beacon in this world of electronics, so I decided it would be necessary to purchase a portable GPS with North Pacific mapping and backup batteries. Killing the electronics would also make flying the plane all that much harder. I would have to allow for a good night's sleep before embarking on this thirteen-hundred-mile flight without electronics or a copilot.

Based on a direct route, and an altitude of thirty-seven thousand feet, the simulator automatically fueled the Airbus for a Memphis landing, a flight to its alternate airport, plus the required one hour of reserve fuel.

However, on the occasions when I flew the simulator without electronics, staying outside of the big island's radar, and at sixteen thousand feet, it was sucking fuel worse than a sixties Cadillac. After I landed at Johnston, I would have little more than the one-hour reserve. It wouldn't be enough to make it to any island other than Wake and Wake was an active military base. I didn't think they would welcome a hijacker with open arms.

With that information in mind, I felt comfortable knowing that weather systems around Johnston Island didn't stay long. With nothing more than a few old and low buildings to slow a weather system, they seldom lasted more than a half hour. I decided I would be good with the fuel.

I heard the garage door opening, so I quickly logged out of the flight simulator, and onto the FAA jobs website.

I was scheduled for an 8:00 a.m. shift on Monday, but after Jewels went to work I decided to call in sick. In the morning I went to a couple of businesses that specialized in actor costumes and makeup. I was pleased to see such wide selections and numerous options, but I was shocked at the prices. It could easily cost five hundred to a thousand dollars to get the makeup and hairpieces I would need.

Before going back to the house, I stopped in at Million Air, one of the largest fixed base operators at Hobby Airport. This business, provided maintenance, fuel, and supplies to pilots – they were the luxury gas stations for the flying community. I was there to price portable aviation GPS units. I was specifically looking for one that would cover the North Pacific area. I was told they could order that for me, and it would take a week or two before delivery.

They ranged in price from a little over a thousand to well over three thousand dollars. Since the unit was going to be used only once, but couldn't fail, I decided to get one of the cheaper units, and a backup battery. I didn't buy anything, but at least I knew I could get what I needed, along with the disguises, and still be well under budget.

I found Earl's plan to be sound—at least so far. But there was still a lot to learn about specific details. One thing that was bothering me was, *could I keep my cool long enough to actually do this thing?* I understood that it would only take a few seconds, and the crew would be knocked out for a few hours without any permanent aftereffects, but those few seconds would be scary as hell. I assumed that if I had a heart attack we would all die in the crash. I just kept telling myself it would be quick and painless.

When Jewels came home from work I didn't want to tell her about calling in sick, so I had to skate around the truth when she asked, "How was your day?"

"Not that bad. All I do is pull flight progress strips off a printer, put them in plastic holders, and place them for the controllers to use. It was a boring job compared to the one I'd had, but it was stress-free."

# Chapter Thirteen

## Details

I had day shifts all week, and in my spare time I was on the Internet researching everything from clothes, to flights, to makeup. I kept flying the Honolulu to Johnston Island run on my flight simulator, and I always shut down all the electronics before turning toward Johnston.

I wouldn't turn the GPS back on to check my position until I estimated myself to be within three hundred miles of Johnston. I was getting pretty good at selecting the right heading for the island when I checked my real position. I always landed on time according to the plan, and it was always before the time the FAA would be starting search and rescue. It was all good.

The standard procedure for overdue aircraft was to try all avenues of communications before starting their search-and-rescue operations. The search area would be defined by starting with the aircraft's last-known position, and following a hundred-mile-wide path to the destination. They would check all airports along the way, plus all within a hundred and fifty miles of the pre-filed destination.

With this U.P.-Ex flight, the search and rescue's last known position would be when it made its last contact with Honolulu Center. I planned that to be the takeover point of three hundred miles east of Honolulu. Without a specific electronic hit from the aircraft, Johnston Island would never be included in the search area.

The FAA would broadcast on emergency frequencies for all aircraft and ships at sea to be on the alert for the missing U.P.-Ex aircraft, or possible debris. All aircraft and commercial marine vessels are required to monitor the emergency frequency of 121.5. Military aircraft would be dispatched to make low flights over the search area.

The week seemed to fly by, and suddenly it was the weekend. I spent the morning doing yard work while Jewels was busy inside. After lunch, she went grocery shopping so I took the opportunity to call Earl. I told him about some of my research, and I quickly got to the problem areas that I thought needed attention.

"About the money; you said it was a five-cubic-foot container of worn currency, but you didn't know a dollar amount. You also failed to mention what protective measures would be in place for the security of the currency, nor how it would be spendable, since I'm sure it could be traced through the serial numbers."

"Good questions Rob, and I have good answers. The Treasury Department exchanges new money for currency that has reached its useful life. Two Secret Service agents are assigned to monitor the exchange, and to record serial numbers of the currency being exchanged. So yes, the currency is traceable."

He cleared his throat. "These shipments of worn currency are sent to the Treasury Department's destruction facility in Maryland where the money is destroyed. It is normally done by burning. That's why I don't consider there to be any victims. We'll only be taking money that's to be burned. These money shipments from Hawaii are scheduled well in advance, and they are bi-monthly."

"As far as the security is concerned, they always place a short-range GPS unit somewhere within the currency. It's big enough that you can't miss it as you're removing the currency and placing it into the suitcases. If you see it, just toss it aside in the cargo area. If you don't see it, then it must be in one of the boxes you haven't opened. Like I said, you can't miss it, so don't worry about it. They never put more than one per shipment, and their signal can't be picked up from inside the cargo bay."

"OK," I said. "So how do we spend this traceable currency?"

"It comes down to the odds, and how we spread it around," Earl replied. "Over four hundred million dollars in currency is stolen every year. A hundred million is from banks. Right now, there's around seventy million dollars of counterfeit currency in circulation across our country. New currency and counterfeit currency are easy to trace because the bills are readable by computers, and the numbers are normally either all the same, or sequential. Not so with worn currency."

"So the numbers aren't going to be sent to banks for them to look out for this stolen currency?" I asked.

"Think about the physical logistics that would go along with the posting of several million different numbers that are in no specific order. Since the worn condition of the currency makes most of the bills unreadable by computerized counting machines. That means it would have to be done manually. When you think about it you've got to know, that is simply not going to happen. It's not cost-effective for money to be burned.

"As long as we watch what we're doing, and keep track of where we're distributing the money, the odds are huge in our favor that no one will ever raise an eyebrow. We can do quick turnarounds of larger amounts under a disguise, and with fake IDs. We can open an account, and deposit up to nine thousand dollars without needing proof of where we got the money. Two days later, we can close the account at a different branch and get paid in cash. If it was all worn currency it might raise a red flag, but if it's well-mixed it won't be a problem.

"The bottom line," Earl continued, "is this: Ten million dollars of worn and mixed-numbered currency, scheduled to be burned within the week, isn't worth the time and manpower of Secret Service agents."

"You asked about the dollar amount of the shipment. Every shipment is a little different, but the average is around ten million dollars."

That got my attention. "Let me get this straight: We're taking about ten million dollars, and you want me to take five hundred thousand for doing all the exposed work? I don't think so."

Earl laughed. "You're a hard man to deal with, Rob. How about if we deduct all the expenses, and then split the balance? That should make our equal shares somewhere in excess of four point five million dollars. Would that work for you?" He paused. "I was just screwing with you about the five hundred thousand to see how hungry you were. You'll get half."

"Earl, I can't believe someone hasn't killed you by now. I've got to go. Jewels should be home anytime now, and I have things to do."

"OK," Earl responded. "I'll need those ID pictures real soon if we're going to get the finished products back to you in time to make this work. Get them to me this week for sure."

I came up with one more question, "Before I hang up, tell me about this person who's going to pick me up from Johnston Island."

"A pilot will pick you up and take you to Princeville airport on Kauai, or some other place if you'd rather, but I think Princeville will be best. I'll need that information this week too. He'll expect you to pay him in cash for his services, and I expect you to do so with worn currency. That's all I can tell you about him."

I was concerned about the Air Defense Identification Zone, so I asked, "What about getting through ADIZ?"

"That isn't your problem, but I can promise you that you won't have to worry about the military scrambling F-16s to greet you. It's going to be taken care of. I think you're forgetting our trust agreement."

I thought about it another moment, and then replied, "I'll trust you, and I'll do this thing, but I'll be your worst enemy if I find surprises along the way."

After disconnecting the call, I just sat there thinking about what I was preparing to do, and the mistakes I had made in my life that had brought me to this juncture.

My biggest mistake was going on strike. The safety issues we were experiencing at the time were both extremely serious and plentiful, but we should have used other avenues to accomplish our goals. Eleven thousand active controllers, including Earl and myself, made the mistake of believing the president's promise of support, and the union leaders' promise of suspensions, not terminations. We were made painfully aware of the strong bond between leaders and lies.

I thought about how Jewels and I should have found a way to live on less instead of using our retirement savings to finance my quest to learn to fly, and be certified in, larger aircraft. Although I reached my goal of becoming a captain for a major airline, it was too little, and too late, to rebuild our savings.

I made a mental note to go to sleep every night, and wake up every morning, reminding myself how there would be no long-term physical, or financial, harm to anyone. If I didn't keep those thoughts ever-present in my mind, I would never be able to do this. It would be totally up to me to make sure this was, indeed, the perfect crime.

My decision was made, and it was time to move on to my next problem: How would I explain my four-day absence to Jewels. I had been thinking about that question for weeks, and I finally decided to fabricate a marginally illegal flight from Atlanta to Freeport, Bahamas.

It was time to have another talk with Jewels.

After dinner, I said, "Earl called, and the December flying job I told you about is going to happen. It will be from Atlanta to the Bahamas and back. I will be gone from Thursday, December twentieth, until the following Saturday or Sunday."

"How much does it pay?" She asked.

"Ten thousand dollars."

Jewels, being cute, replied, "Is your payment going to be in cash, or drugs?"

I gave her a big smile. "I don't know what I'll be hauling, and I don't want to know. I will pick up a loaded Airbus aircraft at the U.P.-Ex terminal in Atlanta, and fly it to Freeport. Once there, I'll taxi the plane to a hangar for customs inspection and unloading. I will be in Freeport until Friday night or very early Saturday, when I'll fly back to Atlanta empty. I should be back here by Saturday afternoon.

"I think there's a good chance that something illegal will be mixed in with that cargo, but I'll just be a last-minute replacement pilot, with no way of knowing what's in the plane. The manifest won't show anything illegal, and I will have no liability."

"We really don't need money that bad, Rob. We'll be OK, and I know you'll find something soon."

"If Earl hadn't forewarned me about the possibility of something illegal being on the plane, I would have no reason to suspect anything. The entire shipment is supposed to be excess freight that U.P.-Ex needs to get to the Bahamas before Christmas. I will be totally clean."

I knew I had to get Jewels on board with this, and I could sense her starting to come around to my explanation.

She frowned. "You might be right, but I'll have to think about that. We knew about the possibility of your not making it through the program, but I never thought you'd have to do something like this to stretch our money. Isn't there another way to get us over the hump until you can get on Social Security, or get another job?"

I shook my head. "Not one that pays that much for so little time. I really hope you'll see your way to understanding how this will help us, with no risk at all. It'll keep us alive for a couple more months while I keep looking."

She sighed. "If you think it's safe, I have to trust you, but keep trying to find a job, and maybe you won't have to do this."

"I'm trying," I replied—to show her I was listening.

# Chapter Fourteen

## Disguises & Saving Grace

I took another sick day, and used it to return to the makeup shops in south Houston. I picked out an array of different skin tones, disfigurements, tattoos, and hairpieces. I also purchased two large bottles of their highest-quality makeup remover. I wouldn't want to be stuck in a disguise because I couldn't get it off when I needed to be myself, or someone else.

As I watched the young man ring up my purchases, I could easily see I was blowing through my five-hundred-dollar estimate. I used a cash withdrawal from a credit card to get enough money to cover these purchases because I knew I couldn't wait until I received my 401K check. I had to get my ID pictures and information to Earl right away if I planned to get them back in time. I hated to obligate myself for the high-interest, cash withdrawal, but if all went well, it shouldn't be an issue.

Back at the house, I mixed and matched the different skin tones and hairpieces before determining which combination looked best. I returned to the mirror time after time until I got what I believed to be the perfect disguises. I put my camera on a tripod, and posed for my new ID pictures. I printed out the pictures, and made up the personal information sheets for each disguise. Once I had them complete, I bagged each ID name with the proper makeup to make sure there would be no mix up along the way. I sent the pictures and info next-day delivery to Earl's home address.

The cleaning solution worked well between disguises, and it became easy to switch from one to the other. I timed myself, and I got it down to under fifteen minutes. That, I believed, would be quick enough for my needs. I had done all I could do for now, so I cleaned out a toolbox, and placed all four of my bagged disguises inside. I knew Jewels would never look in my toolbox.

The following week, I received the check from my 401(k) plan. I knew I couldn't deposit it without Jewels noticing the large balance, so I went to a branch of the bank it was written on, and told them I wanted the funds in cash. I worried a little about keeping twelve thousand dollars in cash, but it would soon be spent.

On November 12, with only a week left before my grace period ended, I was called up to a meeting with the training officer, Jerry Strickland. I had known Jerry from before the strike, and we had remained friends. When we were both seated, he said, "I noticed you're running out of your grace-period time next week, so I talked with the chief, and got approval for a one-month extension. I hope that will be enough because he said he wouldn't be able to approve any more."

With a huge smile, I said, "You couldn't believe how much help that will be for us. I've got a few irons in the fire, both inside and outside of the government, and that would give us time to see them through. Thank you very much."

"That's great. I'm glad I could be of help. That will make December eighteenth your last day at Houston Center. But, hopefully, you would have found something even sooner. If you do make it to the eighteenth it'll be a short day, since all you'll have to do is walk around to the departments to check out. You'll probably be done in two or three hours, and will have time to say good-bye to all your friends."

I stood up. "Thank you again for your help. You're a good man, and I'm sorry I wasn't able to become a meaningful addition to your staff. I must have killed a few too many brain cells along the way." As I walked from his office, I couldn't believe how perfect this was. It would save a month of unemployment, and take me to the doorstep of Earl's plan.

I was excited, and couldn't wait to tell Jewels the good news. I stopped on the way home, and picked up a bottle of wine, and some take-out from our favorite Mexican restaurant.

While waiting for Jewels to arrive, I got a call from our real estate agent. She said we had an offer on our house. With that news on top of the other, I probably should have gone out and bought a lottery ticket because this was certainly my lucky day. Instead, I poured a glass of wine for Jewels and, when she walked in, I couldn't hide my smile.

When she saw my face, she knew I had good news. "You got a job offer?"

"No, I wish I did, but we have an offer on the house, and an extension to my grace period at work."

"Seriously? That's fantastic! How much is the offer on our house?"

"I don't know. She said she'd rather go over it with us in person. She'll be here at seven."

"And your extension?"

"One month. I'm good until December eighteenth. That will take us up to Earl's flight perfectly, and it'll give us the time we need to figure out what's next."

I handed Jewels her wine and, as she walked into the kitchen, she saw the plates of food, and said, "Wow! You went all out!"

I just smiled.

At seven, our real estate representative arrived, and we all sat around the dining room table as she presented the offer. The offer was for two thousand dollars less than our asking price, but we were OK with that. They didn't ask for anything more than normal closing costs, so that was good too; but they did want a quick closing date.

They were under contract to purchase one of the new subdivision homes that was the same model as ours when the builder told them they weren't going to have it completed in time. He told them they would have to push back their closing three weeks. With their current home already sold, and ours newly on the market, it would fit their needs perfectly if we could close early. They also liked the fact that we had put on a deck, and had drapes up in all the rooms.

Their house was set to close on Friday, November 30. They wanted to close on ours on Monday, December 3.

We told our agent we would need to sleep on it. She said, "The offer is only good for twenty-four hours."

That evening we talked it through, and decided we probably wouldn't get a better offer if we waited, and it would give us the flexibility we needed. Since we would be getting most of our equity back, it would free up money to take care of us until well after my return from Hawaii.

I called our agent back the following morning, and told her we would agree to the closing date if they would agree to our full asking price. That afternoon we all reached agreement, and were under contract.

Jewels used her United Van Lines' experience once more to take care of our moving arrangements, while I started looking around for a furnished, short-term apartment for us. I got the easier of our two jobs—there was an extended-stay hotel/apartment only a mile from our house, and they had a furnished two-bedroom unit available.

I scheduled four days off without pay to take care of moving, cleaning and closing. Jewels only needed to take vacation days on Friday and Monday. On Wednesday, November 28, the Suddath United Van Lines pack crew arrived at 8:30 to start packing. While they were taking care of that, I started making trips back and forth between our house and the apartment. We had a lot of clothes, our life history type of paperwork, and a few personal items to move to the apartment. By early afternoon, I had finished with my moving, and had started my next project.

In the garage, I started building a large, six-foot-by-four-foot-by-four-foot wooden box. In a couple of hours I had finished my basic box, but it still needed work. I added supports for a false bottom, and tested it for strength and fit. When I was comfortable with that, I loaded the space above the false bottom with large, but light, unbreakable items from the house and garage. I left the top open for the mover's inventory inspection.

We stayed in our new apartment that night, so I locked up the house, and checked the mail before leaving. I was surprised to see a package from Earl. It held four separate driver's licenses and passports, and one pilot's license with a fairly full logbook. I put everything in with the bags of makeup and hairpieces in my toolbox. I put a lock on it, and placed it in the closet of the spare bedroom.

When Jewels came in, we decided we deserved a dinner out. At that dinner we discussed all the crazy things we had going on in our lives. As always, Jewels kept upbeat and positive about everything. She said, "With the house sold, and nothing really keeping us here, I think we need to make plans to go back to Minneapolis."

I wasn't surprised, since she had family there. "That's OK with me. If you're sure that's what you want to do, I don't see any reason why we can't. I will be back from Atlanta on the Saturday before Christmas, and we've promised to spend that day with our friends. Why don't we plan to be on the road to Minneapolis by the end of the month?"

Jewels replied, "If we were to get on the road as soon as you get back from Atlanta, we could spend Christmas with my family in Minneapolis."

As much as I would like to get out of Houston as soon as possible, I knew that wouldn't give me the time I would need to secure the worn currency, and evaluate the world's reaction to the hijacking. Other than that, her plan for returning to Minneapolis was perfect. It would follow the natural flow of what we would likely do after my losing my job as a controller. It just needed to be pushed back a week.

"We promised Mary, Roger, Debbie, and Carl we would spend Christmas with them, and we may not be able to see them again for some time. A few extra days won't hurt, and you'll have plenty of time to spend with your family after we're there."

"OK," Jewels agreed. "I'll make that compromise."

I was relieved. Things were seemingly falling into place as if they were destined to happen this way. Or, was this just the calm before the storm?

Suddath United Van Lines dropped the container on our driveway early Thursday morning, and the loading crew arrived shortly thereafter. I waited until about half of our household goods were loaded into the container before finding one of the movers, and pointing out the crate in the garage. The mover put it on the inventory, and I secured the top with wood screws. It was loaded a few minutes later. By early afternoon they were done, the container was locked, and it was hauled off to storage.

I moved the rest of our food and personal items over to the apartment. With my moving chores complete, I got on my laptop and started looking for aircraft rentals. I found what I needed in a small airport near San Antonio.

I had a few hours before Jewels was due home, so I put on my makeup and hairpiece for disguise number one. I had named him Roberto, and it was time to take him on a test drive.

I drove north to Conroe, and parked outside a small bank. I was nervous when I walked in, and told the young girl at the counter I needed a prepaid credit card for five thousand dollars. She asked for, and I showed her, my driver's license with Roberto's name. She looked at it, then at me, and asked, "Visa OK?"

A few minutes later, I walked out with a Visa card. Everything went as planned. By the time Jewels came home, I was looking like me again.

Friday morning, Jewels and I were back at our house by 9:00 to start cleaning. The new owners had scheduled their final walk-through for 3:00, and we had a lot to do between now and then. Time went quickly, and we finished our cleaning well-ahead of their scheduled walk through.

Our real estate representative met with the new owners. She called us afterward, and told us all went well. We closed Monday morning at 9:00.

Although Jewels had scheduled the entire day off, she decided to go in and get some work done after our closing. That left me with the rest of the day with no specific plans, so I decided to put disguise number one to work for the second time.

# Chapter Fifteen

## Preparations

Wanting to make it as difficult as possible to follow my trail, I'd decided on three separate legs for my trip to Honolulu. I needed to arrange for a rental aircraft that I would use for the second leg of my trip, so I drove the first leg. It was a boring three-hour drive across the flatlands of south Texas before reaching the hill country, and my destination of Boerne, Texas. It was a small town about thirty miles northwest of San Antonio.

Boerne Field airport was nestled among hangars, homes, and trees. I had found it with an internet search for a Cessna 172 aircraft. I wanted to get everything in order so I would be able to pick up the plane before sunrise on the morning of December 20.

When I arrived, I noticed a small strip mall across from Ralph's Aviation where I planned to rent the plane. I pulled into the mall parking lot, and walked back across the street to Ralph's. It was just the kind of place I was looking for. It had an asphalt runway with hangars and homes spotted around the parallel runway and taxiway.

Inside, there were two, old wooden desks behind a long, wood countertop that separated the lobby from the office area. Both areas were vacant. The lobby had two chairs with a small table between them. The table had a stack of old, curled-up flying magazines. I'd called before leaving Houston to make sure they had the type of plane I needed, and that it would be available for the days I would need it before Christmas.

The door from the office area into the hangar had a window, but it was so dirty I could only make out images. Through it, I could vaguely see a man working on one of the engines of an older twin. When I closed the door behind me the mechanic heard me, and stood up. He started wiping his hands with a rag as I approached. "You must be Roberto?"

His question caught me a little off guard, since this was the first time anyone had called me by that name. I stuck out my hand to greet him, but he held up his greasy palms, and I opted for a more appropriate nod. "Yes, I am. Are you Ralph?" He acknowledged his name, and pointed back toward the office.

Inside, Ralph and I discussed the terms of the agreement, and afterward he made copies of my driver's license, pilot's licenses, and logbook pages showing twenty-five recent hours in a one-seventy-two. The bogus hours showed me to be current, but it had been over a year since I had actually flown one. Ralph said, "How about we take it up for a spin around the pattern?" I agreed.

After flipping a front door sign from "welcome" to "back in thirty," he left the door unlocked, and we went back through the hangar to a large door on the runway side. Along the way, I started reviewing the pre-flight list in my mind. He slid the hangar door open, and there sat the Cessna 172 I had inquired about on the internet. It was tied down outside.

"It's an older plane," Ralph said, "but it's got only a hundred hours since its last major overall. I took the back seats out to haul a piece of furniture my wife bought in Austin, but I'll have them back in place before you need it. Where did you say you were going?"

"Leave the seats out," I said. "I won't need them." I then answered his question, "I'm going to Kansas City—Olathe, Kansas, actually. I went to the University of Kansas in Topeka, and a few of my fraternity brothers and I will be getting together for a reunion in Olathe. I'll be flying into Johnson County Airport, and will be coming back either Saturday or Sunday. I'd like to leave here before sunrise, if that could be arranged. Are there runway lights?"

"There are. They're centerline only, and are activated with clicks from the mike. I'll give you a card with the directions. Are you ready to take her up?"

I nodded, and we started untying the plane. As I was going through my pre-flight, Ralph said, "Don't worry about that. I took her up less than an hour ago."

I shook my head. "It's just for me, I don't like flying anywhere before doing a personal walk-around." Truth be known, I was actually trying to remember everything I needed to do. It easily came back to me because I had flown a one-seventy-two just a few days ago on my simulator. Of course I knew these simulator flights were a far cry from the real thing. After we were settled inside with the engine turning, I asked, "Is there a Unicom here?"

Ralph nodded. "Yeah. The radio's already on the frequency."

I keyed the mike, and announced my intended departure. I had to ask Ralph what the pattern altitude was, but other than that everything went well. After following Ralph's commands for a couple of easy maneuvers, he told me to land and taxi back to the hangar.

Back in the office, I prepaid Ralph in cash, but he copied Roberto's newly acquired Visa for backup. I asked him if he could have the plane ready for my sunrise departure on the twentieth. He said, "I'll have it tied down in its current position, fully fueled, and I'll leave the key in the ignition. We're pretty trusting around here."

Our business was over, but before I left I gave him the number to my prepaid cell in case he needed to reach me.

At the apartment, I put my Roberto look back in my toolbox, and barely finished cleaning myself up when Jewels came in from work.

The closer I got to the end of my grace period, and to Earl's plan, the more I thought an alibi would be good to have just in case something went wrong. I thought it wouldn't hurt to bring Jewels into the small role of providing an alibi for my bogus flight to the Bahamas.

After dinner, we were watching TV, and I said, "Just to be on the safe side, I think I could use an alibi for the days I'll be gone. Would you mind helping me a little with that?"

"I was wondering when I would be called on. Let me hear what you have in mind, and then I'll decide."

"OK, fair enough," I said. "Remember the hotel we stayed at when we went to Galveston last April?"

"Of course. It was The Wave Runner Inn. I really liked that place." Jewels smiled as she thought about the memories. "It had a great pool, a super Gulf view, and nice beaches for walking. Are we going back?"

I smiled too, as I said, "Yes. Or, at least I hope so. Here's the deal. I'll make a reservation for us for Friday, December twenty-first, and Saturday the twenty-second. Of course, you'll have to start without me because I'll be in the Bahamas, but I would like you to check in, and carry on as if I were there. You'll want to get two keys, and you can say I'm parking the car, or something. I should be able to get there by Saturday afternoon, and we can have dinner in their restaurant Saturday evening. You'll want to take some of my clothes with you, including a swim suit and jock. On Friday night, you'll want to make a mess for the maids, to make it look like two people were in the room. Leave our wet swimsuits hanging in the bathroom, some of my dirty clothes scattered around the room, and men's bathroom items where they would normally be expected. You get the picture."

Teasingly, Jewels said, "How about if I just pick up some hunk, and ask him to stay with me until my other guy arrives?"

"Very funny." I was too tense to laugh, so I gave her a weak smile.

Jewels sighed. "Of course I'll do it, but you better be there by Saturday afternoon."

She hadn't asked any questions, so persuading her came easier than expected. I realized how lucky I was to have her, and I knew I was right in not telling her the truth about what I would be doing.

For my next-to-last day of work at the FAA, I was able to work a 5:00 a.m. to 1:00 p.m. shift. That was good because I had a full afternoon planned.

I knew Roberto's credit card could be traced back to Conroe, Texas, where I had purchased it, but I took that risk thinking there would be very little chance of Roberto being tied to the hijacking. That risk, however small, would be the only credit card used by him. He would exist only between Houston and Honolulu, and between Double Eagle II airport and Houston. He would be the least likely to be suspect.

Bill Edwards was a different story. I knew I had to make sure there were no trails outside of the Hawaiian Islands for him. He would show his head in Honolulu and disappear on Kauai – but the world would soon know his name.

Bill would be the new U.P.-Ex employee, and the hijacker of their flight 7-19. His role wouldn't require a credit card since he would be paying cash for everything as he went along.

I didn't want to chance putting Bill Edwards' face on any security cameras before Honolulu, or after Kauai. I donned his makeup and hairpiece to wear around the house for the afternoon. My thought was to make myself accustomed to his look before testing it on the general public and, more specifically, on the flight crew.

It felt weird when I looked in the mirror, and saw someone so totally different, and completely unrecognizable, as being me. I put on a pair of gloves since I knew my role as Bill Edwards had to include gloves. They were out of place for Houston weather, and they'd be even more out of place for Honolulu, but they had to stay on for fingerprint protection.

I was on the simulator most of the afternoon flying from Texas to New Mexico and back. I was finished before Jewels came home. When she walked in she saw only me since Mr. Edwards was safely packed away in my toolbox by then.

My last day of work was, as promised, short and bittersweet. I was glad to put it behind me, but I certainly wished I could have done so under more pleasant circumstances. I made the rounds to all my friends on the control floor and in the offices, but I was still out the door by ten.

Before going home, I went shopping for clothes. With four separate identifications and roles to play, I knew I would need four separate sets of clothing.

I started with Roberto. His day would require him to drive a little over three hours, fly a single-engine plane for six hours, and then board a commercial flight for eight hours. Dressing casual was a must.

I bought tennis shoes, jeans, a short-sleeved denim shirt, and a light jacket. I believed those clothes would be suitable for Roberto's needs, with no second looks.

Along with the clothes, I developed a background story, just in case someone would ask. I decided on his mother being from San Antonio, and his dad from Rome. They had met when she was on vacation in Italy. She had ended up staying there and that was where Roberto was born. When Roberto was only a year old they had divorced. His dad had stayed in Italy, and Roberto had moved back to San Antonio with his mother. Roberto, as my story would go, had no memory of his father. That, I decided, would account for his Italian look, but without the accent. That was it, short and sweet, but all I needed for him.

My second identity would be that of a new employee who would be showing up, unannounced, at the U.P.-Ex hangar in Honolulu with a letter from the CEO authorizing him to ride in the jump seat of their 5:30 a.m. flight to Memphis. This would be a critical step, since the captain had the final authority to accept, or reject, Bill's entrance into the cockpit of the plane.

Bill Edwards would need to make a good first impression if he were to be accepted by a surprised crew with no prior notification. I tried on a nice, tan sport coat, and dark-blue slacks that I believed would do the trick. Next, was a light-blue shirt with a matching, light-blue-and-tan-striped tie. I thought it looked good, but not overly aggressive.

I bought non-descript, black loafers, and socks. When I checked myself out in the mirror, I thought I looked honest, and properly attired for my first day on the job. My letter would be signed by the CEO, and it would explain how I would be working for Earl Baker in the operations department of U.P.-Ex in Memphis.

My third outfit would be for my business jet flight back to Albuquerque. This flight would be, by far, the most-expensive portion of my trip, but it would be pre-paid and arranged by Earl. Since I would be the only passenger on the plane, I knew my role would be one of a person with little regard for the value of a dollar. I would be traveling under the name of Declan Finley.

Thinking about how I would casually dress for a flight such as this, if I could afford to do so, I came up with the name of Tommy

Bahama. I always liked that clothing line, and I had a couple of his shirts. However, for this occasion, I would be paying for a complete outfit that would be worn only once. It seemed like such a waste.

I started with a Bahama trademark flowered shirt. It had a tan background with mostly blue flowers. I liked how the pattern continued across the lapel to both sides of the shirt. My slacks were also tan, and they had the feel of cashmere. The belt I picked out was brown alligator, and it was only a half-inch wide. I found alligator shoes that perfectly matched the belt. Of course, I wouldn't be wearing socks. For my final touch, I bought a medium-brown leather bomber's jacket that was comfortably tight at the waist, and had a collar that couldn't be folded down. Sometimes you've just got to say, *what the hell*. I loved the look, and it fit the flight perfectly.

Since I wasn't sure if my fourth identity would be used at all, and I busted my budget on the last outfit, I decided that was enough shopping for the day. I headed back home.

At the house, I put my clothes boxes away in the bed of my pickup, and locked the cover in place. Inside, I popped the top on a beer to toast the end of my short FAA career.

I called for reservations in the name of Mr. and Mrs. Silvers at the Wave Runner Inn. I was glad to find an even nicer room than the one we'd stayed in last spring. That one hadn't been bad, but I was assured this one would have a much better view of the Gulf, and a bigger balcony. This time, I used my personal credit card. Doing so made me realize how important it would be to double check the IDs I would be using. One slip there could lead to disaster. I made a checklist, and placed one with each identity.

I'd reserved a cargo van a week earlier under the name of Roberto Celestino, but I called the rental company again to make sure it would be available at Houston Intercontinental airport at the time specified. They assured me it would be ready for pickup tomorrow afternoon. I could see how nervous I was getting as I found myself double-checking everything.

I started thinking about DNA, and how that could be picked up from the food or drink I would have along the way. I ran out to a nearby store, and picked up a supply of diabetic food and drink. I wasn't diabetic, but I decided it would be good for the purpose of these flights. It would explain why I wasn't taking the food or drink like everyone else.

I didn't expect anyone to look for DNA on any flight other than the U.P.-Ex flight. The FBI would surely inspect every inch of that plane. As far as I knew, my DNA had never been taken, but they could force me to give them a sample if other evidence was compelling.

Finished with everything on my list for the day, I jumped back on the flight simulator for another run from Honolulu to Johnston Island. I wasn't finished when I heard Jewels come in, but I was close enough to know that I had this flight down pat.

Jewels had given her notice, and her last day of work was the same as my first day of travel—Thursday the twentieth. Friends started calling after hearing we'd sold our house, and would soon be moving back to Minneapolis. They were naturally interested in the details of our plans.

We only told them about moving back to Minnesota. We didn't mention any other plans. Jewels said, "We'll probably stay with my sister for a couple of weeks until we find a place to live." She also used the opportunity to reinforce the alibi by telling friends we were going to spend our last Texas weekend in Galveston.

After Jewels was off to work the next morning I ran through my notes, and double-checked my plans. It was more for something to occupy my mind than anything else. Our unit was equipped with a laundry room, so I washed, dried, and ironed all the new clothes that were washable. I packed them in order of their use, except for Roberto's—I left those out.

After lunch, I did two more simulator flights, and packed and repacked my suitcase a couple of times. Mid-afternoon, I checked to see if my bogus flight from Albuquerque was on time for its arrival in Houston. I had set up my van rental based Roberto being on that flight. It was on time, so I applied my Roberto makeup, and drove to the airport.

I parked in long-term parking, and walked inside the terminal building. I double-checked the incoming flight, and saw that it had landed ten minutes earlier. At the rental counter, she checked my driver's license and insurance before swiping Roberto's credit card. I verified that I would probably be returning the van early Saturday afternoon and she handed me the keys to a new Ford cargo van.

All was in accordance with the plan. When I reached our apartment, I backed the van into a spot near our front door. The rental van had no side windows other than those in the front doors. I checked for a full tank of fuel, and then went inside to remove my makeup and hairpiece. I placed my morning clothes out of sight from Jewels' inquiring eyes, but ready for quick access.

With this being our last night together for a few days, we went out to dinner. We discussed my trip to the Bahamas, and Jewels told me how she wished she could go with me. Of course I told her I wished she could too, but I also pointed out how the weather in Galveston was supposed to be in the upper sixties or lower seventies, and the pool was heated.

Jewels was obviously nervous, and so was I. Neither of us was doing a good job of hiding our apprehension about the weekend. Even my occasional tries to say something funny were falling terribly flat. It wasn't the evening out we were hoping for.

Since I had to get up at 3:30 to keep my schedule, I decided to sleep in the spare bedroom. Before we went to bed I tried to reassure her that all was well, and there was nothing to worry about; but it fell on deaf ears—both hers and mine.

# Chapter Sixteen

## Hawaii-bound

On a night I needed sleep badly; I tossed and turned, and slept very little. I was awake and up before my alarm's 3:30 setting. Before my shower, I used electric hair clippers to give myself a buzz cut. When finished, it was about a quarter of an inch long throughout. During my shower I took care to wash down all the leftover hair.

I applied the olive shade of grease makeup, and followed it with a dusting of olive powder. I took my time to make sure not to miss any spots that would be visible with my clothes on. I applied some small facial bumps to each cheek to give my face a ruddy look. Earl had told me that would serve to keep facial recognition software from matching my face with that of someone identified with the hijacking. I used extra-double-stick tape to hold my hairpiece tightly against my newly shortened hair.

The hairpiece I selected for Roberto was dark blond with the top and sides combed to the back. It doubled the amount of hair I had, even before I cut it; and I couldn't help but be jealous of Roberto's striking good looks. If it weren't for the bumps, my face would be flawless. I looked ten years younger, and my olive skin was definitely good for the Italian look I was after. Part of me wanted to wake Jewels and show her my good looks, but I thought it might give her a heart attack.

I walked out to the van with the confidence that Roberto would never be recognized as being me, and vice-versa.

I was well ahead of schedule when I drove away from the apartment at 3:15. I was armed with four sets of IDs and disguises, plus a pocket full of cash. The next few days, good or bad, were on course to be the adventure of a lifetime. I knew I had to stay focused, yet I was starting out with only five hours sleep.

My first task was to start thinking as I envisioned Roberto Celestino to think. I told myself I was a fifty year-old bachelor born in Italy but raised in San Antonio by my Mexican mother. I kept telling myself that.

As I drove west on the interstate at this early hour I was glad the van had speed control. Without it I would be fifteen over the limit most of the way. There was little traffic, and the highway was smooth and flat. I wondered about what information a trooper would get if he scanned my bogus driver's license, but I sure didn't want to find out. I continued to go over Roberto's life story and even said it out loud to make sure it rolled off my lips smoothly. I was, to say the least, paranoid.

After parking the van in one of the designated spots reserved for Ralph's Aviation, I walked around the hangar with my briefcase and luggage in hand. I had only one suitcase, but it was too big to qualify as a carry-on so I'd have to check it in Albuquerque. The Cessna 172 was sitting as promised, unlocked, with the key in the ignition.

It was still dark, but there was an overhead light shining over the area. I untied the plane, and finished my walk-around before climbing into the left seat for the balance of my preflight. I soon pushed the starter, and watched the propeller slowly start to rotate. The old lady spat and coughed a few times before kicking in. It was loud enough for me to suspect a neighbor or two might be looking out a window to investigate. Wanting to get out of there, I was still working on my inside pre-flight when I started to taxi. I announced my planned departure on Unicom as I rounded the turn onto the runway.

Ralph had told me he lived in a house about midway down the left side of runway three five, so it didn't surprise me when I saw him under his back porch light waving to me as I started my climb. I returned his wave as I continued my climb on the runway heading. The plane was running smoothly.

I used the aircraft's true tail numbers when I called in to San Antonio Approach for flight following. I turned toward Albuquerque as the sun was starting to peek over the horizon behind me. I started seeing faint images of the Texas hill country.

It had been awhile since I'd made a cross-country in a small plane, and I was enjoying the view as I leveled off at my cruise altitude of eighty-five hundred feet. To me, this was the fun of flying. I could see the railways, highways, rivers, and lakes. I compared my view to taking a train instead of an airline. It might be low and slow, but it was a whole lot better than driving. It was soothing to the mind, and I started to release my early morning stress of the day. I felt a calm I hadn't felt for several weeks.

Two hours into my flight I checked my ground speed, and found I was averaging ninety-seven knots. It was about what I'd expected and, if I continued at this pace, I would likely reach my destination of Double Eagle II airport by about noon, Mountain Standard Time.

Double Eagle II airport was about thirty miles northwest of Albuquerque. My plan called for me to land there, pick up another van, and drive to Albuquerque Sunport, the city's main airport. My flight to Honolulu was scheduled to depart from there at 3:00 p.m.

Although my altimeter was still showing eighty-five hundred feet, the ground was coming up to meet me as I was entering the mountainous terrain of New Mexico. The weather was good, as the Double Eagle II tower controller cleared me to land at 11:45. I had reserved a tie-down spot for the plane with Atlantic Aviation, so I taxied to their facility. With my briefcase and suitcase in hand, I checked in, and asked them to fuel and service the plane before tying it down.

I went into their restroom, and was once again shocked as I looked at Roberto in the mirror. He was looking fairly good considering today's wear-and-tear, but I made a few minor repairs.

They gave me the keys to the van I had reserved, and it was sitting next to their entry door. I told them I would be back overnight Friday, but probably after midnight. I had picked this FBO (Fixed Base Operator) because of their 24/7 operation.

I had printed a map to Tom Brown Aviation, so I removed it from my briefcase, and focused on my drive across town. My only purpose at my next stop was to leave the van on their lot so it would be waiting for me when I returned. I asked the young man behind the counter at Tom Brown Aviation if I could leave the van in his lot. He assured me it wouldn't be a problem, so I had him call me a cab.

I only needed to go from one side of the airport to the other so I felt sorry for the cabbie, and I gave him twenty dollars for his one-mile drive. At the main terminal, I checked in for my 3:00 flight with a couple of hours to kill before departure. As much as I wished it wasn't necessary, I checked my suitcase through to Honolulu, but kept my briefcase.

While I had some time, I called to check on the availability of the portable aviation GPS unit. Brewster Aviation had two on hand when I'd called a few days ago, and they were both still available. I told them I would pick one up this evening and I'd need a spare battery, and both batteries fully charged. They said it wasn't a problem and they were open until ten. On another trip to the men's room, I just couldn't get over seeing Roberto in the mirror. He looked marvelous.

There was a bar across from my gate, so I had a couple of beers while waiting for my boarding call. The flight to Honolulu was scheduled for eight hours and, with the time difference, I should be there by 8:00 Thursday evening, HST. With a full day of travel already behind me, and not much sleep last night, I was hoping to sleep most of the way to Honolulu.

We departed on time, and I was glad to see the flight was only about half full. The two other seats in my row were unoccupied so I picked up a couple of pillows and a blanket from the overhead bins, and by the time we reached our cruise altitude I was spread across all three seats. I slept for five hours.

It seemed like the next two hours flew by as I ate dinner and had another beer. I soon heard the chirp of the wheels as we touched down on Hawaiian soil. It had been thirty years since I'd been in Honolulu, and my first impression was how much the city had grown. The sun had set and the lights of the buildings made it look like downtown had tripled in size since I was last there. The buildings seemed to steal some of the grandeur from Diamondhead, but even so, it was all beautiful. My only regret was not having Jewels by my side.

While waiting in the baggage claim area I found something else to worry about. What if my suitcase were to get lost? All my disguises and IDs were in that suitcase. Bag after bag came down the stainless conveyer, but none of them was mine. Suddenly, the belt came to a complete stop, and I was still without my suitcase. I made a quick circle around the conveyer, but still no bag. I started looking at the bags in the hands of others who had gotten off the same flight. None matched mine. This was getting serious, but there were still a few people other than me waiting for their bags.

My nerves were on end as I started walking toward the lost-luggage sign a couple of conveyers over. As I was passing the conveyer next to mine, I heard the loud clunking sound that conveyers always make before starting up again. As I turned to go back I saw my suitcase coming down. I breathed a sigh of relief, and I realized how paranoid I was. The what-ifs were driving me crazy. I needed to calm down, and stay that way.

As I stepped outside, the smell of warm and humid air brought back memories that seemed to be uniquely Hawaiian. I scanned the area for a cab and saw a guy holding a sign that read, "Waikiki Hyatt." I walked up to him, and said, "You must be my ride?"

"If you're Mr. Celestino, I am."

I handed him my suitcase, and stepped into the back seat of the limousine thinking how this was my first limo ride since my high school prom. I wondered whatever happened to whatshername after our one and only date that had turned into an all-nighter.

When I checked in at the Hyatt, the clerk said he had a package for me. It was the briefcase from Earl. All was proceeding as planned.

When I got to my room, I tipped the bellman, and he closed the door behind him. I immediately started changing into my Bill Edwards identity. It took me over a half hour to complete the change, but what a change it was. I went from Italian to African-American and they were two totally different looks.

I knew my time was running out, and I needed to keep moving. I went down to the circle drive in front of the hotel, and grabbed a cab to do the two critical errands I had to complete before sleeping.

My first stop was Brewster's Aviation. It was an FBO on the far side of the airport. It was after 9:00 when I saw one older man behind the counter. I told him I had called earlier, and I was there to pick up a portable GPS with North Pacific mapping.

He introduced himself as the owner, Ben Brewster, and he said, "I talked with you earlier today. I've got both batteries on chargers, and they should be fully charged by now."

He wasn't gone for more than a couple of minutes when he brought out the unit and two batteries. He said, "You should be able to get about ten hours out of each battery."

He put one of the batteries in the unit, showed me how to hook up the suction-cup antenna. He gave me a quick explanation of the controls, and I paid him with twelve one-hundred-dollar bills. I only received pocket change back.

The receipt showed Bill Edwards' name, and a paid-in-cash stamp attested by his signature. Mr. Brewster seemed to be a nice guy, and I was comfortable that he didn't notice any sign of my being in disguise.

My cab was waiting out front with music rolling loudly from the speakers. I didn't recognize the artist, but it was definitely Hawaiian, and I was glad he turned it down when he saw me coming.

Our next stop was to a nearby Wal-Mart for the luggage I needed. By the time I was back at the hotel it was after ten. As I was paying the driver, I asked, "Will there be anyone here around 5:00 tomorrow morning to take me to the U.P.-Ex terminal at the airport?"

He replied, "There is always a cab or two in front of the Hyatt."

I took one of their carts, and pushed my new purchases to my room. Knowing I would need the cart again in the morning, I kept it in my room. I had to be at the U.P.-Ex terminal by five-fifteen so it would be another short night, followed by another long day.

The sleep I got on the plane was a lifesaver, but I needed to add a few more hours. I removed my hairpiece, and showered to make sure I didn't leave traces of Bill on my bedding.

I was still very anxious, so I grabbed a beer from the fridge and stood outside on the balcony. I took small sips, and enjoyed the sights and sound from Waikiki Beach several stories below me. I wished Jewels were here, and that we had a week or two to enjoy it. If all went as planned, I promised myself we would come back.

I set my alarm for 4:00, and I immediately fell asleep.

# Chapter Seventeen

## Friday, December 21

Four o'clock came early, but I was so wired I didn't feel tired. This was the day I had to be at my best all day long. Yet, here I was anxious, nervous, and scared.

I took a shower, and wiped down every inch of the tile and glass. Once more, I put on the ebony makeup of Bill Edwards. I put a wart on my left cheek and a few small bumps on my right cheek. I topped it off with a small scar on my neck. I double and triple-checked my look, and touched up anything that looked out of place. I followed it all with ebony powder to set the makeup. I reminded myself how I needed to take every precaution to avoid rain or tears.

My short, and curly, black hairpiece fit well, and didn't show any signs of being a wig. For my final touch, I put a tattoo on my right arm. I placed it on top of the makeup and blended it in until it looked like tattoos do on black men. As far as I could tell, this was the perfect disguise.

When I took my final look in the mirror all I could see was a black man named Bill Edwards. Not a person in the world, including Jewels, would mistake Bill Edwards for Rob Silvers, and the wart and face bumps should ward off any facial recognition software.

I redistributed my clothes, and packed everything into one of the nested suitcases. I also took everything out of my briefcase, and put it into the briefcase Earl had sent me. I saw a couple of envelopes inside, but I was running late and didn't have time to worry about them now. I would see what was in them on my cab ride to the U.P.-Ex hangar.

Along with the Wal-Mart suitcases, I'd picked up a spray bottle of bleach. I used it to spray down my old suitcase and briefcase. I then took both cases, along with the trash from my room, to the end of the hall where I put them down a trash chute.

I used the rest of the bleach to spray and wipe down everything I could have possibly touched in the room and on the balcony. I left the sliders open to air out the smell of bleach. I couldn't remember where I'd heard about bleach covering up evidence, so I didn't know if it would actually help—but it couldn't hurt.

My room charges were pre-paid, so I used the cart and my luggage as a shield between the night clerk and me as I walked through the lobby. It wouldn't have made any difference anyway since the night clerk was in a heated conversation with someone, and had his back to me. I could have danced naked, and he wouldn't have noticed.

There were three cabs in the circle drive at the front entrance to the hotel. I knocked on the window of the lead cab, and he loaded my luggage. I kept my briefcase with me, and told the driver I was going to the U.P.-Ex hangar at the airport. He knew exactly where it was.

It was time to see what Earl might have in store for me in the two envelopes. I pulled both out, and started reading the one marked, "Authorization Letter" first.

It was, as expected, on the CEO's letterhead. It was short and to the point, as it said I was a new employee who would be working in the operations department. It authorized me to ride in the jump seat of U.P.-Ex flight seven-nineteen, and it offered the reader to refer any questions to Mr. Earl Baker. There was a signature above the CEO's typewritten name, but since I had never seen his signature, I assumed it was as close as Earl could forge. It looked very official, and I placed it in the inside pocket of my sport coat.

The second letter was marked, "Read before landing Johnston." I would have read it anyway, but the cab was already pulling up to the U.P.-Ex hangar. Once my luggage was outside, I tipped the driver, and he wasted no time in his rush to get back to the Hyatt. I moved my luggage close to the glass-door entrance to U.P.-Ex Operations.

The door was locked, but there was a doorbell under an outside light. I pushed the button. After waiting what I considered to be ample time for a response, I nervously rang the bell a second time. From a side office, a sixtyish-looking woman of about 300 pounds suddenly filled the glass before me. From the expression on her face it was obvious she wasn't happy, and had better things to do than to act as a doorman.

There was a speaker above the doorbell, and when her voice came through it she confirmed my worst suspicions of her personality. "What do you want?" she asked in a manner that was obviously reserved for unexpected guests. I wondered if I was at the wrong door.

I used every muscle on my face to fake a smile, and I pulled back my sport coat to show that I was unarmed, before saying, "I have a letter from your CEO. It authorizes me to catch a ride in the jump seat of your morning flight seven-nineteen to Memphis. If you'll let me in, I'll show it to you."

Her only response was in the form of a loud buzzer that activated an electric door lock to allow my entry through the first of two doors. I quickly pulled the door open while I had the chance, and pushed my luggage in before me.

The inside door was also locked, so I moved my luggage out of the way so I could hold the letter to the glass for her inspection. With the speed of a fourth grader, she examined the document. Upon completion, she commanded, "Your driver's license." I held it to the glass. She looked at me, looked at it, and then back to me before she reached up and twisted the lock open.

Remembering that I was a black man, and she was a white woman, I realized that I had just received a first-hand observation of racial profiling. I wondered what it would have been like if I were dressed in a hooded sweatshirt instead of a suit and tie. I felt sure she would have called the cops before letting me in.

I gave her the letter and, while she was giving it her second once-over, I said, "I'm expected to be on flight seven-nineteen to Memphis this morning."

She picked up a phone and called someone, whom I guessed was probably the pilot. She apparently received some sort of permission, and said, "Someone will be down to escort you to your plane." She made a copy of my driver's license but, strangely enough, not the letter.

Knowing we had absolutely nothing in common, we both stood silently for a few minutes until a young man entered the lobby. "I'm Brad, if you'll please follow me, I'll take you to your plane."

He grabbed one of the suitcases, and I took the other along with my briefcase. We passed through a huge hangar with a lot of busy employees scrambling about the loading the planes parked at their gates.

As we walked up the stairs to the cockpit of U.P.-Ex seven-nineteen, I noticed the cargo doors were already closed. At the top of the stairs, we stepped inside and Brad set my luggage aside while introducing me to Captain Austin Alan, and Leslie Vanderlinden, the copilot. Brad handed Austin the letter, and made his exit down the stairs.

While the captain was reading the letter, I said casually, "I'm going to be working in the operations department under Mr. Baker." Austin didn't respond, but looking over to Leslie, he said, "It would be nice if we were given some sort of notice of these things." He shrugged, and then turned to me. "I know it's not your fault. Everything appears to be in order. Put your luggage in the closet behind you, and you can take either of the two jump seats." He handed the letter back to me, and added, "You're just in time. We're leaving early, and we'll be pushing back shortly."

I put my luggage in the large closet and hung my sport coat next to it. I kept my briefcase close as I sat in the jump seat offset behind Leslie, the copilot.

Leslie and Austin were busy going through their final checks when I felt the nudge of the tug as it hooked up in preparation for our push back. I watched the pilot's every move intensely to follow his routine and identify any differences between the Airbus I was sitting in and the Airbus I was accustomed to flying. This was definitely a newer model but, at first glance, it didn't seem to be a problem. Most of the dash looked the same, or had only minor differences.

The copilot received our clearance to push back and taxi to the active runway. Both engines were spinning, and I felt the plane being pushed back. The tug was cleared off, and the captain pushed the throttles slightly forward to taxi speed.

## Controlling – Robert Seckler

There was little traffic on the airport grounds at this hour, so I wasn't surprised when we received our departure clearance well before reaching the runway.

"Cleared for takeoff runway two-six, maintain runway heading until reaching three thousand. Reaching three thousand, turn right heading zero-three-zero, and continue climb to one-two-thousand. Expect further clearance to flight level two-three-zero, one-zero minutes after departure. Leaving two thousand, contact departure control on one-one-eight point three. Have a good day."

Austin bumped up our taxi speed while finishing his checklist with Leslie. We turned onto the runway, and started picking up speed. Leslie began calling off our speed, until saying, "Vee one—rotate." They both eased back on their yokes, and the nose of the plane began to rise. The captain commanded, "Gear up," and Leslie lifted the wheeled handle to its upmost position. After hearing the gear lock into place, and seeing the three dash lights turn from red to green, Leslie said, "We have three green, captain."

Everything was normal except that we'd departed fifteen minutes ahead of schedule, but that was a good thing. I realized that I was lucky to have made it past their three-hundred-pound security system to reach the flight before the doors were locked down. We climbed out per our clearance and, before reaching our assigned altitude of one-two-thousand, we were cleared to flight level two-three-zero, and later on to our final cruise altitude of flight level three-seven-zero. My eyes were still focusing on the instrumentation, and looking for any differences.

There was only one thing that I couldn't find, but it was something that would be very important to this flight. It was the cockpit vent control. This control acts as an air exchanger for the cockpit. The main purpose was to clear the air in the event of smoke in the cockpit. I planned for it to be used to clear chloroform gas from the cockpit.

I was able to see most of the dash, so I thought the control must be blocked by one of the two crew members. If I couldn't find the control, I would have to wear my gas mask throughout the balance of the flight. It wasn't a do-or-die situation, but it sure as hell would make my flight more uncomfortable.

When we leveled off at our cruise altitude, the crew went through their routine of trimming the plane and checking the on autopilot. I kept my eyes on the GPS unit as it counted off the nautical miles from Honolulu. I planned to take control of the flight about three hundred miles east if all final communications with Honolulu Center were complete.

During my cab ride to U.P.-Ex I had put on latex gloves, with nylon gloves over them. It was a little chilly when I first arrived, so it didn't seem out of place, but now, with my coat in the closet, my gloves were very obvious.

As the crew started to relax for the long flight to Memphis, Austin looked back, and asked, "Bill, what are you going to be doing in Memphis?"

I'd almost forgotten my new name, so it took an extra second or two for my response. "I'm going to be a load specialist. I was a dispatcher with Roadway freight, and I'm told my history there would make a good background for this job." I paused, and then couldn't resist asking, "Do you know Mr. Baker? What kind of a guy is he?"

"Yeah, I know him—he's my boss, too. He's all right as a manager, but I think he's a pompous ass as a person—but that's just between us. You won't have any problem working for him, but you might want to skip any social functions."

"Thanks for the heads-up. I'll keep that in mind."

There was a long moment of silence before Austin said, "I couldn't help but notice your gloves. What's up with that?"

I shrugged. "I hate to admit it, but I was doing some gardening, and I thought I was pulling weeds. It turned out the weeds were actually poison ivy. I went to the doctor yesterday, and I told her about this trip. She advised me to wear gloves. She said it would keep me from spreading it to other areas of my body, and it would protect others from getting it. So here I am with my gloves on, and looking like a fool in Hawaii's climate." Both pilots chuckled.

The cockpit became quiet again for awhile before Austin stood and went to get coffee. I took this as a good opportunity to check the gauges I couldn't see with him in his chair. There was nothing surprising to me, but I still didn't see the vent control.

Meeting and talking with Austin and Leslie was making me anxious about what I was going to do. Although I'd considered myself beyond the point of no return when we were wheels-up from Honolulu, I knew I still had the option of completing the trip to Memphis and going to Earl's office to tell him I couldn't do it.

However, that option would only make our financial problems worse because I had wiped out our savings to pay expenses already incurred. I knew I couldn't quit now. I had to move on, but thinking about my next move had me more scared than I had ever been. My hands would shake when I thought about it.

I kept telling myself, *There will be no victims. There will be no victims.* Somehow just saying that made it feel like it wasn't a serious crime. There would be no permanent injuries to either of them and, when they came around and figured out where they were, they would become celebrities telling the world about their hijacking adventure. What could be the harm in that?

It was two hundred and fifty miles east of Honolulu when the crew received a call from Honolulu Center, "U. P.–Ex seven-nineteen, Honolulu Center. Radar contact lost two hundred forty-five miles east of Honolulu, report Duets waypoint to Los Angeles Center on one-two-seven-zero-point-five. Have a good trip, and we'll see you next time."

Leslie responded, "Roger, radar contact lost and report Duets to Los Angeles on twelve-seventy-point-five. Good day!"

I knew that the Duets report wouldn't be expected by the Los Angeles Center controllers for about three hours, and the flight wouldn't be considered overdue until thirty minutes after that. Everything was happening in accordance with the plan, except for my nerves. I felt my hands start to shake again as I thought about triggering the gas. I pushed my hands hard against my legs to get them to stop, and I tried thinking good thoughts of Jewels. It seemed to help.

Austin was comfortably drinking his coffee, and reading a magazine, and Leslie was looking at some aeronautical charts she had spread across her lap. I knew this was the best opportunity I would have.

# Chapter Eighteen

## Taking Control

### Friday – 6:00 a.m. (HST) / Friday – 10 a.m. (CST)

I opened my briefcase, and removed the gas mask. With both pilots busy with other things, I was able to pull it over my head with neither of them seeing me. I closed the briefcase, set it upright on my lap and, with my hand on the trigger, I started mentally counting down from five, four, three, two…

I pulled the trigger.

I was already shaking, but the noise of the gas spewing from the canister scared me even more. Both their heads snapped back to see me holding a briefcase with gas spitting from a nozzle near the bottom. Austin tossed his magazine in the air, and reached out for me. His hand came within six inches of my face, but his seat belt and shoulder harness kept him from reaching me.

As Austin worked to loosen his belts, Leslie's right hand came across her body and grabbed my right arm. I leaned back in my chair and was able to jerk my arm free. She was trying again when, suddenly, as though a switch had been flipped, she fell back into her chair. I looked back to Austin, and he was also slumped over.

I could feel my heart racing like it had never felt before. I knew I had to calm myself, but it wasn't happening. I tried to think of Jewels, but the only image I got was one of my heart flying out of my body like a Meatloaf song. I put my briefcase down, and placed my right hand on my heart. I could feel each pump as I leaned my head back and started taking long and slow breaths. I kept that up for several minutes until I finally began to feel my heartbeat slowing.

I raised my head, and looked around the cockpit. There was no threat from either Austin or Leslie, and the plane was on autopilot. With all threats gone, I started breathing easier and, in a couple of minutes, my composure had calmed enough that I could see and understand what had happened. I just sat there trying to relax for what must have been at least five minutes.

Knowing I could miss my pickup time if I didn't get back on plan, I unbuckled my belts, and went to Leslie's limp body in the right chair. I checked to make sure she was breathing OK before unbuckling her and carrying her to the jump seat. I made her as comfortable as I could while buckling her into the seat I had previously occupied.

I settled into the copilot's chair, and started my search for the cockpit vent control. It had been blocked from my view by Leslie, and I found it in under a minute. I turned it to the on position and I immediately heard the fans kick in. I could feel the air recirculating. It was designed to clear the cockpit air in two minutes or less, but I gave it five minutes before removing my mask. The taste that accompanied chloroform gas was now gone.

It was time to go to Johnston Island. I turned off all electronics, including the autopilot, and got the feel of the plane before pulling back on the throttles enough to start my descent. As the plane began losing altitude I started a ninety-degree turn to the south.

I knew I was on the most heavily traveled route in the Pacific, and I thought about how ironic it would be to have an ex-air traffic controller die in a midair collision. I pulled the throttles back a little further to expedite my descent out of positive-control airspace.

I decided on 16,500 feet as my altitude for the balance of my flight. I would need to keep a close eye on my fuel because at this altitude the air is a lot thicker. Making it even worse, instead of having the jet stream at my back, I would be going against it as I turned to the west. I hoped I would be low enough to avoid most of its effect.

My mind was bombarded with the desperate and frightened faces of Austin and Leslie as they reached out for me. Those were images I knew I'd never forget.

I was well aware of where I was, and how I got there, but my mind still wandered. I found it hard to believe I was actually doing this.

What would make a fifty-nine-year-old man with no criminal record stoop so low as to hijack an aircraft? I had convinced myself that it was all for Jewels, but I knew better. She loved me, as I did her, and we could have lived under any conditions. It was all about me wanting to show her I could keep my promise of a comfortable retirement—a lifestyle she was happy with, but could live without.

I was just trying to overcome all my financial mistakes and the empty promises I'd made her. I just kept telling myself, there would be no victims.

I continued south until I believed it was time for a course adjustment, and the first test of my new portable GPS. I licked the suction cup of the antenna and stuck it to the windscreen. I had preloaded Johnston Island and it came up quickly. I was far enough south to turn directly toward Johnston without fear of being picked up by the radars on the big island of Hawaii. I had all the information I needed and I quickly turned the unit off, and made the necessary route correction.

Although I knew we were burning fuel at a high rate, I wasn't concerned about making Johnston Island, at least not yet. Without electronics I didn't have fuel gauges, and I wasn't about to turn anything on at this stage of my flight.

As I looked down at the ocean I wondered about the ships at sea. At sixteen thousand feet, I didn't think they could see much more than a contrail, but then the plane's fuselage was painted U.P.-Ex's trademark color of bright yellow. The more I thought about it, the more I realized how paranoid I was getting over nothing.

I just wished it were all over.

I suddenly remembered Earl's second letter, and removed it from my briefcase. My part of this hijacking was set in stone, and this letter was written well-before I'd left Houston, so I couldn't imagine it being anything significant. If it were, we would have talked about it before I left. Part of me was saying not to read it at all, but knowing Earl, it could be something he was scared to say to me face-to-face. I opened the envelope.

The letter was typewritten, and it was addressed to the fictitious Bill Edwards. It read:

*If this is to be the perfect crime we both want, you need to dispose of all evidence.*

He didn't need to write me a letter to tell me that.

*The evidence I'm talking about is the U.P.-Ex plane, and the U.P.-Ex crew.*

That came like a big punch in the gut. I threw the letter down in disgust and thought about what a rotten piece of shit Earl was. He was obviously thinking of having me kill the crew. I knew he was an asshole, but I didn't think he was that big of an asshole.

After a few deep breaths, I picked up the letter to read more.

*The plane will be declared lost at sea, and they will only be looking for debris east of Honolulu. You will need to keep the engines running while you unload our cargo on Johnston. With that done, you can follow the enclosed instructions telling you how to setup the autopilot to take the plane off with the unconscious crew on board. It will go until it runs out of fuel and then crash into the ocean unnoticed. This is what it will take to make our plan the absolute perfect crime.*

Tears started running down my cheeks, and I immediately thought about how it could be ruining my disguise. I realized that Earl Baker was capable of murder, and once again, I was sure he was the Houston Center bomber. I could see it was time for him to pay for killing Clyde Roberts.

I had to read the balance so I picked the letter back up and continued to read:

*To make this all worthwhile, I have a bonus for you. There was a late addition to the manifest. One of the largest diamond dealers in Honolulu went bankrupt. Its diamonds were on consignment from Antwerp Diamond Centre, and they are being returned on flight seven-nineteen. They are insured for thirty million dollars and they are in the container closest to the port cargo door. The container number is 763350. They're half yours. Don't let me down on this Bill.*

What a jerk. Had I read his letter last night, I wouldn't be here now.

There was no decision for me to make, because I would never entertain thoughts of killing anyone. Earl could burn in hell, but I had no intention of joining him. I hated Earl for even thinking I would do something like this.

I knew I had to push those thoughts out of my mind, and concentrate on getting this plane on the ground. A weather system was starting to move through the area, and ceilings were dropping.

When I turned on my GPS I realized how I must have been lost in thought, or had even fallen asleep, because we were less than a hundred miles from Johnston. I decided to leave the GPS on until I had the island in sight. I eased back on the throttles, and started a slow descent.

I hoped to make a low pass before setting up to land, but with the ceiling coming down I might be forced to go straight in. I found myself returning to thoughts of Earl's letter. It was keeping me from being focused on what I was doing.

At fifty miles out, I slowed to 250 knots, and put out ten degrees of flaps.

I was committed to staying with the original plan, but the closer I got to the island, the more I found to worry about.

Some components were simply out of my control. One was the possibility of something holding the Fish & Wildlife people over for another day. Unless I actually saw someone walking around the island while I was on approach, I wouldn't know until they came out to greet me.

The gap between the base of the clouds and the ocean was getting smaller by the minute. The GPS showed it directly ahead, but as hard as I scanned the horizon, I couldn't see it. I continued my descent to 1,000 feet. Unless they'd made some changes since I'd been there, I believed the highest building on the island was the control tower, and it was only about thirty or forty feet tall. I was glad to be under the overcast skies.

As I continued to scan for the island, I thought I had spotted it at my ten o'clock position. I adjusted my heading accordingly, and started my descent for landing. The closer I got the more undecided I was about what was before me. It didn't look like the island I'd remembered, but there were no other islands in the area. I was trying to spot the control tower, but I just couldn't make it out.

At two hundred feet, I was almost on top of it before I realized it was a damn ship. I pulled back on the yoke hard, and turned away. I knew anyone in the con tower had to have heard me, and it was more than likely that one of them had looked out to see this canary-yellow aircraft.

I saw enough of their flag to tell it wasn't American, but I couldn't identify what flag it was flying. It was too late to worry about that now, anyway. I could only hope they didn't report it.

As I climbed out from the ship, I glanced at my GPS and saw that the island was behind me now. I'd missed it while chasing down the ship. I was back up to 1,000, and there couldn't be more than another 1,000 feet between me and the clouds above. I made a teardrop turn to line up for landing, and I put out another ten degrees of flaps. I extended the gear, reduced my airspeed, and descended to two hundred feet. I could see the wind sock and it was hanging down loosely.

I was lined up on the runway, and I pulled back on the throttles a little more. I flared over the threshold, and hit the runway at about 160 knots. I pulled the throttles back full, and kicked in the thrust reversers. If there was anyone on this little island they'd soon be running out to see what the racket was about. I was on the brakes, and slowing well.

I probably could have made the first high-speed turnoff, but I didn't try. At the end of the runway I made a slow turn onto the parallel taxiway. As the nose swept from left to right I got a good view of the chalk-colored buildings. The Queen Air was sitting, as expected, on one side of the old terminal building. I taxied to the opposite side.

In what I thought might be nothing more than a feeble attempt to hide the plane from satellite photographs, I nudged it up as close as I could to the terminal building. Part of the left wing was actually hanging over the building's flat roof. The yellow portion of the paint scheme was only on the fuselage, so the wings blended in with the building and the tarmac fairly well. I rationalized that there should be no reason for anyone to be looking at Johnston Island anyway.

Knowing full well that shutting down the engines would end any possibility of fulfilling Earl's request to kill the crew - I shut them down with a smile. As they were winding down, I opened a cockpit window and could feel a slight tropical breeze. It was good to be on the ground. The dreadful hijacking leg of my journey had finally come to an end.

After freeing myself of belts, I stood and went to the captain's side of the plane. When I opened his window the force of the cross breeze doubled. Both crewmembers seemed to be breathing normally, but I saw a slight twitch in the captain's right hand. That worried me.

I decided to close the windows for fear of the breeze causing them to regain consciousness before I was ready. I couldn't take the chance of either of them coming around, so I decided to give them one more blast of gas from a second canister in the briefcase.

I went to the access door from the cockpit into the huge cargo bay full of containers. It was a massive sight, and I realized how it would have taken me all day to find a specific container without the cargo map Earl had given me. I wondered how he planned to avoid suspicion of being the inside-person of this crime. But, like he'd told me several times, I needed to focus on my job, and my job only. Knowing Earl, he would have some sucker lined up to take the fall. Earl wasn't dumb, and he would use anyone as a stepping-stone to improve his version of the good life.

I got all my belongings out of the cockpit and into the cargo bay before moving Leslie back into her copilot chair. I still had my gloves on and I decided to wipe the cockpit down completely, just to be safe. I placed the briefcase inside the doorway facing toward the front of the plane. I closed the cabin door against it and pulling the second trigger.

I let it spew for a few seconds, and then put my gas mask back on, and went back into the cockpit. I opened both windows, and left the cabin door open to air out the crew's space. I remembered to take the radio microphones and satellite phone to the cargo bay.

After opening the cargo doors on each side, I got a good cross-breeze and it felt great. I released the emergency slide, and tossed down a rope ladder.

Standing in the cargo bay door, I looked out over the buildings and palm trees. I gathered my loudest voice, and screamed, "Earl, screw you, and your perfect crime!"

The money container was where Earl had said it would be and, after double-checking the numbers, I broke the seal. I noticed my hands were beginning to sweat. I wasn't sure if it was from my nervous condition, or the heat, but it was becoming a problem. I took off both sets of gloves, and used a rag to wipe down my hands. One at a time I held the gloves open to the wind to let them dry. That reminded me of my need to touch up my makeup before being subject to inspection by my pick-up pilot.

I returned to the cockpit to fix the damage from my tears, and I was soon back on track.

My gloves and hands were dry so I pulled the top cover of the money container back. I could see several rows of cardboard boxes. Each box had a number written on the top. All of the boxes on the top row had the number "One" written with a black marker. Inside, they were full of one-dollar bills. Digging deeper I found fives, tens, fifties, and finally the hundreds. That was as high as they went. Since I needed to put the biggest bills into my luggage first, I unloaded all of the cartons and stacked them by order of the currency denominations.

Once I had my routine down, it went quickly. I filled one suitcase after another, and tossed them down the slide. About half way through the boxes I found the GPS unit Earl had promised to be there. I turned it off and put it aside. The duffel bags were the last to be filled and I was down to five-dollar bills. The final duffel bag ended up with about half five-dollar bills and half ones. As much as I hated to do so, I left the rest behind.

Everything was soon down the slide except me, but I had one more job to do before I was finished. I found the diamond container Earl had mentioned in his letter. Earl was probably one of only a handful of people who knew about the diamonds, so I thought I would give him something to sweat about.

I opened the container and, after moving some top-loaded items, I got down to a locked metal box. This had to be what Earl was talking about. I went back to the cockpit, and took a crowbar from the toolbox. I used it to pry open the metal box.

Sure enough, there were ten soft velvet bags containing individually wrapped diamonds. I looked inside one of the bags, and found several finely cut diamonds in excess of two karats each. As much as I would love to have one mounted for Jewels, I put them back in their bag.

I took all ten bags, and placed them on the throttle console between Austin and Leslie. I checked them both one last time to be sure their breathing was normal. I thought it would be an interesting test of honesty for the crew, but one I believed Austin and Leslie would pass.

I knew my actions with the diamonds could point right to Earl, but he never should have thought I would have done as he requested. He knew me better than that, but he didn't know my plan called for Jewels and I to be in a secure location before he would be able to blame anything on me. I took my first and last trip down the slide.

Los Angeles Center made the call to the chief executive officer of U.P.-Ex to notify him that its Flight 7-19 from Honolulu was overdue its required report of Duets waypoint. Since the CEO was on Christmas vacation in Europe, the call was routed to Earl. The FAA supervisor asked Earl if he'd had any communications with Flight 7-19 today. For show, Earl made a quick check of all people who might have received a call, and he then advised the supervisor that he had not. With that, the FAA supervisor told Earl that search-and-rescue operations would commence immediately.

Earl had the CEO's cell phone number for emergencies, and he called him to pass on the overdue aircraft news. It came as no surprise when he told Earl to stay at work until this was resolved.

# Chapter Nineteen

## Flight to Kauai

Back on Johnston Island, I found a large, four-wheeled cart big enough for loading all the money suitcases, the microphones, the world phone, and my personal suitcase. I pushed it down to the end of the runway where I was scheduled to be picked up. I took the microphones and world phone from the cart, and walked to the water's edge. I threw them as far as I could into the crystal clear water of the North Pacific.

Johnston Island was a coral reef that had been strengthened and expanded when it was decided it would become a launch pad for above-ground nuclear testing. The waters surrounding the island were as clear as any I had seen. The clash of the blue waters and green palms against a background of chalk colored buildings, made the eight-mile island beautiful in many ways. I wished for a camera and Jewels' hand to hold, but not in that order.

While staying within hearing distance of an incoming plane, I walked around the island to kill time. Although in good condition, the runway had several large X's painted on it to indicate it was closed to unauthorized traffic.

I found building doors unlocked but, except for the Queen Air aircraft, there was little of value. The offices were obviously furnished with leftovers from other government offices.

If my pick-up pilot didn't arrive in the next hour, the Queen Air would be my only escape vehicle, so I looked inside. It was an older model but it looked to be in good condition. The key was in the ignition and, when I turned it, both fuel gauges rose to the full position. It looked like the only serious problem I would have would be selecting a safe destination. The closest island was Wake, but it was an active military base. Next would be the Hawaiian chain, and I would have to hug the ocean to sneak through the Air Defense Identification Zone without finding unwanted company before landing.

I heard the distant rumble of the King Air's large twin engines, but it took me a moment or two before I could see him. When I did, I was happy not to be adding a stolen Queen Air to my list of felonies, and happy I didn't have to play cat-and-mouse with armed military aircraft.

My pick-up pilot was a hundred yards from the end of the runway with gear down, and slowed for landing, when I reached my luggage cart. His arrival brought a huge sigh of relief.

The pilot took the first high-speed turnoff and taxied back to within thirty feet of where I was standing. With the engines left running, he opened the door and let the stairs down. Standing in the doorway with his arms crossed, he looked far more like a lumberjack than a pilot. Trying to talk over two idling, and very loud, engines, he hollered, "The cargo door's unlocked, put your luggage in there!"

I didn't like the way he was making his bid for control and, since I held the purse strings, I wasn't going to let that happen without a challenge. He had an intimidating frame of about 6'4" and 280 pounds, but it was going to be a long flight to Kauai. I hollered up my response, "I don't think so. If you want your money, you need to get your ass down here and help."

As he started down the stairs, he grunted something I didn't understand, but I knew I was victorious in our mental battle for control. He reluctantly loaded the lion's share of my luggage. As he was loading the last piece, I made sure to precede him up the stairs.

I was leery enough having to depend on someone else for this leg, and I sure as hell wasn't going to be left on Johnston Island.

As my pilot was wiggling his way into his captain's chair, I was looking in the galley for a drink. I found a beer, and took my seat. I heard the cockpit door slam, and I was lucky to get buckled up before he reached takeoff speed. He was making a point and I knew we'd started off on the wrong foot. I would have to make amends somewhere along the way.

I finished my beer, crushed the can, and put it in my briefcase. We soon leveled off at what would be our cruising altitude. I suspected he would be on a visual-flight-rules flight plan, and I assumed he had filed his return times for crossing into American airspace without military intervention. I decided it was time to give our introduction a second shot.

I knocked on the cockpit door and, after he called, "Come in!" I opened it, and said, "I'm sorry, but we seemed to have gotten off to a bad start. My name's..." I hesitated as I tried to remember... "Bill Edwards. Would you mind if I sat in the right seat for a while?"

He apparently felt the same as I about our beginning, as he replied, "Jim Sellers. Have a seat." I buckled into the copilot's chair, thinking how he was no more Jim Sellers that I was Bill Edwards, but what did it matter? I extended my hand, and he reached over with what I thought was a limp handshake from such a big guy. But, again, what did it matter? It served as another reminder that I was a black man with gloves on. I probably would have had a limp handshake too.

Jim asked about the gloves, and I gave him the same poison ivy story I'd given the crew. It was the first smile I'd seen from him, but I hadn't shared any of mine, either. He said, "You're what, in your fifties, and you don't know what poison ivy looks like?"

"I'm a city guy."

Jim just smiled again, and then said, "What's that plane doing at Johnston?"

"The Queen Air or the Airbus?"

"Are we going to play games again? The huge canary with U.P.-Ex on its tail!"

"Sorry. It had a mechanical problem, and was forced to land here a couple of days ago. The crew's been waiting for a part to be flown in."

"The crew's still on the island?" Jim said anxiously.

I scrambled to answer his reasonable concerns. "No. They went in with the Fish & Wildlife people yesterday. I was the only one left on the island when you arrived. I wanted my departure to be without any fanfare since I'm leaving a month before my contract is completed. I'd had my fill of this rock. I thought island fever was bad enough on Kauai, but it's a paradise compared to Johnston."

His lack of a response got me worrying about what story Earl might have told him. I changed the subject by asking, "I assume you're on a VFR flight plan; what's your plan for crossing ADIZ?"

"I filed outbound on a whale-watching flight with one passenger. We're right on schedule for my filed re-entry time. There's nothing for you to be concerned about." With that said, it soon became obvious that neither of us wanted to share any portions of our lives.

Quiet set in.

My mind started wondering where Earl had gotten off on the wrong track, and I instantly thought it was likely his training as a Marine Corps Special Forces officer. It was our government that had taught him to kill, and it was clandestine orders from the White House that had put him in Cambodia.

Killing from afar is one thing, but it has to be a totally different memory to see blood gushing from your best friend's throat. It was at that time that Earl experienced what he had once called the satisfaction of revenge. He had emptied his magazine into the face of that Cambodian soldier. It must have been those memories that had led to the destruction of Earl's morality. He wasn't born that way. He was taught to kill by our government.

Knowing there was nothing I could do to change the past, I focused on my commitment to finish the plan with no bodily harm to anyone. I put Earl's letter out of my mind, but I saved it.

I knew search-and-rescue operations were under way by now, but we were well outside of the search area. Hopefully, I would be out of Hawaii all together by the time the U.P.-Ex crew made contact with anyone.

Jim broke our silence. "I was told I would be paid in cash upon arrival at Princeville airport. I assume I'll be getting that from you?"

"I have your money."

"I've never landed at Princeville with a King Air." Jim continued, "But I know the runway will be doable, although a little tight. I'll make it work. It's thirty-five hundred feet of rough asphalt so we can expect a few bumps on landing."

"I'll trust you know what you're doing."

Jim keyed his mike. "Honolulu Center, November one-two-eight-six Bravo, fifty miles southwest of Princeville, landing, over."

The center controller responded, "Eight-six bravo, Honolulu Center, roger, squawk one-two-three-six."

"Roger, one-two-three-six. Request flight following and activation of our inbound flight plan." Jim adjusted the dial on his transponder to match the numbers assigned by the center, and waited for their response.

"Eight-six Bravo, radar contact forty-two miles southwest of Princeville. I've activated your inbound flight plan."

"Roger, Center, I'll only be on the ground at Princeville for a few minutes, and I'll then be departing to Port Allen."

The center acknowledged his call, "Eight-six Bravo, roger."

Within a few minutes, I could see the runway. It looked even shorter from the air, but Jim did a good job of setting the King Air down within five feet of the runway threshold.

With no taxiways, Jim turned the plane around on the runway and taxied back. I saw the van I was expecting. It was parked between two hangars. I pointed it out to Jim, and he taxied as close as he could. He kept the engines running as we both unloaded my luggage. I gave him his cash payment in worn currency. He was immediately back in his plane and taxiing across the grass.

We had used most of the runway with our landing, so I was a little concerned about his takeoff since that would take more runway. He gave the engines a strong taste of throttle before releasing the brakes, and heading down the asphalt. With a string of palms as his backdrop, he used every inch of the runway, and a little grass at the end, before I saw his nose lift. I smiled as his gear retracted. He'd done everything he was paid to do, and we were both safely inside the watchful eyes of the military radar.

As per the plan, the van had been left unlocked, and the key was in the glove box. I was soon on the road to Kawai's largest airport: Lihue. Driving south along the coast, I couldn't miss seeing how beautiful the island was, but my concentration was on finding the rest stop Earl promised me would be along this road. As I rounded the next bend, I saw it ahead, and I pulled into an empty parking lot.

I took my personal suitcase inside, and went to the first bathroom stall to start removing Bill Edwards before he became Public Enemy Number One. Once Bill was gone, I started work on disguise number three.

This time I would be Declan Finley, a wealthy businessman who, as my story would go, had been on the island taking care of his mother's estate. I put on my head-to-toe Tommy Bahama outfit. My makeup was courtesy of a bottle of instant tanning cream, and my hairpiece was a neatly trimmed, but recklessly combed, medium brown. I felt confident about this good-looking guy's appearance, and I knew I had to put the thoughts of Earl and Bill behind me. Declan was to be totally cool.

Fifteen minutes later, I pulled up to Bradley Aviation. It was time to return to the mainland… and I would be doing so in style.

# Chapter Twenty

## Regaining Consciousness

### Friday – 3:00 p.m. (HST) / Friday – 7:00 p.m. (CST)

Austin was the first to open his eyes in the cockpit of U.P.-Ex 7-19. He instantly realized that they were on the ground, but where? He reached over to Leslie, and tugged on her arm, but he didn't get a response.

The next thing Austin noticed were the ten velvet bags sitting on the throttle console. He thought he must have been dreaming. Everything still seemed surreal and foggy to him. He opened one of the bags, and looked inside. He couldn't believe the size of the diamonds, and had no idea of how they got there. As he was putting them back into the bag, one dropped to the floor.

Austin tried tugging on Leslie's arm again, and this time he heard a light cough. He was relieved to know she was alive. The last thing Austin remembered was their passenger, Bill Edwards. He was holding a briefcase that was spraying gas. It all went blank from there.

Leslie was opening her eyes and, when she saw Austin, she rubbed her eyes, and said, "What happened?"

"I'm not sure. We're on the ground, but I don't know where."

Their windows were open, and the tropical breeze was refreshing as it flowed through their cockpit. Leslie, still a little groggy, looked out to the island. "There are palm trees and some buildings out there so we know it's tropical."

Austin turned the power on, and expanded the area of the GPS. The identifier of JON was next to their current position and he had to expand his search out to a thousand miles before seeing the Hawaiian Islands well to the northeast of their position. Austin knew the identifier of JON, and he said, "We're on Johnston Island. How in hell did we get here?"

Leslie asked, "Where's Bill?"

Austin was trying to put the pieces together. "It looks like Mr. Edwards wasn't the new employee we thought him to be. I think we've been hijacked." He reached for his microphone to make an emergency call for help, but it wasn't there. "Do you have a mike?" Leslie looked, and shook her head. "How about the satellite phone?" Again, Leslie shook her head as she noticed the bags on the console.

Austin saw her looking at the blue bags, and said, "I don't know if they're real or not, but they sure do look like diamonds."

Leslie smiled, and said, "Bill hijacked our plane so he could leave us diamonds? What's wrong with that picture?"

They were starting to feel more relaxed, and were getting their balance. Neither seemed injured, and there were no obvious threats. But they still didn't know where Bill was.

Austin started to stand. "We need to find a way to tell someone where..." He suddenly fell back in his chair. His balance wasn't as good as he'd thought.

"Are you all right?" Leslie asked with concern. "We need to take this slow. We've been out for a long time."

Looking at his watch, he said, "You're right, it must be close to nine hours. They've got to be looking for us by now, but they won't be looking here. We've got to find a way to let someone know where we are. Let me try this again a little slower." This time he was able to get to his feet by holding onto the back of his chair. Leslie unbuckled her belts, and slowly started to stand. She was also able to stand with the assistance of her chair.

"There's got to be someone on this island. We need to look around."

"What about the diamonds?"

"Just leave them there. We don't want to destroy any evidence. See if the flare gun's still there." Leslie found the flare gun, and handed it to Austin. "We'll take it with us in case we come across Mr. Edwards. A flare to the gut will stop about anyone."

Leslie dropped the bag of diamonds she'd had in her hand onto the console like a busted shoplifter.

Feeling steady now, Austin led the way through the door into the cargo bay with his flare gun ready for action. The first thing they saw out of place was the stack of empty cardboard boxes and loose currency on the floor. "He hit the money container, and it looks like he took most of it. Edwards must have had someone waiting here for him. This is unbelievable."

Leslie was alarmed over the possibilities. "Aren't you worried about them still being here? They could be armed?"

"We can't just sit here." He looked out the cargo door and, after a moment or two, he said, "I don't see anyone, and there has to be some form of communication in one of these buildings. It looks like they went through the cargo door. The emergency slide and rope ladder are down, but I don't see anyone around."

"I'm scared, Austin."

"I'm going down, but if you want to stay here you can pull the rope ladder up to be safe. Just throw it back down when I return."

"No, I'm coming with you."

Austin turned back toward the cockpit. "Your choice, but I've got to run to the bathroom before I do anything."

Leslie said, "Let me have the flare gun"

He handed it to her, and said, "I'm going to get something to drink, do you want anything?"

"Yes, but I'll get it myself. I'm going in when you're through."

"OK, see if you can find any other containers opened."

Several minutes went by without Austin's return. Leslie started walking toward the cockpit just as Austin came through with two cans of Coke.

"What took you so long?"

"I checked the closet to see if Bill took his luggage. He did, but I found the authorization letter on the closet floor. Did you find anything?"

"No. I've been looking out this door to see if I could see any movement before we go down. I haven't seen anything so far." Leslie went to the cockpit for a restroom break before they started out on their search. They both went down the slide.

Still not knowing the whereabouts of Mr. Edwards, Austin had his flare gun ready as they turned the corner to the front of the old terminal building. The sign over the door read: Johnston Atoll – Property of the United States Government.

"The GPS was right," Leslie said while pulling on the front door. She expected the door to be locked, but it opened freely, and she almost fell. The glass door was labeled: U. S. Department of Fish & Wildlife. Inside the door, there was a small table with a phone. It had no dial or buttons, but a sign above it read FAA Flight Service. When she put the receiver to her ear she could hear it ringing. A man's voice answered, "Honolulu Flight Service."

"Is this the FAA?"

"Yes, it is. How can I help you?"

She took a deep breath. "This is U.P.-Ex seven-nineteen, we've been hijacked."

"Stay on the line. We've been looking for you. Is everyone OK?"

An FAA supervisor got on the line as Leslie was holding the receiver out to Austin. Management was now on both ends, and Leslie was glad to let Austin deal with this.

The FAA supervisor said, "We have search-and-rescue looking for you. Is anyone hurt? And, is the hijacker still there?"

"There are two of us, and we're OK, but we don't know where the hijacker is. We believe him to be a black male by the name of Bill Edwards. He boarded our flight in Honolulu with a letter from our CEO authorizing him to ride with us as a new employee."

"Hold on a second." There was a pause. "Can you hear another phone ringing in one of the offices there?"

Austin and Leslie both heard the ringing, and Leslie followed the sound and picked it up." The FAA supervisor said, "It'll be the FBI on the other end."

The special agent in charge of the FBI's Honolulu office was on with Leslie. After introducing himself, he told Leslie, "I understand you are both OK. Is that correct?"

"Yes. We were knocked out by some gas, and we were out for about nine hours. We believe our hijacker to be a black man that looked to be in his fifties. He gave us the name of Bill Edwards. He had a wart on his cheek. We have no idea where he is now. He could still be on the island."

"OK." The agent said, "We need for both of you to stay in the building you're in until we can get help to you. It may take a couple of hours, maybe more, but we'll be there as quickly as possible. Neither of you are to re-enter your aircraft until we can get our agents there to search the plane for evidence. When our agents get there they will allow you access for your personal items. Do you understand what I'm telling you?"

"Yes, I do, we won't go back. I'll make sure Captain Alan also understands."

"Good. We will get help to you as soon as possible but, until then, I believe it best if the two of you stay in the building you're in. One of you needs to monitor this line in case we need to get ahold of you. If possible, I want you to lock all the doors. I'm also going to ask that you make no phone calls whatsoever before we arrive. If you will provide us with the names and phone numbers of relatives or close friends, we will make the necessary calls to tell them you're OK. But we will be unable to provide them with details at this time."

She hesitated. "Well, if we can't call, can you call our operations department, and have them contact our families and let them know we're OK? I think it would be better coming from them."

"We'll take care of those calls. If you need anything else you can call us, but only us, on the phone you are on now." He gave Leslie the phone number, and reassured her they would have people there soon.

When Leslie walked back to Austin she covered everything the agent had told her. They walked together to each door and locked the ones that were lockable. They pushed furniture in front of the others.

Leslie found a VHF radio in the same office where she'd answered the phone. She showed it to Austin, and Austin pushed the power button. It lit up like a Christmas tree, and it was already on the emergency frequency of 121.5. Knowing they weren't to make any calls out, they left it on in case anyone might call them.

To kill some time, they snooped around the offices, and looked at some of the projects the Fish & Wildlife people were working on. It was almost an hour later when they heard a call on the emergency radio.

"U.P.–Ex seven-nineteen. Air Force flight twenty-one, do you read?"

Both raced to the radio, but Leslie picked up the mike first. "Air Force twenty-one, U.P.-Ex seven-nineteen, we read you loud and clear, over."

"Roger U.P.-Ex, we're a flight of two F-16 aircraft, and we'll be landing on Johnston Island in five minutes or less." Leslie acknowledged their transmission, and they both ran to the window to watch the flights land.

They spotted the planes coming in with one aircraft well above the other. The lower of the two had gear down and, as he touched the runway, the upper plane started his moves. Their eyes were glued on the upper aircraft as he pointed his nose toward the sky with throttles full. He did a complete roll and, as he came out, he was perfectly lined up with the runway about a half mile out. He slowed considerably before he dropped his flaps and gear. The first plane was turning onto the taxiway when the second plane touched the concrete.

With a touch of envy in his voice, Austin said, "I guess it's not showing off when you can do it that good."

The two fighters had been dispatched under orders from the White House. They were to search and secure the island while waiting for the FBI to arrive. It had been decided at high levels that this hijacking would be kept under wraps until it was determined if it was, or was not, an act of terrorism. The four F-16 crewmembers searched the island for Bill Edwards, and any associates, but they had negative results.

The island was declared secure.

The FBI landed in a multi-million dollar G-5 aircraft that had become government property as the result of a major drug bust in Honolulu three years before.

Coming off the aircraft first was Special Agent Steve Fair. Seven other agents followed him. All were FBI except for one Secret Service agent, Savanna Anne. She was to oversee the accountability of the currency, since both the currency and the Secret Service fell under the authority of the Treasury Department. Agent Fair and his assistant were to do the questioning of Leslie and Austin, while the rest went to the U.P.-Ex plane to gather evidence.

The four F-16 pilots were questioned briefly about their observations, and then they were released to return to Wake. The questioning of the U.P.-Ex crew took place in the Fish & Wildlife offices, and Agent Fair's assistant set up audio and video recording equipment. Austin and Leslie were called in separately for questioning.

Agent Fair had Austin start with the arrival of Bill Edwards at U.P.-Ex's hangar early Friday morning, and continue in detail until the FBI aircraft landed on Johnston Island. When Austin's questioning was complete, Leslie was called in, and questioned in the same manner. By the time they were both finished they were beat, but Agent Fair wanted to have them repeat what they had just told him.

Austin had had enough, and he said, "I can't speak for Leslie, but I have nothing more to tell you. Unless you have something new to go over, I'm exercising my right to an attorney." Agent Fair apologized, and the questioning was stopped.

Austin and Leslie were allowed to return to the U.P.-Ex aircraft for their personal effects. They were escorted one at a time into the cockpit. Leslie was first, and Savanna escorted her. She took her suitcase from the closet, and Savanna went through it with a fine-toothed comb.

Leslie was then directed to submit to a strip search where she was required to strip down to her bra and panties. Her clothes were then searched thoroughly, and given back to her to get dressed again. She was allowed to leave the plane with her suitcase.

Austin was waiting for his turn outside of the cockpit area when Leslie came out. She said, "Don't worry, it's almost pain-free." Savanna came out, and another male agent took Austin inside. Austin was nervous when it came his time to strip down to his underwear. He protested the reasoning for a strip search, but he was told he must comply. When he was down to his underwear the agent searched through his pockets.

The agent found a carefully wrapped large diamond in his right, front pocket. The agent showed it to Austin, and asked, "What's this?"

Austin answered nervously, "That fell on the floor when we were looking at the bags of diamonds. We had already secured the bags so I put it in my pocket until we came back. I was thinking that if the hijackers were still on the island I might be able to trade it for our release. I forgot all about it. That's the honest truth. I wasn't trying to steal it."

The agent allowed Austin to get dressed, and then escorted him from the cockpit, down the slide, and into the Fish & Wildlife offices, where Special Agent Fair and his assistant were gathering up their recording equipment. The agent told Special Agent Fair of the circumstances of finding the diamond. Agent Fair had ordered the strip searches of Leslie and Austin after it was discovered that a large diamond was missing from the shipment.

Agent Fair looked at Austin, and said, "You've got to be kidding me! You tried to steal one of the diamonds?"

Austin kept repeating his story the same way, and Agent Fair sent his assistant to bring Leslie to him. She was waiting close outside, and was brought in while Austin was taken outside the office. She recounted everything that she had seen, but she didn't know about the diamond dropping, and could only verify that he had gone back in to go to the restroom while she was in the cargo area.

She stood behind Austin one hundred percent as an honest man who had been through a hell of a lot of stress over this long day. She said, "I can see how that could have happened. We were knocked out for nine hours by some sort of gas, and when we were just coming around we saw the diamonds on the console. Neither of us was ourselves. We could barely even stand up. You can't condemn Austin for anything he did in that state of mind, and I'm sure you know it would never stand up in court."

Agent Fair called Austin back into the room. "Your copilot has made a believable statement on your behalf. If you will repeat your previous statement in writing for our record, I will release the two of you to a hotel in Honolulu. Neither of you will be allowed to contact anyone other than your immediate family. They have already been told that neither of you have any injuries, but they haven't been told about a hijacking.

"The hijacking information isn't to be released to anyone outside of our agents, and Mr. Baker, your chief operating officer. You are sworn to secrecy until we get this sorted out. You can have a nice dinner and a good night's rest on the government, but you need to report to our offices tomorrow at one p.m. for either further questioning, or to prepare for a news release, dependent upon the status of the investigation. Our offices are only a block from your hotel."

They agreed, and they were flown back to Honolulu on the G-5.

# Chapter Twenty-One

## Pleasure Flight

### Friday – 6:00 p.m. (HST) / Friday – 10:00 p.m. (CST)

Before going inside Bradley Aviation, I took a look in the vanity mirror, and had a hard time believing how good I looked as Declan Finley. I was expecting a stress-free, luxurious flight to Albuquerque, and I was more than ready. I locked the van, grabbed my briefcase, and went inside.

Immediately, I saw two things that put a smile on my face—a nice-looking, young woman at the front desk, and a Cessna Citation shining on the other side of the glass behind her. She said, "Welcome to Bradley Aviation. I'm Katelyn. How may I help you?"

Looking beyond Katelyn, I said, "I believe that might be my plane."

"Ah," she said, "you must be Mr. Finley. I'm glad to meet you. May I bother you for your identification?" I made sure I had the right ID before handing her Declan Finley's driver's license. She checked my name against her paperwork, and verified that the picture on the driver's license matched my face. Apparently fully satisfied, she asked, "Do you have luggage?"

"Do I ever. My mother passed, and I'm here taking care of her estate. I have several bags of personal items that I'm taking back to my home in Albuquerque."

"I'm so sorry. That's a dreadful job for anyone, especially after a death."

"She was painfully ill for a good while, so it came as a relief for both her and our family. Anyway, I have ten pieces of luggage in the white van parked out front. If you could have someone drive it around to the plane, and take care of that for me, I'd appreciate it." I held the key out.

"We'll take care of that right away. Is there anything else I can do for you?"

"Yes, if you don't mind." I handed her the paperwork for the rental company, and said, "If you can have someone return the van for me, I would be glad to reimburse them for their efforts."

"That won't be necessary. My boyfriend works here too, and he'll be glad to do those things." She made two quick calls. "Your pilot will be right with you." A young man soon picked up the van keys from her, and headed out the front door.

The door to the lounge opened, and a man about my age walked up to greet me. With his hand extended, he said, "Mr. Finley, I'm Captain Randy McClendon. Glad to meet you. It's before your scheduled flight time, but we're fueled and ready to go whenever you'd like."

"I don't want to rush anyone, but I suppose if you guys are ready, I am."

"Great. I'll update our flight plan, and your flight attendant, Melissa, will be right out."

Making conversation while I waited, I looked to Katelyn, and said, "You've got to love your job here on this beautiful island."

"Can you believe it?" she said enthusiastically. "I love it here. My boyfriend is the one out by the plane loading your luggage. He got me this job, and we both like working here. We have to work Saturdays and be on call sometimes, but it's nice to have Sunday and Monday off. Saturdays are pretty busy, but he gets a discount on his flying lessons. He wants to make flying his career. Working here is the best job he could have for that."

The door to the pilot's lounge opened again, and a middle-aged woman with long auburn hair walked out. She was wearing an elegant uniform of black slacks and a white blouse. She carried a black jacket, and pulled a wheeled suitcase. With a huge smile and brilliantly bright teeth, she said, "Mr. Finley, I'm Melissa. I have only one job today, and that's to make your trip to Albuquerque the very best it can possibly be. Are you ready to board our beautiful ride?"

"Yes, I am. And, it's nice to meet you, Melissa."

As we were walking toward the plane, Katelyn's boyfriend was putting the last piece of my luggage into the cargo area. I checked the van to be sure it was empty, as he was locking down the cargo door. I waved him over, gave him two twenties, and said, "Take Katelyn out to dinner; you both do a great job." He thanked me, and Melissa and I boarded the plane.

The cockpit door was open, and Captain McClendon was in his chair reading back his taxi instructions to the ground controller. It looked like we were going to be wheels up about an hour ahead of schedule. That seemed to please everyone, especially me.

The copilot came up the stairs, activated the stair-retrieval control, and locked the door in place. The plane's insulation was obviously excellent because the sounds of the airport vanished. The copilot caught my glance. "I'm Chad Rasmussen. I'm your copilot this afternoon. I see you've met Melissa. She's the best, and you can depend on her spoiling you. Just ask, and she'll deliver." With that, he entered the cockpit and closed the door behind him.

My first impressions of a corporate jet flight were exceeding my high expectations. With the boys up front going to work, Melissa took the seat beside me and, once again, gave me her best smile. She said, "Have you flown with us before, or is this your first corporate flight?"

"Does it show that much?"

"No, not at all, I just needed to know if I should include our "First-Timer Rules of Enjoyment." Here's how it works. If you want anything at all, just wrinkle your nose, raise your hand, or holler my name—whatever it takes to get my attention. I'll be right there. I'll do my best to provide you with anything you need. I've got steak dinners, chicken dinners, fish dinners, and several other dinner options. I have champagne, beer, whisky, vodka, and a large variety of soft drinks. I know how to make most alcoholic drinks, as long as you don't get too wild on me. Now, having said all that, what can I get for you?"

"Melissa, I like you already. And, you and I are going to get along great. For now I'll just have a beer. A Budweiser would be great, but I'm flexible."

As Melissa was serving me my beer, the first engine was starting to turn. The second soon followed. Captain McClendon came over the intercom, "Declan, you and Melissa need to buckle up if you're not already. We'll be taxiing momentarily."

Over the next few hours I would be enjoying what I hoped to be the most stress-free leg of my trip.

The next message from the captain was, "We've been cleared for takeoff, so we'll be turning onto the runway, and picking up speed." My beer was still full so I took a big drink to keep it from spilling, and I was soon glad I did.

The Citation's ability to gain speed and jump into the air quickly was very impressive. There was little traffic from this airport, and apparently little in the center's airspace above, as we were able to climb to our cruise altitude of 41,000 feet without leveling off along the way.

I thought how happy I was to be on this plane with the high-risk parts of the plan behind me. I was sure the U.P.-Ex crew on Johnston was up and about, and it wouldn't be long before they would let their situation be known to the world. I was hopeful I would make it to my next leg before the hijacking became common knowledge. I felt like I could see the light at the end of the tunnel, and I started thinking positive thoughts about seeing Jewels in Galveston tomorrow.

Melissa and I talked a little on the climb out, and she showed me how to change my chair into a fully flat bed with just the touch of a button. I knew I would need sleep, but I thought it would go better on a full stomach. I asked Melissa for one of her steak dinners, and another beer. She soon had a tossed salad before me, and was asking me how I wanted my steak. I was never asked that question on a plane before. "Medium is fine." Five minutes later she served my dinner. Thirty minutes after that I had turned my chair into a bed and was fast asleep.

# Chapter Twenty-Two

## Earl and the FBI

Friday – 7:00 p.m. (HST) / Friday 11:00 p.m. (CST)

It had been some time since Earl had been notified that U.P.-Ex 7-19 was overdue. He had made several calls to the FAA, and each time he was told there was nothing new. The flight was well-beyond its fuel exhaustion time when he called the FBI.

After going through a few lower-level personnel, he finally reached the special agent in charge of the Memphis office. The agent verified Earl's credentials before saying, "The information I'm about to give you is accompanied by a gag order that prevents any further distribution of this information with anyone. I will need to get contact phone numbers for the CEO of your company, and I will tell him what I'm telling you."

"You may discuss operational decisions between each other, but not with others. Both of you are subject to this gag order. Violation of this order is subject to large fines, possible jail time, or both. Are you in agreement with these terms?"

Earl stated that he was.

"Your U.P.-Ex flight 7-19 was hijacked to Johnston Island in the North Pacific. Neither of your two crew members was injured, and they are now safe with our agents. Your plane has no obvious damage, but it will need fuel before it can depart. Due to the recent hijackings of 9-11, we aren't ready to make this information public. Even though all is under control, we don't want to cause any panic. I'm sure you understand."

Earl immediately realized that Rob, for whatever reason, hadn't followed the directions in his letter. He asked, "When were they found, and is the hijacker in custody?"

"They were located several hours ago, but the island they landed on is over seven hundred miles southwest of Honolulu. It will be many hours, maybe even days, before our agents complete their initial investigation. I suspect it will be sometime late tomorrow before we make any kind of public announcement."

Earl said, "It seems to me that I should have been notified much sooner, and I don't appreciate the way this information was kept from myself and our chief executive officer. Under whose authority was this information withheld?"

"These decisions were made in Washington by people well above my pay grade, and I suspect I will get my hands slapped by releasing this to you now. That's why we have the gag order."

"The search-and-rescue operations that were started when the plane was overdue were terminated and explained as a computer problem. If you need to explain any absence of the plane or crew, it should be due to a computer problem that necessitated an unscheduled landing, and they are waiting repairs. That includes notifications to the family members of crew, and those notifications have already been made."

"I understand," said Earl.

"You will be advised as to when you can modify those statements. I hope you understand the need to keep this matter completely confidential until we can get our arms around this thing. We strongly believe this hijacking was done with help from someone within U.P.-Ex. We will need a list of people who had access to any information about a treasury department shipment and/or a shipment of diamonds, both of which were on this aircraft. Can you get that ready for us?"

"Yes, but if I can't disclose any information, it'll take me a while. You want to give me a contact number so I can call you back?"

"I'm going to send an agent to your office. He won't identify himself as an agent, and he won't be wearing a suit, but he's tech-savvy, and he'll be able to help with identifying prospective suspects. He'll be there within the hour."

Earl nodded, but then realized his gesture couldn't be seen. "This whole thing had caught Earl off guard. He said, "What can I tell the families of the flight crew? They're probably wondering why their spouses aren't home yet."

"Again Mr. Baker, That's been taken care of," the agent answered. "But if someone calls in, give him the same story of landing prematurely for maintenance. I need your assurance that this won't go farther than you and the CEO of your company. This includes members of your families. We will let you know when you will be free to release any information, and what you may release. Do you understand this?"

"Of course." He paused. "Do you have a description of the hijacker?"

"Yes, he's a black male in his fifties, about six feet tall, and two hundred pounds. He has curly, black hair, a tattoo on his right arm, and a wart on his right cheek. Does that match with anyone you might have as a current, or previous, employee? He would be a pilot capable of flying the Airbus in question."

Earl had seen the pictures for the IDs, but he had no idea what disguise Rob would use for the hijacking. After hearing this description, he knew he couldn't have done better. No one would ever suspect Rob from that description. He replied to the agent, "I don't know of anyone off the top of my head that fits that description, but I've had a lot of pilots through my office. I'll start checking our personnel files."

"OK. But talk to only our agents and your CEO. We'll keep you updated."

Earl knew this wasn't good, but he was confident he wasn't a suspect… or at least wasn't a suspect yet. The first thing that came to mind was to flood them with names of people who could have possibly had some access. By making the lists as long as possible, it should slow the process.

He started with a list of all the load planners at both Memphis and Honolulu, and then expanded it to include all the clerks who had anything to do with the typing or makeup of manifests. That led him to the insurance underwriters who were provided with shipment values. Next there were the pilots, copilots, and the managers of hangars at origin and destination. He added in the forklift operators and their supervisors. His lists soon included over two hundred employees that could have accessed information.

He started writing down the general categories of personnel for the agent to search through. He thought that would certainly slow things down.

It wasn't long before the night shift receptionist called Earl. "Someone named Terry Higgins is here for you. He said you're expecting him."

"Give him directions to my office, and send him up."

Agent Higgins was surprising. He couldn't be over twenty-five, and he was wearing jeans and a denim shirt. Earl was sure no one would think of him as an agent.

Earl gave him a small office with a computer setup to access any program with the right entry codes. The codes Earl gave Higgins would give him access to the personnel files of employees at Memphis and Honolulu. Earl showed him how to pull up employees by facility, and then by department, and finally by job title. Once he had an employee isolated, he could enter dates and see which shipments that employee accessed.

Earl knew there would be several employees who might have accessed the money shipment, but very few who would have cause to access the diamond shipment. He also knew that when his name was searched it would show him as having accessed both shipments, but many others as well. He hoped they would understand that his position as COO would automatically require him to check these shipments. The agent went to work.

Earl believed it would take four to eight hours to narrow a list down to a reasonable size to start investigations. He was feeling good about slowing down the process – but that feeling didn't last.

The next phone call Earl received was from Douglas Murphy, the national director of the FBI. "I understand you're the person I need to talk to about getting information about the hijacking of U.P.-Ex 7-19. Is that correct?"

"Yes sir, I'm the chief operating officer."

"OK, then you're up to date with the plane being on Johnston Island. That's good. Here's my situation. The president has given several of us notice that we will be called into a meeting sometime tonight, or early tomorrow morning. I need to tell him that we have a person-of-interest list that we are working from, and that we have agents gathering these people into our offices for investigation."

"I understand," said Earl.

"Our Memphis office said they have one of their agents working on that list, but it seems you've given him an overwhelming task that will take several hours or more to narrow it to a functional size. I'm sure you have ways of speeding this process up, do you not?"

"Director, your man could certainly use some help, and I'll be glad to give the agents computers and space if your office can spare more people."

"Mr. Baker, I'm afraid you're failing to understand me. You've got a mole or two in your office, and I want you to put your best people on the job right away. They all will be included in our gag order and I want that list complete within the time it would take for us to get more agents to you. This priority should exceed anything else you have going on. I don't care if it means you have to delay every flight you have. Certainly you realize the tremendous volume of business we give to your company, so I hope you understand the urgency of my request for your cooperation."

"Yes, sir. I'll get right on it."

"Thank you. I'll have my assistant get on the line, and she'll give you fax and phone numbers that will be expecting your results within the hour. I appreciate your full cooperation in this matter. I need this in one hour, not a minute more."

"Shit," Earl said as he hung up the phone. He had four load coordinators and three manifest clerks at work, and he called them all into his office—plus the soon-to-be-exposed agent. Once everyone was present he introduced Mr. Higgins as an agent, and then said, "We are setting aside all other work. We are looking for someone within our organization that has leaked shipment information on containers aboard our flight 7-19. I will divide you into groups of three. As each person completes a list of people who accessed that flight, they will pass their list to one of the others in their group to verify their findings. When finished, each list should be signed off as being correct by every person in your group. Questions?"

Earl paused, but no questions were posed. "I expect my name to be on most of your lists since I access many flights. Don't hesitate putting it on your list. We need the date, time, and container number of each access. This information is critical to the investigation of a major theft from that flight."

There was a mumbling of astonishment across the room.

Earl cleared his throat. "Each of you should consider yourself to be under orders from the FBI not to discuss this matter with anyone, including family or other employees in this building. You can address any questions about that with Agent Higgins."

Agent Higgins said, "We are looking specifically for anyone who accessed information on containers one-two-dash-one-six-three-two, and one-two-dash-one-nine-seven-five."

Earl included himself to be in one of the three groups, and he assigned departments for each. "I expect some of your names to be on these lists. We have forty-five minutes. Get to work!"

Faxes and emails were sent out fifty-five minutes after Earl had hung up with the director. They included the names of eighteen people, and Earl's name was present on all lists. The agencies of both Memphis and Honolulu started sending agents out into the night to question these suspects—regardless of the time.

With the lists complete, Agent Higgins started his investigation of Earl and four other employees who were helping with the search, but were also on the lists of having accessed one or both of the shipments. He talked with Earl first. "I have to ask, it goes with my job, but I'll be quick." He ran through the Miranda rights. And Earl, as casually as he could, waived his right to an attorney.

The agent asked about each specific occasion when it was shown that Earl pulled up information about the containers in question. Earl was ready for this line of questioning. He explained how it was his responsibility to make sure his load specialists had the cargo placed in a manner that would provide safe weight and balance across the cargo bay. He said, "I often need to have containers moved from one location to another because of uneven weight distribution. If the distribution is good, I simply look at it, and move on. It's all on a random basis, but if I see something out of place it can easily lead to a look at most, if not all, containers."

Agent Higgins recorded Earl's responses, and had no reason to question him further. He stood to go to another room to continue his investigation of the other personnel, but Earl stopped him to say, "I'll be going home soon for a few hours rest. Here's my home phone number, and you have my mobile."

When agent Higgins was clear of his office, Earl reached for a bottle of Patron Gold he kept for occasions such as this. He poured himself a good-sized shot, and swallowed it down as he rehashed his thoughts of the day.

He'd known the odds were against Rob following his change of plans to crash the plane and kill the crew, but he'd thought it was worth a try to make this the perfect crime. He wondered if Rob had taken the diamonds. He hadn't heard anything about them being gone.

One of two prepaid cell phones he kept in his briefcase started to ring, and Earl was sure it was Rob. He opened his briefcase, picked up the cell phone that was ringing, and said, "Earl Baker."

The voice on the other end wasn't Rob. It was the only other person who had the number of one of his two prepaid cell phones—Jim Sellers, the pilot who had picked up Rob, and had taken him to Kauai. He said, "So your real name is Earl Baker. That's very interesting. This is your friend in Hawaii, and I have some problems.

"You never told me about a hijacking, but a local policeman knocked on my door, and started asking questions about my flight. It seems he thought I could be the pilot who picked up a hijacker off Johnston Island, but I'm sure you know all about that. I told him I knew nothing and he could either arrest me or get off my porch. He got off my porch, but he said he would be back, and for me not to leave the island."

Earl was starting to sweat, as he said, "Listen to me…" He was cut short.

"You listen! I was going to raise my portion to a hundred thousand dollars. But now that I know your name, my price is one million." He paused, and then added, "By the way, what's the black guy's real name?"

Earl's heart sank down in his chest. He'd really screwed up this time. He couldn't believe what he'd done. He had separate phones for Rob and Jim, and he'd picked up the wrong one.

"Listen to me very carefully," Earl said. "You need to think twice before you mention my name to anyone. If I go down, you can count on me to testify that you knew about the hijacking from the beginning. That'll keep you from ever seeing the light of day. If you're not the dumbass you're sounding like, you'll get more money in about six months, just like the rest of us. If my name surfaces, you'll never see another dollar."

Sellers replied, "I can't wait six months. I'm going to be forced to admit picking up an engineer off Johnston Island, and nothing more. I'll immediately lose my license, and I'll have to get an attorney to fight charges of being an accessory a hijacking that I knew nothing about. I'll accept a hundred thousand within a week, and the balance in six months. Not a dime less."

Earl just wanted to get him off the phone, so he replied, "OK. I'll get you a hundred thousand within a week. Where do you want it sent?"

Sellers gave him the address of a good friend. Earl didn't even write the address down, but he promised the money would be there within a week.

"I'm destroying my phone right now," Earl said, "and I suggest you do the same." Earl disconnected the phone, and opened the back to take out the battery. He put it back in his briefcase. He would save the destruction for a more suitable time and place. He picked up his briefcase and went home.

# Chapter Twenty-Three

## Declan's Update

### Saturday – 2:30 a.m. (CST)

When I woke up, Melissa said, "You must've been really tired. You slept for five hours. We've just started our descent into Albuquerque. Is there anything I can get for you?"

"How about a Diet Coke?"

When she returned with my Coke, Melissa said, "While you were asleep we had a little scare. The captain received a search and rescue alert for a U.P.-Ex flight that was overdue, and possibly lost at sea. We didn't hear anything for a while, but about an hour ago he asked a controller if they ever found the plane, and the controller said the alert was canceled. We never figured out whether it was reported in error, or if they found the plane."

My mind flashed to Jewels. I worried that she might have heard about the alert, but the more I thought about it I realized how these were not made public. I was fairly sure she wouldn't have heard anything. They are given on the emergency frequencies monitored by planes and ships. Unless someone heard it, and passed it on, the media wasn't too likely to have heard anything.

Even though it was over the wrong ocean, I knew it would make her worry if she heard anything about a U.P.-Ex flight. Jewels would worry about everything in general until it was time to tell me, and then she'd downplay them, and look on the bright side. I loved her for things like that.

I'd purposely told her that I would be going to Bermuda to distract her from anything she might hear happening in the Pacific. It was a big lie, but this was one time I knew it would be in her best interest.

Next, I hoped she remembered to keep both of our cell phones in her purse. I thought that might help electronically trace me to Galveston. My mind was jumping from one thing to another, and my next concern was Jim Sellers. The FBI and FAA had surely put their heads together by now. If they ran the radar tapes it wouldn't take long to pick out the possible flights that came from the southwest. There wouldn't be many, and Jim's whale-watching trip would quickly fail the smell test.

I was pretty sure that, if pushed into a corner, he'd crumble like a cracker. I'd found that out when he'd tried to get me to load my luggage. Hopefully, when it happened—and it would happen—it would support their hunt for a black man.

I still had my gloves on, and I had gone through my story one more time with Melissa. However, in my excitement about enjoying a couple of beers and a nice dinner, I hadn't thought about the DNA I could be leaving in the scraps of my food and drink.

As we were making our descent, Melissa stepped into the restroom. I immediately stood and walked to the galley. In the trash, I found my empty cans and the plastic plate holding my leftover food. I crushed the cans and put them, and the plastic plate, in by briefcase. The silverware was in the sink, so I wiped it all and put it back where it was.

I was back in my seat before she came out, but it was scary to think how some little thing like that could have made the difference between walking free and life behind bars.

I was glad to hear the squeal of the tires as the Citation hit the runway at Albuquerque Sunport. Getting five hours sleep along the way hadn't hurt anything. I still had the flight to Boerne Field, and the drive back to Houston.

When the Citation came to a stop, I thanked the crew for the nice ride, and I apologized for sleeping through most of it. As I was about to go down the stairs, Melissa said, "Hope your poison ivy gets better."

I smiled back at her, and waved good-bye.

There was only one person who'd seen me when I had dropped off the van, and I was hoping he worked days, and not the overnight shift. As I went through the office area I saw a young man who was getting ready to go help the Citation crew. He wasn't the one I'd left the van with as Roberto, so I asked him if he could get my luggage out of the plane while I pulled my van around.

"Sure, pull it around, and I'll help you." By the time I drove the van down to an open gate, and then back to the plane, he had only a couple of bags left to unload. He helped me get everything in the van, and I gave him a good tip. I was soon on my way to Double Eagle II airport. I needed to change back into Roberto, so I started looking for a good place to pull over. I remembered a rest stop along the way, and stopped there.

Two cars were in the parking area, and there were a half-dozen eighteen-wheelers out back. I could see this quick change was going to be a little trickier than I'd imagined. I grabbed my personal suitcase and the trash I'd accumulated in my briefcase. I put the trash in an outside can, and went inside.

One man was at the sink, and another in one of the stalls, so I took the handicapped stall at the back. It was bigger than the rest, and there were still two stalls between me and anyone else. It was time for Roberto to show himself one final time. As much as I hated to take off my Declan look and Tommy Bahama outfit, the thought of jeans and a denim shirt sounded comfortable. I changed clothes, and cleaned off as much as I could of the liquid tan, and replaced it with olive makeup. The skin color really wasn't that different.

I had heard a couple of people coming or going while I was changing clothes, but after it was quiet for several minutes, I put on the blond hair and went to the sink to arrange my look back to Roberto—my beginning and ending disguise. I was alone for several minutes, and I was able to complete my look, and return to the handicapped stall before anyone else came in. I wrapped everything up, and went back to the van. My next ID change would be back to being me - Rob Silvers.

I made one more stop at a gas station, and called ahead to the FBO at Double Eagle II. I told them I was running late, and asked if they could have everything ready for me in fifteen or twenty minutes. They told me the plane was ready, it just needed to be untied, and they'd have the bill finalized and ready for me.

When I got there I pulled up next to the plane in a manner that would have the cargo door on the aircraft side, with the van blocking the view from the office. I was able to get my luggage inside the plane before someone came out to help. It was close, but I was closing the airplane door as he arrived. I asked him if he'd take the van back, and he hopped in and drove toward the facility as I started my outside preflight.

When I walked into the office, they had everything ready for me. I gave the man my Roberto credit card, and I signed the charge slip. Once again, I had to stop and think about how the signature went for the person I was disguised to be. He gave me my copies, and said nothing about my gloves. Since the temperature was in the thirties, I assumed my gloves were acceptable now.

At this early morning hour the tower was closed. I called my intended departure, and taxied to the active. It felt good as the wheels left the ground. I called into Albuquerque approach for flight following as I transitioned through their airspace. All was well.

Although I thought the plan was amazingly sound, I still couldn't believe I was flying back to Boerne Field with all this money tucked away behind my chair. It was the unknowns about the authorities and Earl that were driving me crazy. I still hadn't heard anything more about the hijacking, but I thought this was one of those times when no news was good news. I just wanted to hear that the crew was OK. I hoped to be able to find something on my drive between Boerne Field and Houston.

## Chapter Twenty-Four

### Emergency Meeting

### Saturday - 7:00 a.m. (CST) / Saturday 8:00 a.m. (EST)

When the White House was notified that U.P.-Ex 7-19 was overdue and possibly lost at sea, it became more than just an area of concern. Only four months after nine-eleven, the country could ill afford to have rumors of another hijacking panicking the nation. It was decided to keep all news of the U.P.-Ex flight on a need-to-know basis only. When it was discovered that it was indeed a hijacking and not a terrorist attack, the White House placed the gag order in effect until an emergency meeting could address the situation.

The director of the FBI, Doug Murphy, was being pressed hard by the president to determine the details of how this could have happened under the nation's intensified security measures.

The answer was obvious to most in the aviation community. Commercial airlines had little in the way of definable security regulations, and it varied widely from one airport to the next. Box haulers, corporate business jets, and millions of private aviation flights had no security whatsoever.

Following 9-11, airport security was in turmoil with a mixed sense of direction. TSA was still more of an idea than a reality, and there were no conversations that included security for non-airline commercial aviation.

The FBI and Secret Service agreed that if a story broke saying that a person, armed with nothing but an unverified letter of authorization, was granted passage into the cockpit of a fully fueled Airbus, terrorists near and far would be redesigning their next moves.

The president considered this matter worthy of summoning the heads of all relevant alphabet government entities. This included the FBI, Secret Service, DOT, the FAA, and TSA. Since TSA had only been signed into law last month, its yet-to-be-confirmed administrator would attend.

The president's press secretary, Jessica Gibson, took the podium to lay out the situation before them. "It is felt by the president and the chiefs of staff that the hijacking of U.P.-Ex seven-nineteen has the potential to expose a huge security hole that has yet to be addressed by your agencies. Our initial problem is the wording of our media release, which is scheduled shortly after this meeting."

There was no response from the room, so she continued.

"Since nine-eleven, each of your agencies has worked hard to improve the security of the flying public, and many improvements have been made. Many more are still in the planning stage with TSA. However, in the rush to get TSA passed into law, the far less visible sector of aviation, which includes everything outside of airline passenger flights, has been ignored, or pushed aside to be addressed at a later date. Today is that later date."

Ms. Gibson released the floor to the director of the FBI, Doug Murphy. "The way it stands at this moment, box, freight, and corporate business carriers are on their own to police their security. Currently, in the overwhelming majority of these carriers, this plan isn't working. There is virtually no screening of either passengers or freight."

The implications were clear, and everyone in the room knew it. "The question is, do we release the unabridged truth of what happened with this U.P.-Ex flight? I submit that doing so could produce disastrous results."

The secretary of transportation, George Gaddie, brought up the obvious corollary. "How big a lie are you suggesting? And how do you propose keeping it secret?"

The newly appointed administrator of TSA, Robert Smith, suggested, "We could announce that our prime person-of-interest was a pilot for U.P.-Ex. until terminated a couple of months earlier. It is believed that he altered the name on his old ID, and used his inside knowledge to circumvent the company's security systems. He was traveling under the bogus name of Bill Edwards, but his real name is being withheld until our investigation is complete. Since he's still at large, we could release the photos taken from the security cameras at the U.P.-Ex hangar in Honolulu, and request the public's help in locating him."

Director Murphy smiled. "If you just pulled all that off the top of your head, you should have no problem with your confirmation hearings." The room broke into a semi-controlled laughter, and the director waited for it to subside before continuing. "Few people, outside of this room, know how this hijacking actually went down, and they are being kept under a legal gag order. This will give us time to consider our options."

There was a murmur in the room, and he held up his hand to silence them before continuing. "Mr. Smith's story seems feasible to me, and we have no reason to believe that this Edwards guy is currently a threat to society. As a matter of fact, just the opposite—he could have easily killed the crew, who are now our best witnesses. But he didn't.

"Most of you don't realize that Mr. Edwards, or whatever his real name is, had taken thirty million dollars' worth of diamonds from a shipment container, and had placed them on the throttle console between the two unconscious crewmembers. These diamonds could have easily fit into his pockets, but he left them all behind. They have all been accounted for. The first person that can come up with a logical reason for him to have taken ten million dollars in worn currency, yet leave behind thirty million dollars in easy-to-sell diamonds, gets a gold star."

Another murmur drifted around the room.

"This man had to have had insider knowledge as to the location of both the money shipment and the diamonds. He left the diamonds in a location where the crew couldn't possibly miss them. To say this crime is highly unusual is a gross understatement."

"Maybe the guy's real name is Robin Hood," someone in the room joked.

Director Murphy replied, "I know that was said as a joke, but let's be clear about the fact that hijacking is a major crime. The last thing we want to do now is have the media start referring to this guy as Robin Hood. That name isn't to be associated with this crime. Not by anyone.

"What has been said in this room today isn't to be repeated. Each of you are under a gag order until further advised. This meeting is designated as "Secret," and punishable under the laws of confidentiality.

"Unless there is an objection, or other options, we will be releasing a story similar to that suggested by Mr. Smith." He waited for a response before declaring, "This meeting is now adjourned."

# Chapter Twenty-Five

## Earl Goes Home

### Saturday – 7:30 a.m. (CST) / Saturday – 8:30 a.m. (EST)

Earl was home when he received a call from the FBI's Memphis office. "We have several of your employees here who are refusing to answer questions until discussing this matter with a representative of the company. Your name was the one most-mentioned, and we also have some questions we would like to ask you."

"No problem," Earl answered. "I couldn't sleep anyway. Let me get a shower, and I'll be there in about an hour."

Earl had no intention of making that meeting. He knew the accidental release of his name to Jim Sellers had changed everything for him. The combination of that, along with Rob's refusal to carry out his wishes, had him realizing he'd hit another new low in his life. He knew this low wouldn't be one he could recover from easily—and probably not at all. Everything would soon be made public, and his reputation would be ruined. He wasn't ready for that, and he was damned sure he wasn't ready for jail.

Earl backed his Mercedes out of the garage, and down to the end of the drive. He went inside, sat down with his laptop, and started typing. He spent about thirty minutes before he was satisfied with his letter. He printed out two copies, signed each, and placed them in separate envelopes.

Returning to his car, he put the keys in the ignition, lowered the windows, and placed an envelope addressed to the FBI on the front seat. The second envelope was addressed to the Memphis Tribune. He placed it into a neighbor's mailbox, and raised the flag.

Back inside, he gathered anything and everything that could possibly be associated with the hijacking. The electronics were taken to the garage, and placed on the workbench. He opened both his computers and removed their hard drives. With a sledgehammer, he took out his anger by striking them over and over again. It would be impossible to obtain information from these drives. He did the same with the smart keys from his three cell phones. Finally, he crushed each piece to the extent they would be hard to recognize as their previous form. He picked up all the pieces, and placed them in a canvas bag before taking them inside.

Next, he took all the many boxes of paperwork, and brought them to the living room. He started a fire. One by one, he added items to the fire but it was still not the fire he was looking for. He started breaking up pieces of wooden furniture, and tossed them into the blaze.

The fire was quickly getting out of control.

There was no fireplace in the house. His fire was started in the middle of the living room. Smoke was starting to billow at the ceiling, and was getting lower by the second. He knew he could stay and die in the fire, or try crawling to the door to escape, but he'd planned for a third option.

He'd placed a loaded .44 Magnum on top of an end table. He dropped to his knees as he was being consumed by smoke. He crawled toward the table, and reached up for his gun.

Putting his hand on the table, he knocked his gun to the floor. He knew his time was getting short as he blindly searched the floor. He was coughing uncontrollably when he finally found it. He immediately placed it in his mouth, and pulled the trigger. The sound of the hammer hitting the primer in the casing was the last thing he ever heard.

Earl's townhouse shared a common wall with his neighbor, but that townhouse was on the market and unoccupied. By the time the first fire truck arrived, Earl's unit was well beyond any possibility of saving. The firefighters focused their attention on the neighbor's unit, and they let Earl's burn. By the time the smoke subsided, both units were totally destroyed, but Earl's unit was reduced to nothing but ashes, and a few items of brick or steel. Even the aluminum of the computers and phones had melted beyond any ability to read the serial numbers.

## Controlling – Robert Seckler

When Earl didn't show up for his appointment with the FBI, and he didn't answer any calls, they sent an agent to his house. A firefighter had moved Earl's car to make room for fire equipment, and he had found the letter.

When the agent arrived, the firefighter handed the letter to her, and she began to read:

*To whom it may concern: I have endured enough ups and downs in my life, and I'm tired. Although I don't have high hopes, I'm ready to explore whatever comes next. It has to offer more than what I have before me now.*

*I always put myself above all others, and I hurt the ones I loved the most. For that I'm truly sorry.*

*I take full responsibility for the bombing of Houston Center. It was never my intention to hurt anyone and I have regretted the death of Clyde Roberts every day since the bombing. It is, therefore, my dying wish that Clyde Roberts' wife and children receive the balance of my estate.*

*My justification for the bombing was revenge for the president's decision to terminate, instead of suspend, eleven thousand controllers. His decision was undeniably selfish, and purely for his political support of big business. Although it was an impressive show of power, it did nothing to solve the safety concerns that needed to be addressed.*

*I am also responsible for planning the hijacking of U.P.-Ex 7-19. I hired Mr. Edwards for the actual hijacking, and Jim Sellers, a.k.a. Tommy Thomson, to transport Bill Edwards from Johnston Island to Kauai. I am releasing Mr. Thompson's true name because of his threats to blackmail me for more money.*

*Look as you will, but Bill Edwards is now secure in a safe destination where you'll never find him. For all of those who believed in me... Thanks.*

The letter was signed by Earl Baker, former chief operating officer for U.P.-Ex. A call was made to Director Murphy about the suicide of Earl Baker, and the contents of the letter he had left behind.

# Chapter Twenty-Six

## Landing at Boerne Stage Field

### Saturday – 8:15 a.m. (CST) / Saturday – 9:15 a.m. (EST)

The weather was clear, and I was on schedule as I touched down at Boerne Stage Field. I tied down the plane, and immediately pulled my van around to load my luggage. With that done, I went into the hangar to see if Ralph was around. He heard me pull up, and met me at the door. "Roberto, you're early! I wasn't expecting you until tomorrow. How was your trip?"

"It was good until late yesterday. Our host's wife got sick with some sort of stomach virus. We decided to try again next year, and hope for better health. I was glad to get out of Olathe, anyway, because they had snow forecast for this afternoon."

"Did the plane do OK for you?"

"It was great. No problems at all."

"Good. You want me to fill her up so we can finalize your bill?"

"No, don't worry about it. Just debit or credit my card to make it right. I want to get home. It's been a tiring trip." We said our good-byes, and I pointed the van toward Houston.

I was a little surprised that the only news I could find about the U.P.-Ex flight was that there was a computer problem that started search-and-rescue operations, but they were subsequently canceled. I tuned in every station I could but there was no mention of a hijacking.

*Holy shit*, I thought, *this should be on every station by now.* If the crew wasn't able to contact anyone, and they were just sitting on the island waiting for the Fish & Wildlife people to arrive on Monday, the plane would still be declared missing, and they wouldn't cancel the search and rescue operations. This wasn't making any sense.

It was a long drive to Houston, and I kept searching the stations, but there was no new information to be had.

## The Press Release

Saturday – 9:00 a.m. (CST) / Saturday – 10:00 a.m. (EST)

Press Secretary Gibson read her statement from a prepared text:

"Based on information released by the FBI, I can now tell you that a U.P.-Ex flight between Honolulu, Hawaii, and Memphis, Tennessee, was hijacked over the Pacific at around six a.m. yesterday morning. The U.P.-Ex crew, a pilot and copilot, were found uninjured. They are currently working with the FBI in the agency's Honolulu offices.

"After the hijacking, the flight was taken to an island in the North Pacific where the hijacker removed worn currency scheduled to be destroyed by the Treasury Department on Wednesday, December 26. The dollar amount hasn't yet been determined, but it is thought to be between eight and twelve million dollars.

"The suspect is a black male traveling under the name of Bill Edwards. We will be releasing surveillance video and pictures of this man at the end of this press release. The FBI believes this man to be a former pilot for U.P.-Ex who was terminated earlier this year. He was able to breach the company's tight security through the use of a modified U.P.-Ex security pass. The suspect is still at large. If you see this man, do not attempt to apprehend him, but call the FBI immediately. U.P.-Ex is offering a reward of twenty-five thousand dollars for information leading to his arrest and conviction.

"We also have reason to believe this person was working with a minimum of two others who may also have had connections to U.P.-Ex. The FBI is following up on numerous leads, and the president vowed to continue his support of the investigation until the responsible parties are arrested and convicted.

"The president has asked me to assure the country that this hijacking was in no way an act of terrorism. It was a hijacking, and grand theft, but it doesn't represent a threat to our country, or any other country. There is no reason for the general public to be alarmed beyond standard precautions of being aware of someone who has committed a major crime.

"We aren't taking questions at this time, but we will announce additional press conferences as more information becomes available. Thank you for your time."

Secretary Gibson left the platform and returned to her office.

She didn't have time to relax before she was summoned to another emergency meeting at the White House. The meeting was designated only as being mandatory, and immediate.

When Secretary Gibson arrived only Director Murphy and his aide were there waiting for her. Once seated, she was given a complete update on Earl Baker's suicide, and she was given a copy of the letter left behind by Earl. "So what do we do now?"

Director Murphy said, "Well, I don't think we can cover up this mess anymore. We need to blend the story you just released with the additions we received as a result of the suicide. By telling everyone the COO of U.P.-Ex was responsible, the threat of terrorists becoming copy-cat hijackers is diminished to little or nothing."

He paused. "We want to place the blame of both the 1981 bombing of Houston Air Route Traffic Control Center, and the U.P.-Ex hijacking, squarely on Earl Baker. We want to show him as a solo bomber, and the mastermind of the hijacking."

She nodded, knowing it was the only available option she had.

The director continued. "We have notified the press that we've just received significant updates to our ten o'clock press release, and we have asked them to hold their broadcast, and return to the pressroom. We've promised them an update within the next half hour."

Jessica shook her head. "We can't get this ready in a half hour."

"Sure you can. The president and I are in agreement that only a few changes will be necessary. We still have Bill Edwards at large, and now we can expose Earl Baker as the inside man and mastermind of the hijacking. We can also tell the public that he was responsible for the bombing of Houston Center in 1981. You'll probably want to add that we are happy to finally close that case."

He paused, and glanced over to Jessica. "Tell them the suicide was the direct result of intense pressure by the FBI on Earl Baker as a suspect. We found his recent trail of numerous accesses to specific freight locations on the hijacked flight. When we confronted him with this information he retreated to his rented townhouse. He set it on fire, and died in the flames. You can wrap it up by saying the FBI is still in pursuit of the hijacker, and would appreciate the public's assistance in locating the man known only as Bill Edwards. He remains our prime person-of-interest in this case."

The director's aide cleared his throat, and handed Murphy a handwritten note. "Good," he muttered, and then looked at Jessica's notes. "You won't need those, the press room is full, and we'll have to wing it. I'll let you take the reins, and I'll be your backup. This time, we'll answer any questions at the end." He stood, looked over to Jessica, and said, "Let's do this."

In the pressroom, Director Murphy spoke first. "I'll take questions after Secretary Gibson's remarks." He turned to Jessica and with a fluid motion of his hand, threw her under the bus. But this wasn't the first time, and she was a very accomplished speaker.

"First off, I'd like to welcome all of you back for this update. Information was just coming in as we ended our last release, and we felt it important enough to call all of you back. If I seem a little disorganized you'll have to forgive me as I have had no time to polish our statement."

She took a deep breath and released it. "With that said, I will first report that Mr. Earl Baker, the chief operating officer for U.P.-Ex, committed suicide this morning in his home. In doing so, he left a letter addressed to the FBI. Mr. Baker confessed that he was the mastermind of the hijacking of U.P.-Ex flight seven-nineteen."

She paused as the room erupted in a rumbling of mumbles. She held up her hand until the room settled back to normal.

"In the past hour, the Honolulu office of the FBI has arrested a person of interest who is suspected of flying the pickup plane from

Johnston Island to Kauai. We have agents on Kauai searching Bill Edwards. As you heard in our previous release, he is a black male of about six feet tall, and two hundred pounds. He has a wart on his right cheek and a tattoo on his right arm. We would appreciate the public's help in locating this suspect. Do not try to apprehend this man. Instead, call the FBI immediately."

Secretary Gibson paused to change the subject. "On a separate matter concerning Earl Baker—he confessed to the 1981 bombing of Houston Air Route Traffic Control Center. He stated he was solely responsible for that bombing."

"We all owe a debt of gratitude to the quick response and investigations that the Memphis and Honolulu offices of the FBI have put forth as this story started to unfold. The president realizes that, although we still have work left to do, the FBI has stepped forward to a good start in exposing two of three major suspects. FBI Director Murphy will now take your questions."

Director Murphy took, and answered, several questions, but he eluded any specific answers about where they were in catching the hijacker. Jessica went back to her office as he was speaking.

# Chapter Twenty-Seven

## Rob's Back

### Saturday – 12:15 p.m. (CST) / Saturday – 1:15 p.m. (EST)

I had given up on finding anything on the radio and I listened to CDs for the last couple of hours. I pulled up in front of our apartment at noon and I quickly unloaded my luggage into the spare bedroom, and touched up my Roberto look for his last outing. I had to return the rental van under my Roberto disguise. I tried the news again and tuned the van radio to CNN. Their latest report came out of the speakers and I got a lot more than I bargained for.

They were replaying the press releases, and I was only two blocks from the apartment when I heard the news about Earl's confessions and suicide. I immediately pulled off the road and stopped. I was devastated, and the more I heard, the more I cried. I blotted my tears knowing I had to keep Roberto intact for another half hour.

I reached down and turned the radio off. On the way back from San Antonio I'd worried about why the hijacking hadn't been on the news. But now that it was, I wasn't ready to listen. I had to keep my focus until my job was done.

I returned the van to the airport lot, and made the last charge to Roberto's card. I avoided looking at the monitors, but I couldn't help catching a glimpse as I walked through the terminal building. When I did, I saw pictures of Earl and a U.P.-Ex plane filling the screen. One scary scenario after another rushed through my head. I was frightened, but I pushed on.

I picked up my truck from long-term parking, paid with cash, and headed back to the apartment. I took a hot shower, and scrubbed off all traces of previous disguises. It was, bar none, the best part of my trip. When I looked in the mirror I was actually happy to see my balding head again. But I knew more than ever that I couldn't stop until I reached Galveston.

I took $10,000 of the worn currency, and placed it in a shoebox in the top of the entry closet. I loaded my suitcase full of disguises and clothes into the bed of my pickup, and followed it with all the money suitcases and duffel bags.

I had rented a mini-storage unit a few blocks from the apartment, and I placed the money suitcases inside, and locked the unit.

Instead of driving south toward Galveston, I drove north to an isolated bridge over a cove of Lake Conroe. The road was gravel, and seldom traveled, but when they built the lake they agreed to bridge out to what became an island with only five houses.

I parked on the crest of the bridge, took out my suitcase of disguises and clothes, and cut several small slits in both sides. I dropped it into the lake, and watched the bubbles as it sank into forty feet of water. I felt my hijacking history was being buried deeper and deeper with each bubble.

It was time to head south for my reunion with Jewels, and time for me to catch up with the latest news of the hijacking. I tuned in a national news station, and it was all about the death of Earl Baker, and his suicide letter confessions to both the U.P.-Ex flight and the bombing of Houston Center.

I was relieved when I heard the portion of his letter that said the hijacker was already in a safe place, and wouldn't be found. With Bill Edwards being a black man, and the final traces of Declan and Roberto at the bottom of Lake Conroe, I felt more comfortable than I had since this whole thing started —except for Jewels.

I couldn't help but think Jewels had heard the news of Earl's death, and the hijacking of a U.P.-Ex plane. She was a bright girl, and I was sure she would put things together and think I was the hijacker, but I had to convince her otherwise.

Sticking to my story about my flight from Atlanta to the Bahamas and back had to be my plan. I had to claim my innocence until proven guilty. I hoped she had heard, and believed, that the hijacker was a black man. That would go a long way in proving my case, and I had the ten thousand dollars in cash to support my claims.

I was happy to be without makeup, and it made my life simpler as I broke into tears several times on the road to Galveston. I cried about Earl, Clyde Roberts, and about the people that I left terribly inconvenienced.

About a half hour from Galveston, I turned off the news, and turned on the music. Somehow, I had to pull myself together enough to sound positive in front of Jewels. I couldn't wait to see her, and could only hope she would greet me with love, and not as the criminal I was.

There was a CD player in my truck, and I had numerous CDs behind my seat. I would tell her that was why I didn't hear anything about Earl. I played music all the way. I had to be totally surprised about the hijacking, and I had to make it believable.

It was 4:00 Saturday afternoon when I reached the Wave Runner Inn. I picked up a house phone in the lobby, and asked for the Silvers' room. When Jewels answered, I said, "I love you. Did you miss me?"

"Where are you?"

"I'm in the lobby…" was all I could say before hearing the phone drop. I walked toward the elevator just in time for her to burst out toward me. She wrapped her arms around me, and gave me a long, passionate kiss. We were both very excited to see each other, but I couldn't help checking the area to see if we were being watched. This reunion was far too exaggerated for a mere separation of an hour or two. It was more like we hadn't seen each other for years.

I didn't see anyone watching us, and from her reception, she had no knowledge of the hijacking. This was great.

As we turned back toward the elevator, Jewels said, "This shit ends today, you're going to get a regular nine-to-five job."

On the way up to our room questions were flying right and left about my trip. How much money did I get? Did they pay me in cash? I answered her questions as if I had made the Bahamas' trip, but I needed to be sure she hadn't heard about the hijacking. I asked, "Tell me about your day so far."

Jewels replied, "I know you told me everything was fine, but I couldn't help but worry about you. I took a long walk on the beach to clear my head. It was relaxing, and I even waded out waist-high in the ocean. For a girl that doesn't swim, that was fairly adventurous. I got back a couple of hours ago, and I turned on a movie to pass the time. I guess the sun had made me sleepy, because I fell asleep and woke up when you called."

I decided it was time to let the elephant into our room. I sat on the bed next to Jewels, put my arm around her shoulder, and proceeded to tell her the news about Earl. "During my drive between Houston and here, I heard some very sad news about Earl." I paused to let that sink in, and could see Jewels was hanging on my every word, "I'm afraid it's the worst kind of news. Earl is dead. He committed suicide."

Jewels put her hands to her mouth, and took a large gasp of air.

I continued, "While I was making my flight back from Freeport, Earl was busy on the other side of the country. He'd left a suicide letter, and in it he'd admitted to hiring a black guy to hijack a U.P.-Ex flight between Honolulu and Memphis."

Jewels said, "I knew bad things would happen after he told you about that four-hundred-thousand-dollar flight one of his pilots made out of Dubai. What about your flight to Freeport? Wasn't that another one of Earl's trumped up flights? Should I be worried about that now?"

"No, you shouldn't. My flight was fine, and I'm OK, but I was a little worried about that flight too, so I took some extra precautions. I made the trip under a disguise, a bogus name, and fake IDs. With that, along with my alibi of being here with you, there is absolutely no reason to be worried."

"Rob, you're scaring the hell out of me. Is Earl really dead?"

I picked up the remote from the end table and, after scanning through a few channels, I found what I was looking for. An all-news channel was about five minutes into their report about Earl and the hijacking. Jewels paid close attention.

She started crying as she heard the description of Earl's suicide in a fire, and cried even more when she saw the old videos of the Houston Center bombing, followed by pictures of Earl as the bomber. I pulled her closer to me, and whispered, "I know you're scared, but this isn't about us."

As the report wrapped up, they showed pictures of the hijacker, Bill Edwards, and gave his description as, "A mid-fifties black male, approximately six-foot-tall, and two hundred twenty pounds. He has a wart on his right cheek and small scar on his neck. If you see this person, don't attempt to apprehend, but call the FBI immediately."

Jewels responded, "The Earl that did those things wasn't the same Earl we knew. Somewhere in the back of my mind, I sort of suspected Earl for the bombing, but I was always able to find some reason why he didn't do it. This hijacking is something I would have never expected from him."

I continued to push forward with my lies. "I guess I was lucky with my trip to the Bahamas." When we made eye contact, I could see she wasn't totally comfortable with the story I was telling.

We decided to take a quick walk on the beach before going to dinner. As we walked past the pool I stopped at the bar and got us a couple of beers to sip along the way. I tipped the bartender ten dollars. It was one more memory to add to my alibi.

As we walked along the beach, Jewels asked, "OK, how much did you get paid?"

I replied, "Ten thousand dollars. I'm banking on it to take care of us until we get settled in Minneapolis. After Christmas, we'll focus on wrapping things up here before hitting the road north. Of course, with all that's going on, we need to be strong with my alibi of being here from Friday afternoon." Jewels looked at me with obvious disapproval of my alibi comment.

I took another shower before we went to dinner, and it was nice to put on clean clothes from the suitcase Jewels had brought down for me. As we walked to dinner I mentally reviewed my plan for a little something extra to make our stay more memorable. At dinner I ordered a steak medium rare. When it was delivered, I told our waiter it was overcooked.

Jewels urged me to just eat it, but I politely asked for a replacement. It was less than five minutes later when I received my new rare steak. I was almost afraid to eat it, thinking it was probably spit on a couple times on its way to me. I took note of our waiter's name, and I gave him a thirty-percent tip. It wasn't a huge thing, but it was enough to be remembered.

We enjoyed our evening by making love, watching a movie, and making love. I tried to avoid the news, but Jewels wanted an update. I agreed, but I later wished I hadn't.

They showed the ashes of Earl's townhouse with his corporate Mercedes still sitting out front. Neither of us could stand the thoughts of Earl burning. Jewels was the first to cry, but I wasn't far behind. I grabbed the remote, and changed the channel away from the news.

After we kissed goodnight, I closed my eyes and fell asleep immediately. I must have slept soundly, because when I woke up, Jewels had our suitcases packed and was ready to go. I looked over to the clock and it showed 10:00.

Jewels said, "Check-out is eleven."

We put our suitcases in Jewels' car and, when we checked out, I questioned a couple of items on the bill—just to add one more memorable moment. We were back at our apartment about 3:00 Sunday afternoon. Jewels wanted to check the latest news about Earl, and although I knew it wouldn't lead to anything good, I agreed.

# Chapter Twenty-Eight

## National News

Jewels flipped through the channels until she settled on a report that was just beginning. I sat down beside her and tried to hide my nerves.

"Arson inspectors have verified that Mr. Baker started the fire in his rented townhouse, and he elected to stay inside as it burned to the ground. They further verified the fact that his death was caused by a self-inflicted, single shot to the head. Two identical suicide letters were left behind. One was addressed to the FBI, and the other to a Memphis newspaper. The signature on both letters has been authenticated as that of Earl Baker. The FBI has confirmed that their investigation supports Earl Baker's confession of his role in the bombing of Houston Center, and the hijacking of U.P.-Ex seven-nineteen."

They broke for a commercial.

I looked over to Jewels, and said, "If I'd reported my suspicions of Earl's actions in 1981, I might have prevented not only the bombing, but also the hijacking."

Jewels became immediately angry with me. "Don't even talk like that. There was nothing you could have done. I was there and you told me your thoughts. You have no reason to feel the least bit guilty. If you're at fault, so am I, but I refuse to think that way, and I don't want to hear any more of that from you."

The news continued, "It's rumored that Earl Baker revealed the name of the pilot who flew the hijacker between Johnston Island and Kauai. The FBI will neither confirm nor deny that rumor, but their Honolulu office does have a person-of-interest in custody at this time."

As more information came out, I started feeling sick to my stomach. I knew my name could very well be the next one released. The reporter continued, "Also not confirmed, but rumored…" My heart was pounding… "the hijacker was reported in the letter to be…" My hands were starting to shake… "already in a safe place where he wouldn't be found."

Jewels looked over to me, and asked, "Are you OK?"

"I just don't like listening to this shit."

The reporter continued, "Although we cannot confirm these rumors, our source is an individual who personally read the entire letter. He is considered by this network to be very reliable."

As the broadcast broke for a commercial, I fell to the floor, and on my knees. I said, "Thank God!"

It was quiet for a moment as I got back on the sofa. That proved to be enough time for Jewels to put the pieces together.

"You son of a bitch!" she screamed, jumping to her feet. "You're the damn hijacker. How could you do that to us Rob? What the hell were you thinking?" She burst into tears as she turned her head away from me.

I didn't think I could do or say anything that would change the way she was feeling, and I knew I couldn't lie my way out of this. If I wanted to save my marriage, I had to be honest from this moment on.

Jewels was getting louder, and the walls of our apartment were thin. I said, "Jewels, you need to calm down, and lower your voice before someone hears you. I'm sorry to have to tell you that you're right. I was the one who did the hijacking." She started breathing heavily, and I knew she was becoming hysterical.

I tried to put my arm around her shoulders, but she pushed me away. I said, "When you're ready, I'll tell you everything." Her crying was growing even louder, and I tried again to move closer, but she stopped me. I turned off the news, and sat on the other end of the sofa.

Between tears, she called me numerous obscenities, all of which were justified. I knew I'd taken the worst of wrong roads in my attempt to cure our retirement problems, but I also knew I couldn't change what was already done.

A few minutes later, as her tears were starting to subside, I said, "When you're ready."

"You can go to hell as far as I'm concerned. I'm going to Minnesota."

"I understand, and I can't blame you, but we really do need to talk about this. I kept my promise, and there were no victims. But I must have lost my mind to follow Earl's lead with his plan to cure our retirement problems."

She was sniffling, but she seemed to be listening.

"Most importantly, nobody was physically injured, and the money I took off that plane was worn currency scheduled to be destroyed by the treasury department. The net effect of taking this money is zero until we spend it, and then it will serve to provide a very modest boost to our country's economy. My actions might even force the government to take a hard look at the country's aviation security systems, and that would be a good thing."

Jewels said nothing.

"Earl wrote me a letter that I didn't have a chance to read until after I was in control of the plane. In it he told me that after I removed diamonds and currency, I should set the plane up to take off from Johnston Island, with the unconscious crew on board. It would crash at sea and kill the crew.

That was his idea of the perfect crime. Had I done as he wished, I would have been guilty of murder. For that, he offered me half of thirty million dollars in diamonds on the plane. I didn't take the diamonds, and I didn't kill the crew." I paused before continuing, "Honey, listen to me. I promised you no victims, and there were no victims."

"What about Earl, wasn't he a victim?" whispered Jewels.

"I guess he was," I conceded. "And maybe he killed himself because I didn't do as he wanted, but the reality is… that was his choice, not mine."

That was it. I'd said what I had to say, and it would be up to Jewels as to what she would do next. If she were to call the FBI and tell them how she had no part in this, I would stand behind any story she wished to tell.

I went to the closet where I'd put the ten thousand dollars. I put Earl's second letter on top of the money, and handed both to her. I said, "This is the letter Earl gave to me. If you want to give it to the FBI, you can. Otherwise, I'll mail it to them from some remote post office."

Jewels said nothing, but she did start reading the letter. I took that as a major step in my direction.

For the next hour there was little conversation between Jewels and me. Finally, she went to the kitchen, and returned with a spiral notebook and pen. She started asking questions, such as, "How much money do you have, and where is it now? Where do you plan to keep this money? Is it spendable? I already helped you with the trip to Galveston to establish your alibi, how is that going to affect me when you go to jail? Did you think at all before you made me an accomplice to your hijacking?"

The questions about the money were easy enough to answer, and I did so truthfully. When she got to the questions about how I considered, or failed to consider, her involvement, and possible jail time, I could see how the conversation was changing from factual to personal. I hoped that might lead to new avenues of discussion.

I said, "You tell me what you want me to say, and I'll say it. If you're going to turn me in, your best bet would be to cut a deal with the FBI. There's little doubt that you'll be able to walk away with nothing on your record, and certainly no jail time. You might even be able to collect a reward. Of course, I hope you don't do that, but I love you enough to make sure you don't get punished for something you had no knowledge of."

Her face was impassive. "If I was to stay with you through this, and I'm not saying I will, what is your plan to avoid arrest and prosecution?"

*Oh, my God, she's going to stay.*

"You'll remember, the hijacker's a black man. Only you and Earl know differently, and Earl's dead. If the FBI thought for one moment that the hijacker was a white guy, I'd be in jail already."

"I have to admit that when I saw the pictures of Bill Edwards on the news," Jewels said, "I immediately ruled you out. But don't you think they'll figure it out sooner or later?"

I shrugged. "I really don't think so, but just to be safe, I hope we're in Dubai before that happens."

Jewels didn't respond, so I continued, "After hearing the news of Earl's suicide, along with his letter, I knew we needed to move an overseas vacation to the top of our priority list. For numerous reasons, Dubai would be my first choice. It's a very modern city with a warm climate, and there's no extradition agreement with the U.S. It would just be until this hijacking news went away and all our newly found currency is cleaned. Dubai also has a reputation as one of the best places in the world to launder money."

With Jewels still seemingly interested in my plan, I decided to use this opportunity to its full advantage. "To make this all work, I suggest we call Suddath United Van Lines, and tell them we want to split our shipment into two separate shipments. One will be shipped to Minneapolis to be placed in storage there. The second shipment will be just enough to furnish a two-bedroom apartment, and it will be shipped to Dubai. It will probably take between six months to a year before this all blows over, and we will have enough money to bring family members over there for visits. I'm pretty sure any of them would jump at the chance if we pick up their airfare."

I walked to the kitchen to give Jewels a moment to think about what I had said, and returned with a drink for each of us. Her only response was, "Thank you," and that was for the drink.

"At any rate, Jewels, I've already built a crate big enough to hold the money under a false bottom. It was loaded with our household goods. When we sort out our two shipments, I plan to fill the bottom with the worn currency, and send it with the Dubai shipment. American dollars, worn or new, are easily converted to dirhams. I've looked at the laws of the United Arab Emirates, and I found none that place a limit on the amount of dollars that can be brought into the country. I don't believe we will have any worries there."

"One more thing," I continued. "If the Treasury Department releases the serial numbers of the stolen currency, it will be a week or so before they get the list, and it will be about ten thousand numbers long because the numbers aren't sequential. Even American banks would have a hard time with that, and Dubai banks aren't likely to give a shit one way or the other."

Jewels was staring at me, mesmerized.

"As soon as possible, we leave for Minneapolis. We'll catch a flight to Dubai out of there. I found out we can get temporary visas that are good for sixty days at the airport when we arrive. After that, we can apply for extensions up to one year, and if we want to stay longer we can get dual citizenship. That's my plan in a nutshell."

Jewels nodded. "You say 'we' a lot but you shouldn't get your hopes up for my going with you. But I'll think about it." She picked up her purse and jacket, and said, "I need some time to myself. I'm going out, and I'm not sure when I'll be back. Don't worry about dinner for me, but I'll either be back before midnight, or I'll call."

I didn't know what to think, but I understood her need to get away for some personal time. I decided to do a little shopping of my own just to keep my mind off all that was happening. I left Jewels a note in case she came home while I was out.

My shopping was only window-shopping, but it did help clear my mind. I stopped for some fast food, picked up a six-pack of beer, and a nice bottle of champagne. The champagne was in case Jewels came home in a good mood. When I got back to the apartment I was still alone, and there were no messages.

I turned on the tube, and opened a beer. Here I was with ten million dollars, sitting alone in a cheap apartment, and watching the ads about the last shopping days before Christmas. To top it off, the FBI was under pressure to find me—the hijacker. This wasn't what I had envisioned.

With the help of a few beers, I fell asleep on the sofa with the television still on.

After tossing and turning most of the night, I finally got up about five-thirty, and opened the door to the bedroom. Jewels was sleeping soundly.

I took a shower and, when I came out, Jewels was sitting on the sofa watching the news. I put on some coffee, and went in to join her. "Does this mean we're OK today?"

Jewels responded, "I've been thinking about what you said yesterday, and I think I can understand why you didn't tell me about doing this. You knew I would have done everything I could to keep you away from Earl and his wild-ass plans. Maybe I would have succeeded, and we wouldn't be in this mess. However, since you did do this thing, it was probably better that you didn't tell me. I'm not sure how I might have responded if I'd heard the hijacking news if I'd thought you were the one doing the hijacking. That said, the lying has to stop right now."

I started to say something, but she waved me off.

"I doubt I'll be going to Dubai, but I'll stay with you until Minneapolis. After we get there, I'll make my final decision. But one lie, and I'll collect whatever reward the FBI will give me."

I replied, "I can live with that, but the honesty has to be a two-way street. It will be crucial that we share everything with each other."

"That's fine with me—I haven't been the one lying. You can start right now by telling me the whole true story about your trip."

For the next hour, I went through every detail of my trip to Johnston Island and back. I ended my story by telling her the location of the mini-storage where I put the money.

She seemed satisfied with the truth of what actually happened over those three days.

# Chapter Twenty-Nine

## Final Move

I didn't know if Suddath United Van Lines would be open on Christmas Eve, but I gave them a try, and they answered. My salesperson was in the office getting caught up on some paperwork, and there were two operations specialists staying until noon.

I told him we'd be splitting our shipment, and sending most of it to Minneapolis, but a small shipment would be going to Dubai. He chuckled, "What's the deal with Dubai? You're the fourth shipment going there this month."

"It's all about the oil," I replied. "They're paying the big bucks, and they've got a lot of job openings. Most people are getting at least double what they would be making here."

"When do you want to split the shipments?"

"I'd like to do it on Wednesday if possible. We'd like to have our container set out on the back lot so we can go through everything. Once we finish with that we'll leave it to your guys to re-inventory, and reload everything into the two separate containers."

"That sounds good," he replied. "I've got another shipment going to Dubai, and it's scheduled to be picked up on Friday. I'll try to get them both in the same pickup. If I can, it'll save you guys a good chunk of change."

"Sounds good. So everything is set for Wednesday?"

"Yes. I'll have your container set out first thing Wednesday morning so you can start any time after eight."

All was good.

After we disconnected, Jewels asked if I needed her help. I told her I would until we had the two shipments separated, and then she would need to come back to sign the paperwork. "You can take my pickup to run around while you're waiting for the final inventories to be complete. I will call your cell when we need you." She agreed.

Knowing we would be having a late Christmas dinner, we ate a good breakfast, and went for a walk around the neighborhood. Our conversation was very civil, and I filled in a lot of gaps that Jewels had concerning Dubai. Although she continued to profess her non-commitment, her curiosity was a good sign.

Back at the apartment, we watched the news but there wasn't anything we hadn't heard. The FBI was still in pursuit of the elusive Bill Edwards, but there were no indications they suspected him to be anything but black.

We were having dinner with friends, and arrived at Mary and Roger's house, as planned, at two. Our mutual friends, Elaine and Stacy, and Carl and Debbie were also joining us. We all shared the common ground of not having relatives in the area, and not wanting to spend Christmas alone.

Mary, as usual, made a great dinner, and there was plenty left for a second round later in the day. We played games, and talked throughout the day and early evening. Much of our conversation was about the hijacking, and specifically, Earl Baker. Everyone there knew Earl, and thought it was inconceivable that he, with his doctorate in management, and his quarter-of-a-million-dollar wages, would stoop to hiring out the hijacking of a company plane.

However, everyone seemed even more surprised that he was the bomber of Houston Center. Jewels caught me off guard by saying, "We were a little suspicious of him, but we didn't see enough to warrant a call to the FBI, which, in hindsight, is what we probably should have done. The main thing we noticed was the change in his personality after the bombing. He shifted from being totally pissed because nobody took revenge for the strike, to being happy because someone finally did. He mourned very little about Clyde."

Mary said, "At least he felt enough guilt to leave whatever estate he had to Clyde's family."

Roger added, "There probably won't be anything left after U.P.-Ex settles their claims."

We all agreed with the statements about Earl. It was after 9:00 when we headed toward our apartment. We told the group we were moving to Minneapolis, but we made no mention of Dubai.

On the way, we re-hashed some of the day's conversations. I told Jewels, "I was at first surprised when you started talking about our suspicions about Earl, but then I agreed with what you said. I was glad you didn't mention his visit in August. I didn't tell anyone about that."

She replied, "Don't you think the FBI has found out about his trip to Houston by now?"

"Maybe so, but they must not have linked it to us. At least, not yet."

When we got back to our apartment we broke out the bottle of Champaign, and we did our Christmas gift exchange. It was interesting how minds sometimes work in the same way. Knowing we were going to Minneapolis, we'd bought each other leather jackets. We even exchanged a few kisses for the first time since she'd discovered the truth.

Jewels said she'd taken some time out from shopping, and had looked up some things about Dubai. It came as good news when she said, "It's a very Americanized city, with plenty of condos and housing areas that are over fifty-percent American. But it's not cheap. Everything there is very expensive."

Next, she looked me in the eye, and added, "I was just looking around. I haven't made a decision on going, and you need to be ready to accept the fact that I very well may stay in Minneapolis. I don't want you to push me on this."

"I won't push you one way or the other. It's your decision to make. But I'll need to know sometime before we reach Minneapolis. Are you OK with that?"

"This is all still scaring me," she admitted. "I never would have thought you would go to this extreme, and I'm worried how it may end. I need breathing room and I still wish it would all go away. It should have never happened. We would have been fine, Rob."

Wednesday morning, we dressed in jeans and T-shirts for a work day in the mid-seventies. We decided to just take one vehicle, and it had to be my pickup because we needed room for the money. Our first stop was the mini-storage unit. Jewels went in to close my account while I loaded the money suitcases in the bed of my truck. I locked it down as Jewels finished with our rental business.

We were on time at Suddath's warehouse, and our container was ready for us. I borrowed two dollies, and we went to work. We had unloaded about half of our household goods before we reached the money box. We were somewhat hidden behind the warehouse, and it was just the two of us, so I took everything out of the box, and removed the false bottom. After making sure we were alone, I had Jewels watch for anyone coming, while I started loading money into the bottom of the box.

It took me about five minutes to get the money in place and, because I held some out, it didn't fill the space. I placed moving blankets at both ends to keep the currency from shifting. I secured the false bottom and put the garage items back in. I left the top off for the mover's inventory inspection.

When we had the two shipments completely separated, we walked around to the office to tell them we were ready. Bob Kane, our salesperson, was in his office with another man. I knocked to tell him we were ready when he was. He introduced us to the man in his office, "This is Tim Joseph. He's a U.S. customs officer, and he's just finished inspecting the other shipment we have going to Dubai."

Mr. Joseph shook my hand, and said, "We have a new reciprocity agreement on shipments to Dubai that will arrive after January first. Your shipment qualifies under that agreement with the United Arab Emirates. Let me explain how this will work. I will inspect your shipment this afternoon, and it will be sealed here. By doing this, you will save a lot of time and inconvenience at the other end. The backlog in Dubai this year has been between three to six months before delivery."

Tim seemingly paused to look at Jewels and I, before continuing, "We have been schooled as to what they will allow, or won't allow, and we have assured them of compliance on all shipments sealed by us. They have numerous religious restrictions that call for us to remove some books and religious artifacts that aren't allowed in their country. Do you have any of these items?"

I felt like the agent was looking at us to see signs of nervousness that might indicate we had something to hide. With that thought in mind, I responded, "I'm sure we don't, but if you see anything you can feel free to throw it away."

Tim replied, "That sound's good and, if all goes as planned, you should be able to get your shipment within a few weeks of its arrival. This is a win-win situation, but keep in mind, your shipment will be one of the first under this agreement so we'll have to keep our fingers crossed."

"It's got to be better than waiting around forever for our stuff." I said as I looked at Jewels, and continued, "That sounds great to us." Jewels was nodding her approval as I spoke.

Tim said it would probably add about an hour to our load time, but Mr. Kane offered up a couple more people to help speed the process.

As we were walking back around to our shipment I asked Tim if my wife would be needed. He said, "Only to sign the documentation, and that'll probably be in a couple of hours."

I was concerned that Jewels might be overly nervous when Tim got to the money box, so I said, "Why don't you do some shopping, and I'll call you when we're getting close to finishing here." She jumped on the opportunity.

Counting Tim and I, there were a total of six of us to finish loading the two shipments. I stayed with Tim as he inspected the shipment to Dubai while the guys were loading the Minneapolis shipment back into the forty-foot container. The Minneapolis shipment was soon loaded and returned to the warehouse.

The crew then started loading what was already inspected by Mr. Joseph. When the loading crew got to the money box, they asked Tim if they could load it next because of its size and the ability to stack other items on top of it. Tim went to the crate and started his inspection.

I was glad Jewels wasn't here because I knew if she saw how nervous I was, she'd be even worse. Tim looked over at me and said, "You need to wrap some of these items in paper pads or you're going have some damage." He then turned to the crew, and said, "Put the top back on and load her up."

I was afraid my voice would crack so I just nodded, and picked up some paper pads. With the help of a couple of the guys, we wrapped some of the items and I attached the top for shipment. It was loaded a few minutes later. I called Jewels when we were close to being finished and told her she could come back now.

I hadn't felt so relieved since I had touched down on Johnston Island. It was one more heart-attack moment. I didn't know how much more my body could take.

Jewels came back, and the Dubai shipment was sealed and locked with U.S. Customs specific seals. The paperwork was signed, and I was told the overseas shipment would be picked up tomorrow.

I came close to maxing out two credit cards paying for the two shipments, but the paperwork was signed, and we were on our way.

On the way back to our apartment, I told Jewels about the significance of having our custom's inspection out of the way. "We just shipped close to ten million dollars in cash to our new home in Dubai. It's not a total free pass, because they will spot-check shipments. But our odds are a lot better now. You've got to realize how important that is."

"From your smile I assume it's a big deal, but you need to stop saying our, and we, or you could be in for a big disappointment in Minnesota. I'm serious, Rob. I'm not leaning in your direction."

I didn't respond, but I was reminded to be careful about how I chose my words. "Tomorrow, I need to sell my pickup. There's a good full-service car wash on the way home. I'm going to stop there unless you want me to drop you at the apartment first." She agreed to the stop.

With the truck waiting in line at the car wash, I started reviewing our next two days. "I think we're both in agreement that it would be best to get on the road tomorrow."

Jewels agreed.

I continued, "I'll check for opening times for the string of car dealerships along I-45. I hope to get enough out of my truck to pay most of our expenses along the way to Minneapolis, and my expenses to Dubai. I'll need you to come get me, and take me to the bank to cash their check. While I'm selling the truck, maybe you can start getting things packed and ready at the apartment. Anything we don't really need can go into the dumpster."

"I'm fine with that. I thought I'd give any leftover food or drink to Alice, our busybody neighbor. We'll have to forfeit our deposit, but I'll take care of everything before picking you up."

"OK. We're good, and it looks like they're through with the truck."

On the drive to the apartment, Jewels dropped her own bomb. "When we get to the apartment, I need you to go through our financials. I want to see exactly where we stand. You'll need to include how much you will need between now and the first month in Dubai. I want half of the balance given to me without any worn currency.

"It's not that I don't trust you," Jewels continued. "It's that I don't trust you completely. You've done some things lately that I would have never thought possible from you. You're going to have to earn back the trust I once had with you, and I feel terrible having to say that."

"I feel terrible about your having to say that, too, but I'll do that for you." It was quiet for awhile, and I knew tomorrow would be a long day, so I suggested we go to bed. She handed me my blanket and pillow, and she went to bed.

I didn't sleep well, and woke up early Thursday morning. I did a rough draft of what Jewels had asked of me through the first month of Dubai. It took me the better part of an hour, but I still had it completed by the time Jewels got up.

She looked it over, and said, "Thank you. Your expenses are higher than I expected, but so is the amount of money we will have available. I can live with this."

We sat down with our coffee, and a look at the morning news. The reporter confirmed that Earl Baker's body was the one in the burned townhouse, and the coroner stated that the cause of death was a single bullet wound to the head. The townhouse was a total loss, but the FBI still had agents on site looking for additional evidence.

I looked over to Jewels and said, "I think it's time for me to destroy my laptop and the prepaid phone I used to talk with Earl."

"I can't believe you haven't done that already. Is there anything else you're hanging onto for God-knows-what reason?"

"Let me know if you see anything when you're getting things ready for our trip. I'll take the memory cards and hard drives out of these, and put them in the dumpster of the apartments down the street."

"What about your disguises?"

"They're already at the bottom of one of the deepest channels of Lake Conroe."

Back on the news, the reporter said, "The special agent in charge of the Memphis office of the FBI told us that although they don't have any additional suspects in custody at this time, they are making considerable progress. This hijacking remains the agency's number-one priority."

Jewels said, "I can't believe they haven't knocked on our door. You must know that day will come, even if it's just because of your friendship with Earl, or his trip to see us. If they were to knock on our door with a search warrant they would find the ten thousand dollars in our closet. You need to know I would deny any knowledge of that money. I'm scared, Rob."

I put my arm around her shoulders. "Like you said, I expect them to come around sooner or later, but every report I've heard still has them looking for a black man. The only thing they would want from me is answers to questions about Earl, and our past friendship. I'm going to get my truck sold so we can get a good start on our way to Minneapolis today. If someone knocks on the door, don't answer."

"That won't happen. I don't want to stay here alone, and I'm going with you."

"OK. We can take a cab to the bank, and back to the apartment." She agreed.

We hit several car dealers before finding one willing to give us what we thought was a reasonable offer. We took his offer, and they had a young man drive us back to the apartment. We didn't go inside, but went directly to Jewels' car. We stopped at the bank to cash the check and, with that done, we were glad to check one more thing off our to-do list.

Back at the apartment, Jewels and I worked together to get everything either into the car or into the dumpster. Jewels gave all our extra food to our neighbor. We checked out, and told the manager we'd call her with a forwarding address as soon as we landed somewhere solid. We told the post office to just hold our mail until we sent them an official forwarding address. Jewels made arrangements for us to stay with her sister in Coon Rapids, Minnesota by Friday night.

It was mid-afternoon on Thursday when we were finally leaving Houston and on the road to Minnesota.

## CHAPTER THIRTY

### CONTINUING INVESTIGATIONS

At Princeville airport on Kauai, the owners told the inquiring policeman they'd agreed to allow Bill Edwards to spot a rental van at the airport.

"We received two hundred dollars in the mail for letting a van sit there for a couple of days. We thought that was a pretty good deal, and since we were paid in cash, it didn't bother us that we never actually met anyone. Our living area is in the back of our house, so we didn't see anything, but we heard a plane land - and then take off a few minutes later. When we finally got around to looking outside, the van was gone."

At Lihue airport, officers pulled videos and went to the commercial flight counters to interview all who might have seen Bill Edwards. They remembered one black man boarding a flight to Honolulu, but they didn't believe him to be as tall as listed in the description of Bill Edwards. The videos confirmed their memory.

Their final stop at Lihue airport was the fixed base operator where Declan departed. They were told about the Citation that departed to Albuquerque, but with the only passenger being an Italian man with wavy hair, they dismissed any connection. They filed their report of negative results in the search for Bill Edwards.

Back in Memphis, FBI agent Kostelnik and Secret Service agent Matt Haglund were interviewing Earl's dispatch manager, Randy Rappe. Randy said, "We have ten active pilots that come close to the description of Bill Edwards. We also have numerous African-American pilots who have applied for positions with U.P.-Ex, but we don't have photos of these people.

Agent Kostelnik took the personnel files of all current pilots, and the résumés of prospective pilots, and took them back to his office for review. Agent Haglund stayed behind to discuss security measures for past and future treasury department shipments.

The FBI believed that Earl Baker provided the letter of authorization and all necessary insider information to Bill Edwards. They had identified hundreds of black men under that name, and they were in the process of weeding through them. They also believed Earl Baker hired the pickup pilot, but doubted that pilot knew anything about the hijacking.

The pickup pilot remained in custody, and the hijacker remained at large. With Earl dead, Edwards was the FBI's number one suspect. They continued to show the pictures of him and asked for the public's help finding him.

The U.P.-Ex board of directors scheduled an emergency meeting to discuss an upcoming media release concerning Mr. Baker. The meeting had been delayed slightly while waiting for their chief executive officer, Mr. Severson, to return from Europe. The media was already chastising him for his failure to return immediately upon notification of the flight being overdue. The board was to meet at 1:00 to prepare for a planned media release at 5:00.

Mr. Severson called the meeting to order, and gave his opening remarks. "As you all are aware, we have scheduled our media release for five this afternoon so we don't have too much time to work through the numerous problems Mr. Baker has laid in our laps. The popular saying, 'It is what it is' seems applicable to what's happened to our company over the past week. There is nothing we can do to change that. We need to focus only on what we can do to make this whole ordeal go away as quickly as possible. We are charged with damage control, and placing our company in the most favorable light possible."

The board discussed different options, but in the final analysis they agreed to hang everything on Earl, but they knew they had to show his background to be squeaky clean or face lawsuits. They would announce upcoming new and aggressive security measures throughout the company. They would include updated, and annual, background checks on all current and future employees.

The CEO would express his deep regret for the problems resulting from this unfortunate incident. But they all secretly hoped the hijacking dirt would be overshadowed by the horrific 1981 bombing of Houston Center.

# Chapter Thirty-One

## Cartwright Returns

When agent Cartwright heard the news about Earl Baker's suicide letter he felt he was finally redeemed for all the hard work he'd put into the Houston Center bombing case, which had ended with his demotion. It was late in the '81 investigation when he came to the conclusion that Earl could have easily bombed the center. Due to the lack of solid evidence, he was stopped from pursuing his gut feelings.

Now, with Earl's admission to being the mastermind of the U.P.-Ex hijacking, agent Cartwright decided to pull the cold case files on Earl to see if he could find a connection to Bill Edwards or Declan Finley. It was close to midnight Thursday when Cartwright was looking through old files for known associates of Earl Baker. The first name that came up was Rob Silvers, Earl's roommate in Houston. He remembered that Mr. Silvers had solid alibi for the bombing, and he was at the end of a long day, so he placed the file on his desk and went home. He set his alarm for 6:00 a.m.

Cartwright came in at 7:00 Thursday morning to start tracking down Rob Silvers. He did a current background check and couldn't believe what he found. Rob had made captain for Northwest Airlines, and he was certified and current on Airbus aircraft. Next he found that Rob had moved to Houston, and was re-hired as a controller at Houston Center. He made an early morning call to Houston Center and was routed to the duty officer, Dave Robichaux.

When he asked about Rob Silvers, Mr. Robichaux replied, "He failed to make it through the training program, and he was terminated on December 18. Like many of the re-hires, he was either too old, or he killed too many brain cells, to keep pace with today's traffic. I believe

Rob was even a little older than the rest. He was certified on a sector or two, but that was about it. Last I heard, he was looking for another government job, but I don't know if he found anything. Our human resource people come in at eight and they may be able to give you more information. Is he in some sort of trouble or something?"

Cartwright said, "No, I don't think so. I'm just following up on some of Earl Baker's friends, and his name came up."

Mr. Robichaux said, "I never met Earl Baker, but Rob was a nice guy and well-liked. I think it was just a matter of being 59 in a job best suited for those in their 20s and 30s. His age proved to be his nemesis. Last I heard he and his wife are still living in Houston, but I think they sold their house and moved into one of those extend-a-stay apartments."

After disconnecting, agent Cartwright, talking out loud to himself, said, "You tricky old bastard. You're the damn hijacker!"

Agent Cartwright and his partner, Don Woolsey, were both planning their retirement soon and they decided to make this their last hurrah. Cartwright found six apartment units like the one Robichaux had told him about, and they started knocking on doors.

They hit pay-dirt with their second stop. The manager there told them the Silvers had left a few hours ago. "They didn't leave a forwarding address, but they told me they would call with one as soon as they settled somewhere."

Cartwright and Woolsey had been chasing the Silvers most of the day, and they were both tired, but they decided to try one more door before calling it a day. They went to unit number 133 to see Alice, the Silvers' next-door neighbor for the last few weeks.

When Alice answered their knock agent Cartwright immediately thought her to be in her mid-eighties. He introduced himself and Agent Woolsey and then asked her what she knew about her recent neighbors, the Silvers.

The term, "too much information" soon came to mind as Alice said, "What a nice couple they were. I miss them already. You know I often watched over their place when they weren't home. A week ago I got their mail and newspaper while they were in Galveston for the weekend. You just missed them – they moved out and haven't been gone more than a few hours. They gave me a bunch of food, and a lamp for my bedroom. They were very nice people."

When she stopped talking, agent Woolsey jumped in, "When did you say they went to Galveston?"

Alice replied, "They left sometime before noon last Friday. I didn't see them, but I noticed their car was gone when I came back from playing cards with my friends. I got back a little after noon. We play cards every Friday morning. There are usually four of us but one had a doctor's appointment, and she couldn't play."

It was agent Cartwright who cut in this time, "When did they come back from Galveston?"

"They came back Sunday afternoon. I saw them drive up. First it was Rob, and then Jewels pulled in. I don't know why they came back is separate cars."

Cartwright said, "You don't happen to know where they stayed in Galveston do you?"

"I sure do, they stayed at the Wave Runner Inn. I remember, because I asked Jewels and, when she told me where they were staying, I told her my husband and I stayed there forty years ago. It was our favorite place to stay but we never went back. I'm not sure why." The look on her face changed to one of sadness as she said, "He passed about ten years ago."

Cartwright looked at his watch, and said, "We're running late. Thanks for everything. You were a big help." They were walking before she could start talking.

Cartwright decided they would go to Galveston Friday morning. He thought it was possible for Rob, disguised as Declan, to get an early morning flight from Albuquerque to Houston, and make it to Galveston by Saturday afternoon. If both the Silvers were there on Friday his gut feeling would be wrong—but it seldom was. He told Woolsey, "Right now, my gut feels the same as it did when I thought Earl Baker did the bombing."

Although Woolsey was on the phone with their office, but Cartwright continued to talk. "Have our specialists check flights from Albuquerque to Houston last Saturday morning to see if Declan or Rob can be found. Send the pictures of Bill Edwards and Declan Finley to our guys in Albuquerque so they can pull their camera footage for a match. I'm thinking Bill Edwards, Declan Finley, and Rob Silvers could be the same guy. See if anyone can find out how these guys got to Honolulu or Kauai."

As Jewels and I were driving north on I-45, we were listening to the U.P.-Ex news conference. I was pleased to hear that the CEO had made no mention of Bill Edwards. He talked about how Earl Baker was a man of secret lives, with multiple wives, quiet divorces, and infidelity. But he followed that with, "Earl was an excellent manager of people, and he kept his financial and marital problems separate from his work. We were totally unaware of the deep financial hole he was in, and we now realize that it was that debt that drove him to plan this crime. We feel fortunate that no one was seriously injured, and over ninety-five percent of our cargo was left intact."

I could see how the CEO was working hard to be politically correct as he continued, "We realize that on occasion an employee could have a drastic change in their life during their employment with U.P.-Ex, and we know it only takes one person to cause a problem such as this. We are taking measures to ensure this doesn't happen again. We will immediately start updating all employee background checks, and we will continue to do so annually. I'll take your questions now."

I had heard all I needed to hear. They were obviously trying to cut their losses. I put a soothing CD in the player to help us relax. Our stress relief came easier now that we were out of Houston. We had distanced ourselves from doors the FBI could knock on and we soon started to relax as we headed north on the road to Minneapolis.

When our gas gauge dropped below a quarter of a tank, I started to look for a motel. We were well north of Dallas when I saw a Holiday Inn. As I pulled in, Jewels woke up from a nap. I didn't feel like anyone was breathing down our necks, and our departure from Houston was well-planned in advance, so we believed our behavior would seem acceptable to anyone that might be interested. I used my personal credit card when we checked in.

I had given Jewels her share of our money in clean cash, but it was understood that if she decided to make the trip to Dubai, she would have to pay her airfare out of that money. We had enough cash to pay for our airline tickets and our living expenses through our first month, maybe two, in Dubai. If we didn't have our big supply of worn currency by then, we'd have to look for jobs.

As I lay there trying to go to sleep, I couldn't help but think of how this was going to end. I had done everything I knew to do to persuade Jewels to come with me, and I knew putting more pressure on her would make things worse. The bigger question now was, "Could I leave without her?" I decided I could go long enough to get setup in an apartment, change the American money into Dirhams, and, hopefully, I would be able to make trips back to Minneapolis. With that satisfaction, I finally fell asleep.

# Chapter Thirty-Two

## Galveston

At 7:00 Friday morning, agents Cartwright and Woolsey were on their way to Galveston. The manager of Wave Runner Inn was expecting them, and had set aside a conference room for their investigation.

The desk clerk that was on duty the afternoon of December 21$^{st}$ was the first to be questioned. He remembered Mrs. Silvers checking in, "She didn't have any luggage with her, but she said her husband was parking the car, so I assumed he would be taking care of that. I gave her two room keys and she went out through the front door. I didn't see her again that day."

Cartwright asked, "Did you see Mr. Silvers on Friday?"

*"No, I didn't see either of them again until they passed through the lobby* on their way to dinner Saturday evening."

The lady responsible for cleaning the Silvers' room was the next to be questioned. She said, "It was about nine o'clock Saturday morning when I cleaned their room. I knocked on the door, but there was no response. I used my key, found the room empty, and cleaned normally. I remember seeing both men's and women's clothing in the closet, and also in an open suitcase on the floor. There were two swim suits in the bathroom hanging on the shower railing to dry. One was a man's suit and the other a woman's. The man's suit had a wet jock strap next to it. That's all I remember about their room."

Cartwright asked, "Did you ever actually see Mr. Silvers, or any other man with Mrs. Silvers?"

"Yes sir - I saw Mr. and Mrs. Silvers leaving their room a little before eleven Sunday morning. They had their suitcases with them so I asked if they were checking out. Mr. Silvers said they were, so I went to clean their room. Inside I found they had left me a twenty dollar tip."

Woolsey showed her a picture of Rob Silvers, and asked if she was sure this was the man. She told him it was. There were a few other employees who remembered seeing both of them late Saturday afternoon, and Sunday morning, but none saw either of them after check-in Friday afternoon.

Cartwright asked about security cameras, and the manager told him that the hotel was fifty years old, and much of their draw was due to its well-preserved historical look. They didn't have security cameras.

The waiter who served them dinner said, "Mr. Silvers said his steak was overcooked. I got him another steak that met with his satisfaction. I agreed with him that the first steak was lacking the red center expected of a medium- rare steak. He gave me a good tip."

Cartwright was expecting much better results from their trip, but while they were in Galveston they checked some security cameras around the area. They were unable to find any views of the Silvers or either of their vehicles. At noon they stopped to eat, and Agent Woolsey said, "It looks like we've hit a dead end." Agent Cartwright didn't respond.

As they were driving back to Houston, Cartwright said, "The way I see it, Mr. Silvers has a weak alibi and he has no one other than his wife to confirm that he was in Galveston before late afternoon on Saturday. He could have made connections from Albuquerque to Houston, and made Galveston by Saturday afternoon. Call into the office and have our guys check all the flights, private or commercial, from any airport around Albuquerque to any airport around Houston or Galveston. I still think Silvers had a hand in this."

While Woolsey was on his cell with the specialists, Cartwright remembered the Silvers lived in the Minneapolis area while he was with Northwest. He asked Woolsey to check and see if either of the Silvers had relatives in the Minneapolis area.

After Woolsey hung up with the office, he said, "You may be right about Rob being able to make it from Albuquerque to Galveston by

Saturday afternoon. The first flight out of Albuquerque was at five forty-seven a.m., and it arrived at Houston Intercontinental at eleven thirty. If he had a car spotted at the airport, or if someone picked him up, he could possibly get to Galveston by mid-afternoon on Saturday. But with ten pieces of luggage the gate agents would have surely taken notice of that. So far we haven't found any."

"There aren't any commercial flights out of Albuquerque into Hobby or Galveston Saturday morning. The guys checked under the names of Bill Edward, Declan Finley, and Rob Silvers, but there were no hits."

Woolsey continued, "I've had the specialists look for private flights from Albuquerque into any airport in the Houston area, but no luck. He could have flown a small plane without filing a flight plan, but that's going to be even harder to find. It's going to take some time."

Back at their office Cartwright asked for overtime on Saturday for him and Agent Woolsey. He said he had some leads on the U.P.-Ex hijacking that he needed to follow up on. He was told that as long as it was about the hijacking, there was a green light for agent and specialist overtime.

With that free pass, Cartwright asked Woolsey if he would come in on Saturday, one of his days off. Woolsey said he'd like some morning time with his family, but he would come in about eleven. They agreed to an 11:00 a.m. start.

Friday morning, Jewels and I were watching the morning news while having our coffee in our room at the Holiday Inn. The anchor said, "This is a special report on the hijacking of U.P.-Ex 7-19. The FBI has just released photos of a new person of interest. The person now shown on your screen boarded a chartered flight from Kauai, Hawaii, to Albuquerque, New Mexico." The picture shown was one of me in disguise as Declan Finley.

"This person, known as Declan Finley, boarded a Citation jet aircraft with the same ten pieces of luggage Bill Edwards transferred from Johnston Island to Kauai." I took a deep breath, but said nothing.

"The van used by Declan Finley was returned to a rental agency at Lihue airport, and is now being investigated by the FBI."

"The Memphis office of the FBI has tracked three separate money transfers, totaling twenty-three thousand dollars, between Earl Baker and the owner of the Citation aircraft. It is believed the suitcases were transferred from Bill Edwards to Declan Finley on Kauai. With the trail of Bill Edwards ending on Kauai, and the trail of Declan Finley starting where Edwards' trail stopped, and ending in Albuquerque, the FBI is investigating the possibility of these two men being one and the same—but under excellent disguises."

"The FBI continues to ask for the public's assistance in locating either of these men." They showed a split screen picture of Edwards and Finley. Although they looked totally different, they were of the same height and weight. Their mannerisms, walk, and speech, were reported to be identical.

Next they showed pictures of the luggage as it was being loaded into the Citation. This luggage has been verified as being the same luggage unloaded, from the King Air aircraft flight between Johnston Island and Kauai. Rob turned off the television.

It was totally quiet in the room for a long moment or two before Jewels said, "Rob, that picture of Declan looks a lot more like you than the pictures of Bill Edwards, but I'll give you credit—both disguises are very well done. Let's leave right now. I want to get to Rita's house before they catch up with you."

I replied, "I want to be in Dubai."

We loaded the car, filled the tank, and headed north. When I was established on I-35 and crossing the state line into Oklahoma, Jewels had a bewildered look on her face. She said, "I know you want my decision, but you need to realize the position you've put me in. I love you, Rob, you know that. I'm just not sure if I can love Rob the hijacker, like I love Rob the pilot, or Rob the controller. Under normal circumstances I'd jump at the chance of going to Dubai with you, but I'm afraid how this whole hijacking thing has changed you. You seem more callous now."

"I know that's true, because I don't feel like myself either," Rob replied. "It seems like there's a new threat around every corner, but I'm confident the threats will all go away when we're in the safety of Dubai.

We can relax there. I assure you the old Rob will return as soon as our flight is over international waters. We'll be good there, and you'll be surprised how quickly this will all blow over."

"Are you sure of that? I'm afraid of our being stuck there with no way out."

"That's not going to happen because they'll never find enough evidence to arrest me. I took every precaution to make sure I didn't leave any physical evidence behind. No DNA, and no fingerprints, to prove their case. They may have their suspicions, but with our Galveston alibi there will be far too many unknowns to make it worthwhile to chase after someone - especially someone who physically hurt no one, and stole nothing of value. It's like stealing a car for a joy ride, and bringing it back undamaged. It's just on a much larger scale."

"I wouldn't advise you to use that totally ridiculous analogy in court," Jewels replied.

"OK, that's over the top, but they won't find the evidence they need, and it will blow over. Don't forget, they still believe a black man did the hijacking, and they see Declan as an accomplice. Roberto's name hasn't come up at all. We're going to weather this storm."

"Another important thing to consider: By going with me to Dubai, you'll put yourself out of reach of questioning by the FBI. If you stay, you'll have to make the decision of lying to protect me, or telling the truth to convict me."

Jewels listened, but she didn't say anything for a couple of minutes. When she finally spoke it was worth the wait because she said exactly what I wanted to hear. "It is only because I don't want to live without you, and I certainly don't want to be faced with questions about you, that I have no choice but to go to Dubai. But mark my words Rob; I won't stay a day more than one year. With or without you, I will come back to Minneapolis."

It was like someone had suddenly lifted a huge weight from my shoulders. I took her hand and squeezed it as I said, "I promise, you won't regret this decision. I'll make sure of that."

We made a stop for gas in Kansas and found a branch of our bank. Jewels and I had separate accounts so we made separate deposits.

We kept the deposits low enough as to not raise any red flags and we could justify the money as coming from the selling of my truck and closing of a 401K. Her deposit was all clean money but mine was about fifty-fifty of worn currency. We wanted to have enough in our accounts to pay for our flights with our debit cards.

As we were closing in on Jewels' sisters' home I asked Jewels to tell her sister and brother-in-law, Rita and Bob, that we were going to Mexico City for a few weeks' vacation. She agreed it would be better than telling them we were going to Dubai for a year.

It had been a long day on the road but we stayed up and talked until about eleven before we went to their basement for some sleep. As tired as I was, I took a few minutes to use a computer in Bob's office while Jewels was in the bath. I looked up information on flights to both Mexico City and Dubai. I also checked on the value of Jewels' car. We planned on selling it Saturday. It was almost midnight before we fell asleep.

At breakfast Saturday morning the conversation was focused on our trip to Mexico City. With the weather outside hovering around zero, they had no problem understanding why we picked that city.

After breakfast, we were talking about our need to sell Jewels' car. I said we were planning to replace it, but we didn't want to buy anything until we got back from our trip. Jewels said, "We aren't sure how long we'll stay in Mexico, but it could be a couple of months if it works out for us."

Rita immediately showed an interest by asking, "How much are you asking for it?"

Jewels replied, "We looked up the average value for its year and mileage and it was listed at $11,500 – Why? Are you interested?"

Rita looked over to her husband, Bob, and said, "What do you think? It would sure be a lot better than mine."

Bob said, "Why don't you guys just leave it with us while you're in Mexico? That way we could have time to sell Rita's car. If you can live with $10,000, we can pay you half now and the other half when you get back."

Jewels looked over to me and I said, "It's your car, and your decision." "Okay, that'll save us a lot of trouble." Rita gave Jewels a check for $5,000 and later in the morning when her and Rita were grocery shopping for the evening dinner, Jewels was able to deposit the check.

Saturday afternoon, I booked reservations for us on a Sunny Air flight to Mexico City. I used one of my personal credit cards, knowing full well it could come up on the FBI's radar, should they be looking. The flight was scheduled to depart at 9:00 Sunday morning, and their website reminded me that, due to the events of 9-11, international flights required check-in two hours before departure.

Saturday evening, Jewels' other two sisters and their spouses, who also lived in Minneapolis, joined us for dinner. With it being a long time since the four sisters got together, the evening ran into the night, and it was almost midnight before we laid our heads on a pillow. Before going to sleep I called a cab company and arranged for a cab to be sitting outside of Rita's house at 6:00 Sunday morning. We set our alarm for 4:40, knowing that tomorrow would be one hell of a day.

# Chapter Thirty-Three

## Leaving on a Jet Plane

Sunday morning I hit the shower first and, as soon as I was out, Jewels went in. While she was getting dressed, I was getting everything packed for our trip. I put most of the remaining cash in my briefcase and carried our suitcases to the front door. Rita heard us, and brought out coffee and rolls while we waited for the cab. It pulled up at exactly 6:00. We said our good-byes and gave our hugs as driver was helping us with our luggage.

Our flight on Sunny Air was out of the Hubert H. Humphrey terminal, which was across the field from the main airport. I told our driver to take us to the main terminal first, and wait while we took our luggage inside. We were only in the main terminal long enough to put our suitcases in the lockers there. Our cabbie waited for us, and then drove us to the Humphrey terminal.

Jewels thought we were just wasting time and money buying tickets to Mexico City. I agreed, but I also knew the FBI would certainly be looking for us soon. By putting everything on my personal credit card it would be obvious to the FBI, and we would be in Dubai before we got the bill.

It was 7:00 a.m. when we checked in and picked up our boarding passes. Because of 9/11 there was a two-hour advance requirement and the clerk at the check-in counter noted that we barely met the guidelines. When she saw we didn't have luggage, another red flag was raised. I explained how we shipped it with U.P.-Ex., "We had two large suitcases come up missing about a year ago, and we were only paid three hundred dollars each from the airline. That didn't come anywhere near the value of what we lost. We found that we could eliminate that possibility, plus have full replacement cost for our belongings by shipping them in advance. They also ship directly to our hotel so we don't have to carry them around."

She replied, "That makes sense."

We went through security with only my briefcase full of money and Jewels carry-on luggage. Both were X-rayed with no questions or comments.

Having flown out of the Humphrey terminal a few times, I was aware of their gate procedures. The person at our gate counter was the same person who gathered up the boarding passes during the loading process. That fit perfectly with my plan.

When the boarding started, the gate agent stayed at the counter collecting the boarding passes. From there the passengers traveled between two lines of red velvet ropes that extended without break to the ramp going down to the plane. We gave the clerk our boarding passes and, while she was attending to the people behind us, we ducked under the velvet rope and passed behind her counter. We walked slowly to the next gate and joined in with the people coming off an incoming flight.

We went back to the terminal building and found a window that looked out to the tarmac where our flight was parked. We were getting worried when our flight didn't push back on schedule. It was a long fifteen minutes later before it finally made its move. We couldn't help but wonder if the flight delay was due to a problem with their head count. We grabbed a cab, and went to the main terminal.

We had some time to kill, since our flight to Dubai didn't depart until noon, but it had a 10:00 check-in. We knew we would be taking a chance by showing up with no reservations, but we also knew the flight was only about seventy percent full when I checked it Saturday night.

# Chapter Thirty-Four

## Chasing the Silvers

Agent Cartwright was at home reading the paper and finishing his morning coffee when his home phone rang at 9:45 Sunday morning. A specialist from his office said, "I found the Silvers."

"Where are they?"

"They boarded a Sunny Airlines flight to Mexico City about a half hour ago. They're probably over Iowa by now."

"Are we sure they got on the plane?"

"Yes. They were confirmed as having boarded the plane, and their names are on the passenger manifest."

He nodded. "Call Agent Woolsey, and tell him what you told me, and tell him I'm on the way to the office. Call the FAA at Kansas City Center, and find out exactly where they are and find out what is required to force the plan to land at Houston. I'll be there in a half hour. Call me on my cell to keep me advised of your progress."

From his car, Cartwright called his boss, Barry Vaughn, the special agent in charge of the Houston office. He reached him at his home. "Barry, I've got a problem. It looks like my suspect, Rob Silvers, is on the run. He and his wife boarded a Sunny Air flight to Mexico City this morning, and he's somewhere around Kansas City now. I want to force the plane to land in Houston."

"What do we have for evidence?"

"I believe Rob Silvers is the same person known as Declan Finley, and maybe even the same person as Bill Edwards. We checked times and flights out of Albuquerque, and he could have flown into Houston in time to make Galveston by mid-afternoon the Saturday after the hijacking. That is the first time Rob Silvers was seen in Galveston. I'm sure this guy's got the money, and he's on his way to Mexico City."

Barry replied, "I know your gut's telling you this is our guy, but we need something more than circumstantial evidence to force a plane to land. Do you have any idea of the lawsuits we'll have, especially if you're wrong?"

"I was right with Earl Baker, and I'm right now. You and I both know we've gone to court with less than this, and won our cases. Let me divert the plane and pull his ass off."

"I'll call Director Murphy and see what he says. I'll call you back."

"OK, but the Silvers will be in international airspace within the hour."

"I'll call you back as soon as I have something for you. Don't do anything before then. We can always have the Mexican authorities pick them up as they come off the plane, and hold them until we can get the extradition paperwork in place. You'll hear from me soon."

It was a long twenty minutes, and the Sunny Air flight was getting closer to Mexican airspace by the minute, when agent Vaughn returned Cartwright's call. "It's not going to happen. The director said, and I agree, it's too big a risk to divert the plane based on circumstantial evidence. It would come at the expense of numerous lawsuits, and the Silvers' attorney would probably be the first to file."

Cartwright ended the call, cursed, and looked over to Woolsey, who had just arrived. "This isn't over. Have the Mexican authorities pick the Silvers up when they walk off the plane. We'll need them to hold the Silvers until we can get there and work out the extradition requirements. It may take a little longer, but we'll get this done."

Woolsey soon talked with the airport police in Mexico City, and they agreed to meet the plane. He then faxed them photos of both Rob and Jewels. The Silvers were scheduled to land at Mexico City's Benito Juarez International airport at 1:00 p.m.

Cartwright knew he would need more evidence, or the authorities in Mexico would have to release the Silvers after twenty-four hours. Cartwright started the process of pulling the security camera tapes at the Humphrey terminal. Cartwright knew their facial recognition software would show a match with the Silvers since they were traveling under their true names. He could only hope that it would also match with Declan Finley and Bill Edwards.

When the recognition software paired Rob against Bill Edwards, and Declan Finley, it came up with only a sixty-three percent accuracy rating against Declan Finley, and it didn't get a hit at all against Bill Edwards. The sixty-three percent against Declan wasn't enough to stand up in court and the specialists were still unable to link Declan Finley to any commercial, or private, flights between Albuquerque and south Texas.

They did find a Cessna 172 that departed from Double Eagle II airport without filing a flight plan, but the pilot was a Roberto Celestino, and he didn't match Declan Finley's description. The pilot told Albuquerque approach his destination was Olathe, Kansas. The people working at Double Eagle II airport said they didn't see him load any luggage.

The Mexican airport authorities posted two men at the gate of the arriving Sunny Air flight. The flight was running late because of a late start and some re-routes around weather. It was 1:40 when the passengers started coming off the plane. Both airport police assigned to locate the Silvers looked closely at each passenger but found none matching the pictures of Rob and Jewels.

They then boarded the plane, made a complete search, and questioned the flight attendants. Only one remembered seeing the Silvers, and that was in the waiting room at the gate in Minneapolis. No one had seen them on the plane.

A call was made to Agent Cartwright in Houston to relay the results. They went over the extent of their search, and explained how the Silvers were definitely not on that plane.

Cartwright, frustrated and disappointed, said, "What kind of operation are you guys running down there? You can't even pick out a passenger when you have good pictures, and they're passing by your people in single file?"

The Mexican policeman snarled, "Next time, use your own people!" He hung up the phone.

Cartwright was convinced that Rob Silvers was the country's best suspect for the hijacking, but he didn't know what to do next. He called Special Agent Vaughn, and explained the situation. Agent Vaughn said, "I guess I have no choice but to call the director and explain, but he's probably going to wonder how this kind of a mistake could happen. It's a damn good thing we didn't force that plane down as you suggested."

Cartwright sat at his desk for a few minutes before typing a letter of resignation on his computer. He printed out a couple of copies and put one on Agent Vaughn's desk.

He told Woolsey about his letter of resignation and said, "You can have this shit; I've had enough of the FBI, and I'm well past my retirement age. I'll stay around to finish out my two weeks' notice, but then I'm gone."

# Chapter Thirty-Five

## Dubai

Jewels and I were both nervous when we took off, but the comfort of the soft leather seats of first class eased our fears of capture. First class was all that was available when we had bought our tickets.

As we climbed out over Canadian airspace I felt better, but when we were over the Atlantic, I gave Jewels' hand a squeeze, and we both felt a happiness we hadn't shared in sometime. The smile on Jewels face was all I needed to know our relationship was on the road to recovery.

Six months later, Jewels sent her sister Rita a package. It contained two first-class tickets, 7,346 United Emirates dirhams, and a note that read:

*Dubai is beautiful any time of year. Come visit.*

*Love, Jewels & Rob*

## About the Author

Robert Seckler was born in Houston, raised in Tulsa, and after high school was off to see the world via the Navy.

He used Johnston Island in his novel because he had personal knowledge of the island in 1962 when his ship was temporarily assigned there. He was present when the government detonated its largest above ground nuclear test about 50,000 feet above their heads.

After the Navy he received his education at the University of Tulsa and Prairie View A & M University. He received his pilot's license at Riverside airport in Tulsa, and it was this training that sparked his interest in becoming an air traffic controller.

He was a controller at Kansas City Center, Houston Center, and Seattle Center. In 1977 he was accepted as an Instructor at the FAA Academy in Oklahoma City.

In 1981 he was one of over eleven thousand controllers terminated by President Reagan during the massive air traffic controller strike.

During the following 18 years he served as Vice President/General Manager of agencies for United Van Lines and North American Van Lines.

In 1999 Bob became one of less than a thousand ex-controllers who was re-hired by President Clinton. He was first assigned to Oakland Center, but in 2000 he transferred back to Houston Center as an air traffic controller. He retired from air traffic control in 2007, and currently lives with his wife, Julie, in Coon Rapids, Minnesota.

CPSIA information can be obtained at www.ICGtesting.com
Printed in the USA
LVOW05s0312230714

395515LV00002B/3/P